*Katy King*

# The Seventh Life
# of Pauline Johnson

Thanks to all the friendly storytellers who let me use their anecdotes about 'the good old days;' thanks to the kind people who answered my questions and the helpful readers who encouraged me and made suggestions. Thanks to the Burnett County Historical Society for preserving the material on one-room schoolhouses.

I dedicate this book to the real Pauline. I named my heroine after her because she was a joy to be with.

# Cast of characters

Pauline Johnson, was crippled in body and spirit by three strokes, but then . . .
Maggie O'Neill was Pauline's helper, friend, instigator and co-investigator
Pauline's children:
    Stuart, a good family man
    Mary, an artist and grandmother
    Sara tried to get along with Pauline because Pauline was rich, and her mother.
    Alec, a forty-four-year old divorced alcoholic
    Dorothy, a good doctor, a good daughter, single

Adele Pinch liked Pauline's nice things.
Dixie Dowling melted men's brains to get money for gambling, until she died mysteriously

Suspects:
    Jim Dowling, Dixie's apathetic husband
    Cal, Dixie's obnoxious teenaged son
    Alec, one of Dixie's dupes
    Vern Fitzelditz, an alcoholic who admitted he'd been there when Dixie died
    Nimrod Clapquist, a boil on the nose of humanity, another of Dixie's pawns
        (Nimrod's drinking buddies: Zeke, Bleek, Nels, Nork and Willard)
    Fast Eddie Olnitz and Jake Kleidaker, two more of Dixie's patsies

Pauline's friends
    Doris Doppler had the world's best radar for gossip
    Brownie, a woman who did everything and knew everybody
    Pierre, a one-hundred-year-old story-teller

Marion, everybody's Grandma
Myrna, a fellow-teacher and card player
George Dogoodly, former student of Pauline's, now
  sheriff
Kathy and Dave, Pauline's helpful neighbors

Maggie's friends:
  Teresa and Jo

Swimming friends:
  Adeline, Beatrice, Betty, Betty Ann, Carol, Catherine,
  Ellie, Florence, Jan, Jenine, Karen, Laverne, Lois,
  Mary, Pat, Ruth, Sharron,

Joan Lefair, friend of Alec Johnson and Jim Dowling
Patty Brown, Cal's friend
Pete Jenkins an organizer of burglars

# 1

Pauline was well up in years when she sold her mansion and bought back her family's old farm in northern Wisconsin. Her five grown children had protested mightily.

Her baby, Doctor Dorothy, didn't want her living alone, so far from help. "I'll get one of those trouble beepers and Dorothy, you will be only twenty minutes away at the hospital."

Stuart worried about who would do the heavy work, like mowing the lawn. "I'll rent my fields to Dave, on the next farm, in return for handyman help from him and his sons."

"What about the furniture and china and all the other valuables?" Sara squawked.

"I have listed what I'll take with me," Pauline said. "If you want some of my things, this is how we'll do it. You can take turns choosing from the other things. If anyone gets disagreeable, we'll stop and I'll auction all of it and give the money to charity."

"But you can't . . ." The cat was already at the cream -- she'd outflanked them again -- their protests died.

Predictably, Stuart chose things like his father's desk and artistic Mary picked paintings and art work. Sentimental Dorothy wanted the old Christmas tree decorations  and the thimbles Pauline had collected traveling with her second husband, Tom. Alec selected several good paintings and antiques, enough to get him out of his current financial difficulties. Sara, the little princess gone sour, flinched every time someone picked an expensive item, but she managed to acquire most of the costly pieces.

Pauline put the mansion on the market and hired remodeling done at the farm: new wood floors, a new furnace, reroofing, wallpaper (a quiet floral pattern in greens and blues for the living room), a bigger bathroom, fresh white paint on the outside; reluctantly she replaced the old six over six windows with their wavy glass -- new triple-paned windows would be much more energy efficient and she needed warmth that she hadn't needed when she was young. Creaking steps and doors brought back memories; those she kept.

She moved back in the spring, in time to put in a garden, and took up housecleaning again, after years of having servants do it; she tended the garden, canned, read, and entertained old friends. Pauline enjoyed ten quiet years. Then the strokes came and she had to have help with everything, even getting in and out of the shower.

Sandy pushed Pauline's wheelchair into the grocery store out of the nasty weather; it was one of those cold, wet, windy days in September when people wondered how they would ever survive the sub-zero temperatures of January. "Now get the footrests out," Pauline ordered. Sandy tried to move the left one into position as a woman almost backed into the right side pulling a grocery cart loose.

"Oh, I'm sorry." She noticed that Sandy couldn't get the footrest around, so she reached down, flipped the lever and pushed the right footrest down and around.

Pauline spoke gruffly, "Thank you. How did you know what to do?"

"I'm a home health aide. I worked with a woman in a wheelchair last year until she had to go into a nursing home."

Pauline stared at the tall woman; she had a grandmotherly plumpness and a bit of gray mixed in with her dark brown hair. "Can you cook?" Pauline asked.

She laughed. "Can I cook? Well, I'm definitely not a gourmet cook, but I make a fantastic bean soup and beef stew and things like that."

"You want to work for me?" Pauline asked.

The tall woman sized up the shriveled body, the wrinkled skin, the gray hair and settled on the feisty, gray eyes. "Yeah, I think I'd like that."

Pauline grinned. "I'm Pauline Johnson. This is Sandy Gray. And you?"

"Maggie O'Neill."

Pauline told Sandy to go ahead and start shopping. After she left, Pauline said to Maggie, "Sandy is a very good cleaner, but she's about as colorful as her name and so is her cooking. You can be my cook-helper; she can clean and do laundry."

"Sounds good to me," Maggie replied. "I'd like to work just five days a week. Could she do the other two?"

"Yes. She could do the cleaning and laundry on those days. I'll start you out at the same pay as the agency. If I like you after two weeks, you name your own pay."

Maggie grinned. She decided. She said, "$20 an hour plus expenses would be nice, though if I like you after two weeks, I'd probably be willing to work even for agency pay."

# 2

"Pauline, it's me, Maggie O'Neill," she announced as she came in the back door for the first time. (Everybody had always used the back door except those who didn't know better). Maggie walked to the small bedroom, which barely had room for a dresser, chest of drawers, a catchall kitchen chair, a commode and hospital bed. Lying in bed, Pauline blinked when Maggie turned on the bedroom light. "Hi, Pauline. How are you this morning?"

"I'd be much happier if I was meeting you for a card game instead of needing your help," Pauline answered.

Maggie looked at the spunky little woman. "So would I," she said quietly. Maggie moved the commode away from the bed, then said, "Tell me what to do."

"First, turn the heat up to 75 in the dining room and 80 in the bathroom. And open the curtains."

"Okay."

After Maggie came back, Pauline sat up, using her left arm and the railing; she swung her left leg over the edge of the bed and dragged her right leg after it. Maggie reached over and pulled it around.

"I can do that!" Pauline protested.

"I know you can because you used the commode by yourself last night. Do you *want* me to do it?"

Pauline frowned. "Oh, all right. Now bring that towel off the dresser and put it on the back and seat of the wheelchair. Put the wheelchair next to the bed where the commode was and set the walker in front of me."

Pauline scooted forward off the bed, stood up, and used the walker for balance as she turned her backside to the wheelchair. Maggie held the walker in place as Pauline sat/fell in the wheelchair. Maggie wheeled her toward the bathroom. Outside the bathroom, Pauline ordered, "Stop here. Bring me the walker."

While Pauline used the toilet, Maggie checked the bedding, which was dry, and gathered Pauline's clothes.

"I want a shower this morning."

"Okay."

Pauline used the walker to get to the shower; then she used her left hand to move her right hand to the floor-to-ceiling pole just outside the shower. Maggie moved the walker out of the way. With her left hand, Pauline took hold of the grab bar just inside the shower and lifted her left foot into the shower. With her left hand, she moved her right hand from the pole to the grab bar across the shower and took hold of the other bar with her left hand again. "Now lift my right foot into the shower." Maggie did. Pauline pulled herself in and sat on the plastic chair.

Pauline washed wherever she could reach and Maggie did the rest. Maggie had such a very gentle touch that Pauline found herself enjoying her shower. "Do you want me to shampoo your hair?"

"Yes."

"This movable shower head is handy. I can rinse you off without you moving at all."

Pauline bragged, "My son Stuart put that in. He added the grab bars, too."

"How many kids do you have?"

"Stuart is the oldest and then there's Mary, Sara, Alec and Dorothy."

"And your husband?" Maggie asked.

"My children's father, Andy Anderson, died in 1960. Six years later, I married Tom Johnson. He died in '86."

"Sounds like you've had some tough times."

After her shower, Pauline sat in her wheelchair at the dining room table. It's well-made simplicity, which accentuated the beauty of the wood, had made it one of the few pieces of furniture she had brought from the mansion. The matching chairs and china cupboard came too, though the cupboard contained lovely, inexpensive treasures here.

"What would you like for breakfast?"

Pauline knew exactly what she wanted. "An orange, oatmeal with raisins and brown sugar, cranberry juice, cocoa, water."

"Coming right up."

After breakfast dishes were done, Maggie set Pauline's hair. "What shall I fix for lunch?"

"I haven't had any good stew for ages!"

"What do you want in it?"

"Beef, potatoes, carrots, onions, celery and plenty of spices."

Maggie checked the refrigerator, the freezer and the cupboards. "Pauline, you have garlic, parsley and salt, but that won't make stew. All you have is frozen pot pies, TV dinners and the like. How about if we make out menus for a week and go shopping? I'll fix a simple lunch today and tomorrow I'll cook up a storm. Oh, that won't work. Your hair's still wet."

"There's a hair dryer in the bathroom cupboard. I know what we'll do. I don't really like shopping at Mackerel Market. Their prices are high and their selection is poor. Let's go to Little Fork, have lunch there and then shop."

Maggie found a pencil and paper. "What are you hungry for?"

"Beef stew, meat loaf, ham and rutemas, fried chicken and mashed potatoes, a cheeseburger, barbecued pork ribs, . . ."

"Slow down! Ham and what?"

"Rutemas are mashed potatoes and mashed rutabagas mixed together, topped with white sauce."

"Got it."

After listing everything they would need for dinners, they did breakfasts and suppers, which Pauline liked light. Maggie checked to see what was on hand -- the grocery list was long.

Maggie pushed Pauline's wheelchair out the front door, down the ramp and next to the rear door of her Toyota. With the wheelchair's brakes on, she opened the front door and put the walker in front of Pauline. Pauline stood up, took hold of the walker and Maggie pulled the wheelchair away. Pauline used the walker to turn backside to the car; then she sat down. She lifted her left leg in and Maggie lifted the right leg in.

After Maggie sat down in the driver's seat she grinned at Pauline and said, "It's crisply cool and grandly sunny, a great day to be out and about."

As they drove past a small, old white building, Pauline said, "That's where I went to school. Stuart went there, too, until they closed it down and they all went to Cranberry Town to school, then. Cranberry Town has grown a little since then, but not much; I heard the other day that they had about thirteen hundred people now.

"Anyway, when I was in school, we always had a Christmas program, at night. We would sing and recite poems; Santa would come with his presents, then. We each received a bag with a little maple sugar candy, an orange and other rare treats. I think my mother got the maple sugar candy from the Indians. That was the best present, that and the orange. Long after I knew the truth about Santa, I still looked forward to his special gifts. Now I can have oranges every day, but maple sugar candy, I haven't had that since my school days."

"When did the school close down?"

"1955."

"I didn't know that one-room schoolhouses were being used that recently." Then Maggie asked, "Shall we buy gas in Mackerel? It's usually cheaper than in Little Fork." Maggie groaned. "You know, when I moved to Bear County nearly thirty years ago, gas cost only thirty to thirty-three cents a gallon; now it's about *two dollars* a gallon. But why am I acting so chintzy about pennies, when you're paying for it?"

Pauline laughed, too. "My second husband was as rich as my first one was poor. Tom wanted me to feel free to spend his money. But I was forty-odd years of set in my frugal ways and now I'm even more so. Let's get gas in holy Mackerel."

After Maggie put gas in the car, Pauline said, "The population of Mackerel hasn't changed much over the years, but not a store or office in Mackerel is the same as when I was young. The grocery store was on Main Street, the post office was two blocks west of where it is now, the Mackerel Mercantile Store was torn down, Moren and Anderson's furniture and hardware is gone, the library is in the old bank building.

"Even the Community Center has changed. During the Depression, when I was a child, Roosevelt had pushed through a bill providing money for government work projects; the jobs and the money helped stimulate the dormant economy. They built the Community Center as a WPA project. People used it for town meetings, club meetings, political meetings, dances, and socials. In the sixties and seventies, it was a movie theater. Then the Lions remodeled it. You can see the old windows used to be about eight feet high; they covered over the top halves, to save on heat. They fixed it up inside and now it hosts meetings, wedding receptions, luncheons and Lions' Bingo."

"I've never stayed in one place long enough to see that much change. That's mind-boggling!"

"I don't mean to say all changes are bad. When my parents were young, just after the turn of the century, most folks around here walked the twenty miles to Cranberry Town for groceries and mail. Rather than carry a hundred-pound bag of flour for twenty miles, my father made a cart with wooden wheels which he could pull along the path that used to serve as a road. And a hundred years later, here we are, driving fifty miles to a grocery store in an hour."

They were driving along County Road A when Pauline saw another one-room schoolhouse. "There's the Orange School, where my mother went to school. She used to talk about the O'Hara kids. Their father donated land for the school and for a church and started the local post office. Where we now have three schools and three post offices, when I was young there were dozens of each, because people still had to walk everywhere.

"Mr. O'Hara was French, Irish and Indian but his wife spoke mostly Norwegian; so their kids had an Irish name, with French and Indian blood; my mother said the O'Hara children knew more of the Norwegian language than some full-blooded Norwegians. There was an article in last week's paper about Pierre O'Hara celebrating his one hundredth birthday. I wonder if he remembers my mother. Would you take me to visit him some day?"

"Sure," Maggie said. "I'll bet he can tell a lot of great stories. I'd like that," Maggie said. "A lot of the homes along here are new since I moved here. The whole county has a lot of new homes."

"You're right. The towns haven't increased their

populations much, but Bear County has; the population has gone from nine thousand to over fifteen thousand in the last thirty years." They drove past more small woods and small farms. Most of the farms provided a place to live and work; both husband and wife probably had a job in town or ran a small business out of their home in order to earn a living. Modest to grand retirement homes surrounded the larger lakes.

After breakfast the next day, Maggie chopped the beef into small chunks and started them boiling with the onion, garlic, parsley, sage, oregano and thyme. Then she tidied up and did the breakfast dishes.

"Pauline, do you want to help me with vegetables for the stew?" The question surprised Pauline, so Maggie said, "I'll clean and peel; you can chop." Pauline realized she could chop so she readily agreed.

At the small kitchen work table, Pauline used her right hand to hold the celery in place and cut with her left hand; it was awkward, but it worked. Shared kitchen work is conducive to confidences. As she chopped, Pauline told Maggie about selling her mansion. "You know, I was tempted to modernize the kitchen when I bought this place. I thought I might miss all the gadgets I had in the kitchen at the mansion. But I never did much cooking when I lived there because Tom had a cook and even a cleaning lady. Maybe that's why the mansion never seemed like home to me. Well, I did bring my microwave and a few other time-savers, but this is my kitchen, the heart of my home. Until a year ago, I used my wire whip instead of a blender and I mixed meat loaf with my fingers instead of with a heavy-duty mixer: neither machines nor hired cooks came between me and my work."

Of course, they sampled before it was quite finished. "It needs a bit more garlic." "Maybe more salt."

At lunch, Pauline relished every bite of the stew and the baking powder biscuits they had made. Her great pleasure was so contagious, it turned the meal into a celebration. When she finished, she sat back in her wheelchair and smiled with great satisfaction. "Best stew

I ever ate," she told Maggie.

"It's fun cooking for someone who enjoys a meal as much as you do."

"I don't have to wait two weeks to decide. You're hired if you want the job. Twenty dollars an hour, you said?"

Maggie grinned. "Can you afford that?"

"I can. I'm quite rich."

"All right. I think I'm really going to like working with you."

Pauline sighed, greatly relieved.

Maggie asked, "What is it?"

Desolation passed across Pauline's face. "This last year has been very difficult. My third stroke put me in a nursing home for six months. When I could finally come home, my doctor daughter insisted that I have help. She went to the agency, which provided six women a week to do two four-hour shifts a day. Just about every week there was someone new; it was an endless parade of well-meaning, underpaid helpers."

Pauline seemed reluctant to criticize the women who had helped her. "So there I was, useless, dependent on strangers for my basic needs, a burden to my children; I didn't want any of my friends to see me when I was so miserable. In other words, I was suffocating myself in self-pity. I woke up two days ago and realized I was tired of being miserable. I decided to change things. Choosing you to help me was a deliberately impulsive decision, and definitely serendipitous." Pauline smiled at Maggie. "Now, I think things are looking up."

Maggie sensed that the strokes had not only stripped Pauline of control over her life, but had even stolen all her small pleasures because few of her helpers had bothered to find out what she liked. She resolved to give Pauline bushels of reasons to smile every day, starting with food that Pauline liked at every meal. Maggie smiled back at Pauline, "Things are looking *way* up."

After supper that night, Maggie said, "Pauline, I noticed you have some great old children's books in your bookcase."

"Yes. When my children moved out, they didn't want the books, so I kept them. I've read them often; now my eyes aren't good enough to read anymore, but I still can't throw them out."

Maggie asked, "Would you like for me to read them to you?" Pauline's delighted smile was her answer. Maggie walked over to the bookcase. "What would you like first, Wizard of Oz, Pippi Longstocking, Secret Garden, Wind in the Willows, Anne of Green Gables . . .?"

"Anne of Green Gables!"

Maggie read with great Irish gusto and Pauline reacted vigorously. She shook her head from side to side, silently scolding Rachel for disapproving of the orphan coming to help Marilla and Matthew. She nodded in sympathy as the passionately talkative little red-haired Anne overwhelmed poor shy Matthew with her wildly imaginative chatter.

Pauline's daughter stopped in. "Dorothy, this is Maggie. She'll be helping me now. Maggie, is there any stew left?"

"Yes. Shall I warm some up for Dorothy?"

Dorothy protested, "No, I can do it. You keep on reading."

Eating at the dining room table, Dorothy saw her mother's frown as Maggie read that Matthew thought Marilla would make him take Anne back; Pauline almost cried when Marilla made it clear that Anne must return to the orphanage. When she finished eating, Dorothy went to sit on the sofa, opposite Maggie in a rocking chair and Pauline in her lift chair. "Don't stop." Maggie read on. Of course, her audience wouldn't let Maggie quit reading until Marilla finally decided to keep Anne; that was fifty pages into the book. When she stopped, no one spoke for a moment; they let the charm of the story fall gently away.

Pauline looked at Dorothy. "I've found a kindred spirit. And she can cook, too."

"Did you make the stew, Maggie?" Dorothy asked.

"We both did," she replied.

17

"I haven't had stew that good since I was a kid! Mom, you're terrible. You told me you'd picked up a stranger in the grocery store to be your helper. You had me all worried." Pauline just grinned. "Well, Maggie, maybe you can talk Mom into doing her exercises." Pauline quit grinning and put on her stubborn face.

When she left that night, Maggie remembered Pauline's comment. "Goodnight, kindred spirit."

"Goodnight."

### Pauline's Beef Stew

1 lb. chuck roast, cut in chunks
1 medium onion
1 t salt
1 t beef soup base
2 t garlic
2 t parsley
½ t thyme
½ t sage
½ t oregano
Cover with water, simmer until beef is almost tender, 2-3 hours, then add the following
2 large potatoes, in chunks
2 carrots, sliced thinly
1 stick celery, chopped
Add enough water to cover vegetables. Simmer until tender, about another hour. Drain, put liquid in separate pan. Put ½ cup cold water and 2 T flour in a tightly covered jar, shake until well mixed, add flour-water to stew-water, boil for 1 minute, wire whipping constantly. Pour over meat and vegetables.
To make *Maggie's Irish Stew*, substitute lamb or mutton for the chuck roast, omit spices except salt and pepper

# 3

The next morning at breakfast, Maggie said, "I know you don't want to do your exercises, but how about going to the water exercises at the pool?"

"What?"

"At the pool, ten o'clock Tuesdays and Fridays, there's an exercise hour. Jenine says to move your arms this way and that and move your legs here and there. You can move just as fast or slow as you want. There's even a chair lift; you sit in it and it lowers you into the water and lifts you out again."

Pauline found an excuse, "But what if I have another stroke?"

"Do you really want to stop having fun because you *might* have another stroke? Besides, the water is so relaxing it's very unlikely, but I'll be right next to you all the time, just in case."

She had another excuse too, "I don't have a swim suit."

"We'll get you one."

Trying on swim suits was a very trying experience, but Pauline had made up her mind and nothing could stop her. Pauline said, "I think I'll like swimming again. I used to love it, but I haven't been since I was first married."

In the pool, Pauline exclaimed, "Brownie, Betty Ann, I didn't know you'd be here! It's been a long time!"

"Hi Pauline. Good to see you."

Pauline held onto the edge with her left hand and Maggie held her right arm. She walked very slowly along the shallow end. "Oh, this feels so good. You said the water was warm and it really is." They walked along the edge into deeper water, until it was chest-deep for Pauline. "Remember, Pauline, just do what you can. If you feel tired, you can stop, any time," Maggie said.

Jenine started. "Face the deep end, cross your leg over and push your hips toward the edge; keep your shoulders level."

Maggie stood right next to Pauline, helping her understand how to move, laughing with her over nothing.

Jenine called out, "Roll your shoulders."

After a while, Pauline told Brownie, "We passed the Karlsburg school on our way here. It seems like another world, back when I went to school there."

Brownie agreed emphatically, "It was another world! When I was a year old, our house burned down. The neighbors helped my father build a new one. Nowadays, nobody builds his own house and the neighbors aren't there helping. Our bedroom was upstairs. In the winter, Mother would put the Sears' catalogs in the oven and then in our beds to warm our feet; if it snowed at night, we woke up with snow on our bed; it would blow in through cracks between the windows and the frame."

"Stand tall," Jenine said.

Brownie went on, "Our new house was only two miles from the Orange School, so I had to walk. We wore long johns and knee stockings. On really cold days, our teacher had to start the fire in the wood stove by six o'clock so it would be warm when we got there. It seemed warm to us then, but it was probably only about fifty or sixty degrees.

"There were two outhouses, one for the boys and one for the girls; they each had three holes. I always hated to go out there in the winter because it was so cold and the boys always threw snowballs at us girls when we went to the outhouse; then our teacher found out about it and kept all the boys in the schoolhouse whenever the girls went. I learned never to complain about the outhouse to my cousin Jane, though. She went to Trade Lake school and they had indoor flush toilets! She loved the opportunity to tease me about our outhouses."

"Right leg out to the side and down; left leg out and down," Jenine directed.

Betty Ann added her memories. "I was too young for school when my friends started at Jackson School, the next school west of the Orange School. I made such a fuss that my sister Gertrude, who had finished school, talked to her friend who was the teacher. The teacher gave Gertrude the books and my sister taught me at home. Mr. Nelson, our superintendent of schools, said that if I could pass all the first grade tests, I could start in second grade. I passed and skipped first grade. They'd never let kids do that now.

"When I went to high school in town, I found that those of us who went to country schools were way ahead of the 'town kids.' During the war, World War II that is, we had school on Saturdays and we had very few vacation days. That way school could go from the end of September to early May and the boys could work the farms to get in the extra crops needed during the war."

"Circle your whole leg." Jenine inserted the next move into the conversation as Betty Ann paused.

Betty Ann continued, "After I graduated from high school, in 1946, my Dad saw an ad: bookkeeper wanted at the creamery in Mackerel. I was good in arithmetic, so Dad thought I should try it. I don't think they would have hired me if they'd known I was only sixteen, but I got the job. At that time, the creamery had a full grocery store upstairs and a feed store; they bought milk and shipped it out; some farmers brought in only cream (they fed the skimmed milk to pigs and calves) and the creamery made that into butter.

"I kept the books for everything. The adding machine would only add, not multiply. So to multiply 654x32, I had to add 654+654+6540+6540+6540. I did my job well and after a year, they bought a new adding machine that would also multiply. When I wasn't working on the books, I would wrap butter in parchment paper or help with other odd jobs."

"Could we interrupt these great stories long enough to can-can?" Jenine asked the women. She started singing, "Ta-ra-ra-boom-de-ay, ta-ra-ra-boom-de-ay . . ." Then, "Rotate your arms and your legs,"

Joan told a little story. "When I started school, the kids teased me about my freckles rather than about my red hair." Her tanned arm was *very* freckled. "But my grandmother told me the freckles were where angels had kissed me, so I never minded."

Adeline remembered, "I went to a one-room school, too, down near Ellsworth. I liked learning about famous artists. Our teacher received a monthly magazine with short biographies of artists and small copies of one of their paintings for each of us students. I still have them, mounted in a homemade scrapbook."

"Row, row, row your boat . . ." Jenine started singing, which was the signal for jumping jacks. Jenine had explained that she really wanted everyone to sing with her, because then if she went off-key, they wouldn't notice; usually the exercisers cooperated, though it interrupted their conversations. After that, "Lunge forward"

Catherine had another ingredient for the story stew. "I grew up in the thirties on a farm which is now part of St. Paul. My father was a wonderful storyteller and a very poor provider. My mother grew strawberries, apples, asparagus, anything she could sell. Fritz Kreissler, the world-famous violinist, came to the Cities in 1940 for a concert. My father used his storytelling magic on a friendly merchant, who loaned him money to buy third-row seats for the concert. My mother nearly had a heart attack! Until his turn came, Fritz Kreissler watched the orchestra with his tongue sticking out. He looked like the village idiot. But when he played, it was magnificent, the most wonderful music you could ever imagine. My father's foolishness enriched my life."

"Lunge to the side."

Florence smiled shyly; Pauline could see the 18-year-old in the 95-year-old woman. Florence told them, "I was born and raised in Chicago. Every summer, I would visit my cousins who lived on a farm near Tony, Wisconsin. I helped with the gardening, cooking, and doing dishes. Every Saturday night we went to a dance. My parents never allowed me to go to dances in Chicago, so I felt a little wicked, but I went anyway. The dances were fun and that's where I met Chuck, when I was 18. My cousin and I double-dated; we went to an ice cream social at the Baptist Church in Tony. Chuck was with my cousin and I was with Alvin. During the evening, Chuck said, 'Let's change partners.' We did, and we became life partners, but not right away. At home, I dated Jack. I liked them both, so Jack was my winter boy friend and Chuck was my summer boy friend, for ten years. I didn't want to marry yet and then the Depression came. I finally married Chuck in 1933; we were both 28 years old."

"Frog jump." Jenine said.

"Sure and it was all Judy's fault," Maggie claimed, shifting into a bit of brogue as she told a story about her childhood. "I always got to my Catholic school in plenty of time for Mass. But in Kansas City, where I grew up, we didn't have much snow, don't you know. I was a wee lass in the late forties when we woke up to several inches of snow on the ground. Dressed in snowsuit and galoshes, I was, as I studied the snow on my way to school: what it felt like making new footprints in the snow, what the bushes looked like in their snowy dresses, what it sounded like when a tree dropped a snowball on my head. Judy caught up with me just as I reached Quivira Lake Road. After that, the houses sat up on a steep hill, fifteen feet high it was. Judy ran up the less steep driveway, sat down at the top of the hill, pushed off and down she came. It looked like fun, so I tried it, too. What a thrill! I never had so much excitement in all my life. Up and down, up and down, giggling all the while.

"We missed Mass and the first half hour of school. Sister Hildegarde asked why we were late. I was scared and embarrassed to be sure, but Judy didn't seem a bit worried; she said it was the snow. Sister Hildegarde wanted to know how our uniform skirts got so wet. Judy told her we fell down.

"I *knew* our teacher knew that Judy was bending the truth a bit, but she just told us to stand by the radiator in back until we were dry. The shame of our wickedness was terrible, but then I looked at Judy, thinking, 'We got away with it!' We both started to giggle. Sister Hildegarde stopped talking and gave us a stern look. Somehow, we both knew that our punishment was stiff indeed: we had to work very hard and behave perfectly or else!"

Jan said, "I remember some summer mischief, before I started fifth grade, about a hundred miles west of here; it must have been about 1940. One hot summer day, my friend Ellie and I decided we just had to have a watermelon. We didn't have any money. We could swipe one! We walked the two miles to Mr. Finstad's farm, getting hotter, thirstier and less excited as we went.

"We were almost to his watermelon patch when he drove up in his ancient car. 'Hey girls, why don't you go over to my watermelon patch and pick one out for yourselves?'

"We did. We had to carry it all the way home because we forgot to take a knife with us. After all that, it wasn't much good. Mr. Finstad had ruined everything by giving it to us."

When Pauline looked tired, Maggie helped her to the lift chair where she sat for a few minutes. When the hour was over, Pauline said, "I'd like to stay until next week." They laughed and got out anyway.

On their way home, Pauline said, "Stories like the women were telling today bring back another life." After a moment, she continued, "It seems to me that I've lived many lives: in my first life, I was a child; in my second I was a teacher; in my third I was a wife with a charming, irresponsible husband and five children; in my fourth, I was a poor widow trying to be father and mother to my children; in my fifth, I was a rich wife and mother and in my sixth a rich widow who arranged her own life; after the strokes, I gave up, but now, I think there is a fine new life ahead."

Several weeks later, Maggie told Pauline, "There's a concert of Shostakovich music in Minneapolis next month. I've noticed you have some of his records. Would you like to go to the concert with me?"

Pauline just stared at Maggie. Then, "Do you really mean that?"

"I don't say things I don't mean." Maggie grinned.

Pauline's eyes went teary. "My husband Tom and I went to concerts; we learned to appreciate good music together. I'd love to go, but are you sure you can manage . . . Of course you are. Yes, let's do it."

"I thought we could go early, have dinner and then go to the concert, if that suits you."

"We can take my old Buick. Now that Norm has fixed it all up, it runs beautifully and it's easier for me to get out of."

On the way to Minneapolis, Maggie said, "You told me that you named your daughter Sara after The Little Princess' Sara. What about your other kids?"

Pauline replied, "Let's see, that goes back to my third life, when I was married to Andy. He ridiculed the name I gave our firstborn. 'You can't name a kid after a mouse!' But I did. Stuart Little had a great sense of adventure and a wonderful zest for life. I told Andy we didn't have to tell anyone. He could say we named the boy after the English and Scottish Kings if he wanted. I never did tell Stuart where his name came from. By the time he was old enough to understand, it was obvious: Stuart was considerate, helpful, generous -- he was loaded with tons of virtues, but not an ounce of adventure."

"Where did you get Dorothy's name?"

"From The Wizard of Oz, of course. And my Dorothy did come back home. She settled in the nearest town here and she is a doctor at the hospital. It's ironic. She was only six when I married Tom and we moved to Minneapolis, so she hardly remembers those rough times. Maybe that's why she moved back."

Maggie asked, "Why were those rough times?"

"Andy and I had a few good years together, but then I became pregnant the third time and he lost his job. Responsibility always was his short suit. He worked on and off after that, but he didn't mind too much because he'd found his true love, booze. After Sara was born, I went back to teaching. My father had died, so we moved in with Mother and she took care of the kids for me. Alec and Dorothy were born after Sara and while I was pregnant, they wouldn't let me teach. We had some hungry days. Six years we lived like that and finally Andy killed himself, in a car accident; he drove drunk once too often.

"After Andy died, we had some quiet years. With Mom helping at home, I kept teaching. Back then, even with degrees and experience, teachers' salaries were low and they paid women even less than men; there wasn't much money for seven of us, but we got by."

"Was Alec named for The Black Stallion's Alec?"

"You guessed it. Alec in the book was a strong resourceful boy. When life handed him a problem, he solved it. Just the opposite of my Alec."

"And Mary?"

Pauline answered, "Why, Mary of The Secret Garden."

"Of course."

"My Mary doesn't garden, but she does get out of herself when she paints."

Maggie said, "Of all your children, I like Stuart best."

"He has his father's easy charm which balances all those virtues. Everybody likes him."

Maggie commented, "But no Anne of Green Gables."

"Anne is my favorite, but I was afraid to name a child after an orphan."

At dinner, Maggie said, "You know, Pauline, one of the many things I like about you is you know when to talk, when to listen and when to concentrate on eating. I'm glad you talked me into getting lobster. This is 'supermelagorgeous beyond which there isn't any whicher.' And with that nice raise on top of an already nice wage, I can even afford to have it again. But we aren't being very frugal." Maggie didn't sound a bit worried.

"Frugality is for necessities; we save on them in order to have our delightful splurges. Now be quiet and eat." Maggie obeyed.

Maggie used the handicapped parking, so she

didn't have to push Pauline's wheelchair as far. Because of the wheelchair, they sat in the back for the concert, separate from the others, which was fortunate, because as the orchestra galoped, waltzed and polkaed merrily and gloriously along, Pauline whispered to Maggie, "The sleighs are having a wild race in the moonlight." Maggie listened then nodded in agreement. Maggie felt the next piece as a circus parade; Pauline did, too. Then Pauline heard the coffee pot perking; company was coming. A sad piece told of Father out of work in the middle of winter with a sick child and no one to help.

As she tucked Pauline in bed that night, Maggie squeezed her hand and said, "Pauline, I've been to other concerts, but I've never enjoyed one as much. Sharing it with you was so special, I don't even know how to say it." She kissed Pauline's wet, smiling cheek.

"I know."

# 4

As she walked into Pauline's bedroom a few mornings later, Maggie said, "Hi, Pauline."

Pauline noticed that Maggie seemed sad. "What's wrong, Maggie?"

"My dog had a seizure last night. He's old and arthritic and he hates going to the vet. Keeping him alive would be cruel. So I took him to the vet and had him put to sleep." Maggie pushed a tear away. Pauline reached out and took Maggie's hand. They were quiet for a few minutes and then Maggie said, "You're a good friend, Pauline." After that, they moved on to the daily routine.

The next morning, Maggie told Pauline, "I was feeling all alone in my house last night without Rusty. I opened the windows as usual and went to bed. About three o'clock this morning, a noise woke me up. I figured it was a bat flying around and I hoped it was outside. I turned on the light. It was in my bedroom. Bats are good because they eat mosquitos and other bugs. But I *don't like them in my house*. It flew around the bedroom a few times and then flew out to the living room.

"Back when I was in college, I spent some evenings in the dorm, studying for tests with my friends; if a bat came flying along, all the girls would scream and hide under a desk or something dumb. So, just to be different, I'd take up a broom or a dust mop and swat at it until I killed it or it disappeared. Now there's nobody to show off for and I feel just as scared as those girls felt. So last night I shut the bedroom door and stuffed rags across the bottom so I could sleep in peace. And I yelled at the bat to get out of my house. Do you think it will leave?"

Pauline laughed. "I couldn't begin to count all the bats we've had in this house."

"What did you do about them?"

"Sometimes we chased them out. Sometimes we just let them be, especially if they were in the walls."

"I know it's silly, but I really don't like them. They're fine outside, but not in my house." A moment later, Maggie said, "I almost forgot. My friend Jo and I picked blueberries last summer and I froze most of them. I brought some with me this morning. Would you like blueberry pancakes for breakfast?"

Pauline exclaimed, "I love blueberry pancakes!"

Monday morning, Maggie told Pauline about another problem. Rust collected in the pipes because she lived alone and didn't use much water. Every now and then it broke loose as air in the pipes caused the faucets to spit and sputter; for several days her water would be so rusty she couldn't see to the bottom of the toilet bowl. But the bat hadn't come back.

Maggie said, "My friend Teresa told me if I hold my tennis racket up instead of swinging it, I can stun the bat, scoop it up on a dustpan and take it outside to let it go

28

free. That's better than killing it. She and her husband came over to get rid of Rusty's chair. He dripped urine on it lately and the upholstery was worn, so I was glad to get rid of it. I thought of saving the mattress (it pulled out into a bed) but I found the urine smell had penetrated that, too. That didn't matter, but then I realized that my hide-a-bed sofa would smell, too. Thanks to your great pay, I could afford to buy a new one, but the colors of the new ones are just plain *ugly*! I guess I'll see if sunshine and baking soda will take care of it." Then she asked, "Pauline, how about scrambled eggs and my special blueberry muffins for breakfast?" She grated half an apple into the batter, which accentuated the delicious flavors.

"Yes!"

A week later, Maggie's water was still rusty and the hide-a-bed mattress and cushions still stank, but at least the bat hadn't come back. A snake snuck into her garage. She chased it out but knew it would be back if she didn't block its entrance.

Rusty's death had slowed her brain, but she finally searched around the outside of her house. Her dead patio tomato plant sat in a large, rusty pan. She found several boards with rusty nails in them and an old truck tire on a rusty rim. She couldn't budge the tire, but got rid of the other rust-makers. She talked to Bruce at the hardware store; he told her to  take the old thingumgoochie off the water tank and put on a new one. She did and the faucets stopped spitting.

She remembered when she was small, she would follow her dad around as he fixed the toilet or put in a new doorbell. He had all the gadgets he wanted from his hardware store and he loved working with them. Maggie loved to watch her father tinker, but after a while, her father laughed her away, because "This is man's work; go help your mother." As a grown-up, sometimes Maggie felt as handy as a raccoon taking things apart and other times as handy as a raccoon trying to put them back together.

That night as Maggie sat reading at home, a bat flew into her living room from the kitchen. As she stood up, she grabbed the tennis racket off the coffee table. She intended to stun the bat but when it flew toward her, she swatted. The bat circled anxiously. Maggie swung and missed, six times before she got mad and determined. Then she missed it six more times before she finally hit it. She put the racket on top of it, just in case it wasn't dead and went to get the dust pan to pick it up.

As she reached to the floor of the kitchen closet, movement caught her eye. Another bat! Bad enough to kill one bat, but two, and how many more? She grabbed the dust mop, swung it and missed three times before the bat flew down the open staircase to the basement. Maggie scooped up the dead bat and threw it outside, then grabbed her book and barricaded herself in the bedroom for the night.

Maggie told Pauline about the bats the next day. She growled and swung an imaginary tennis racket as she told about the first bat and whimpered as she described the second one. "I was feeling so put upon that if some man had come along and said, 'If you marry me, I'll be your fixer-upper,' I probably would have agreed. Sometimes the emotional cost of independence seems as exorbitant as today's gas prices!"

"I think it was Will Rogers who had the answer to that; only cars that are paid for should be allowed on the road. That would bring gas prices down."

Just before she left Pauline, Maggie asked her, "Pauline, what do you do to me? Lately when I come here, I've been feeling very sorry for myself and swamped with all the things I have to take care of. But when I tell you about my trials and tribulations, pretty soon you have me laughing at myself. I just can't take myself too seriously when I'm around you."

Maggie called Tim. "I have bats in my house. Could you please come over and fill all the holes so they can't get in?"

"Sure. Will you be home tomorrow evening?"

"Yes."

"I'll come over and see what we need to do."

"Okay. Thanks."

Several days later, Tim brought three young men to caulk and nail all the holes. His assistants worked inside, efficiently and quietly, except when the nail gun belched. Outside, the peaked sides had flat boards from the roof down to the round logs. The boards had warped; Tim squirted caulking behind them and nailed them tight. He put a new rubber seal at the bottom of the garage door to keep the snake out. And he put the old truck tire onto his pickup.

They finished in two hours. Maggie was greatly relieved to have it done and to have someone else do it. She told Pauline all about the bat man and his three robins.

Maggie took the cover off one of the sofa cushions to see about cleaning it up and found that the foam rubber was crumbling. She decided to wash the cushion covers in the washing machine, replace the foam and use a rinse-'n-vac to clean the rest of the sofa. That night, she thought "About the only thing that hasn't gone wrong is that my water bed isn't leaking." So she checked it and sure enough, it was leaking. She put vinyl glue on the holes, cleaned out all the water that had leaked and added more water.

When Maggie put the vinyl glue back in the junk drawer, she decided to clean it out. She threw out this and that, things she had forgotten the uses of. She found an adapter that would screw in before the light bulb; it had a short chain attached. Just what she'd always wanted, and it had been there since before her husband had died! When she bought her home, the second light in the basement had no switch or string; she had to reach up and screw the bulb in tightly to turn it on. She hadn't been able to reach it for years without standing on something, which was a nuisance. Maggie tied a string to the short chain, went to the basement, took out the bulb, screwed in the adapter and then the light bulb and pulled on the string a few times just for the fun of it. Eventually, she had everything in order. That evening, she asked

31

Pauline, "How should we celebrate?"
"Pineapple upside-down cake?"
"Yeah!"

# 5

A few days later, Maggie answered the doorbell at Pauline's. "Hello. I'm Adele Pinch. I'm here to talk to Pauline." Adele was tall and skinny with a skinny, shrill voice. Maggie stepped back to let her in and Adele barged right past her. Pauline sat in her wheel chair, watching Jeopardy; she knew the question for the answer and wanted to see if the contestants knew it.

Adele didn't wait. "I'm selling tickets for the library-sponsored salad luncheon to honor Local Living Legends; I brought you tickets here because you can afford them, even if you can't come to our fund-raiser." She inspected the china cupboard as she spoke.

Amazed, Pauline just looked at Adele.

Impatiently, Adele demanded to know, "Well, how many do you want?" She glanced at Pauline, then at the TV and the stereo.

"Mrs. Pinch, your rudeness is offensive. Leave my house."

"But you have to buy some tickets."

Adele was determined, but Maggie stepped toward her, with a mean look in her eye. Adele looked at Pauline. Pauline raised her arm and pointed to the door. "Out."

"But . . ."

"Out."

Maggie took a firm hold on Adele's arm and pulled her toward the door. Adele jerked loose. "All right, I'm going." But she paused at the back door to look at the lock.

Pauline called her friend, Doris Doppler, who had

an excellent radar for gossip.

"How are you doing?"

"Well, I'm having a terrible time. The arthritis in my hands is so bad, I can't do dishes or knit or anything."

After a while, Pauline switched Doris to her second favorite topic, gossip. "Who's president of the Friends of the Library these days?"

"Edna Dogoodly. Why?"

"A rather fierce woman, Adele Pinch, just stopped in to sell tickets for the salad luncheon. Her rudeness was appalling. I thought I'd better tell Edna to put her out to pasture before she scares everyone away from the luncheon."

Doris replied, "I've heard of Adele. She and her family moved up from the Cities about ten years ago. She knows all the answers and she demands that everything be done her way. She has a husband and two kids in high school, all pretty much browbeaten into little nobodies."

"Thanks, Doris. What else is new?" Twenty minutes later, Doris finished relating the recent gossip.

Pauline called Edna. "Edna, did you send Adele Pinch over here to sell me tickets to the salad luncheon?"

Edna laughed. "She ordered me to give her a job. I thought I'd send her to you because I knew you could handle her. Did you buy any tickets?"

"I did not. She was rude so I told her to leave. I had to repeat myself several times. She's less welcome here then mosquito bites on top of a bad sunburn. If you promise never to inflict her on me again, you can send me two tickets. What's it all about? She was so busy ordering me around that I forgot to listen to her."

"The Friends of the Library and the HCE clubs are giving a luncheon to raise money for a new copy machine for the library. Maxine, our ingenious and industrious librarian, suggested that we make it special by honoring some of the people who have been the backbone of our community, our Local Living Legends."

"I like that idea very much. Send me the tickets, then and I'll mail you a check." (Pauline sent a check,

33

which not only paid for two tickets, but also gave a sizable donation.)

"Thanks, Pauline."

As they ate lunch, Maggie said, "I didn't like the way she was looking at the things in your hutch."

"Yes, I noticed that, too."

Pauline thought for several minutes and then asked, "Maggie, would you help me prepare an ambush and stay tonight to see if it works?"

Maggie grinned. "Sure."

"You could leave your car at Dave's, down the road, so intruders won't see it. Would you also bake a batch of those peanut butter, chocolate chip cookies?"

Sitting back to back on the dark enclosed porch, Pauline watched the road to the south and Maggie watched to the north. They talked quietly to stay awake. At 2:30, Pauline saw car lights from over the hill, but then they went off. "They're coming."

They went into the living room. A few minutes later, a pickup with no lights drove up the driveway and in back of the house. The full moon, obscured by clouds, gave just enough light for Pauline and Maggie to see a dark shadow at the door; they heard the "key" unlocking the door. Pauline activated her trouble beeper, identified herself and the problem. When the door opened, a dozen pots and pans fell on the intruders' heads, clattering and banging. All the lights went on. "@#$%^& *%&$# %$#&%," a woman's voice shrieked.

Pauline held her trouble beeper in plain sight and spoke into it, "The intruders are Adele Pinch and a man I presume is her husband." To Adele, she said, "They have called the sheriff."

"How do you know who I am when I have a mask on?" Adele whined.

Pauline ignored her question. "What I don't understand is why you want to rob me. All those pretty things in the china cupboard were worth only a few hundred dollars when they were new. None of them are more than ten years old. Hardly worth the risk, I would think." She was stalling. "At any rate, the sheriff won't be here immediately, but there isn't enough time for you to rob me, because my neighbor will be here in a minute. If you look out the kitchen window, you will see that his lights are on. You might want to leave now."

Adele looked at the cupboard, as if she didn't believe Pauline. Her partner yelled, "Let's get out of here!" He grabbed her and pulled her out the door, rattling through the pans as they left.

When the pickup was gone, Dave came in, carrying his deer rifle. "That was perfect, Dave. Thank you so much." Pauline said.

"You planned it; I just followed orders."

Fifteen minutes later, Sheriff George Dogoodly (Edna's son and Pauline's former pupil) came with his deputy Henry and the two intruders; unmasked, they were as expected, Adele and Horace Pinch. "I found these two just over the hill from here, fussing about their flat tires. I brought them over to see if you might know them."

"Yes, they broke into my house a little while ago." Pauline answered the sheriff's questions. Dave told them he'd flattened the tires and written down the license plate number. Before they left, Pauline gave a bag of cookies to the sheriff, to his deputy and to Dave.

The next morning, Pauline visited Adele and Horace in jail. After talking to each of them separately, she decided that they were only sorry about getting caught, but that they weren't stupid enough to bother her again, so she didn't press charges.

# 6

As Pauline cut up celery and onions for bean soup, she said, "You know, Maggie, whenever I make bean soup I remember the first time I made it for Andy. I had everything in the kettle and the burner down low when Andy came in, full of high spirits, wanting to go joy riding. This was after the war, they didn't ration gas anymore. Our car was a '38 Chevy, but it still ran well nine years later. It was a day when spring was busting out all over and we laughed and sang and wandered around.

"When we finally came home, there was a fire truck in our driveway! And my soup kettle was a black ugly mess there in the yard. A neighbor down the road was going home and saw smoke pouring out the kitchen window so he called the fire department. It seems funny now, but at the time, I felt terrible about all that wasted soup and on top of that, *everybody* would know about it. I scrubbed that kettle for days until it was usable again."

A while later, the bean soup gurgled quietly on the stove as Maggie pulled the ingredients for cornbread out of the cupboards. Pauline's son Alec came in the back door and sat down with Pauline at the dining room table where she'd been enjoying the parade at the bird feeder outside the window. The goldfinches' feathers were turning dark and the chickadees wore their usual somber coats.

One look at Alec told Pauline that he was in trouble. Again. His six-foot frame curled up under the weight of his problem, his anxious face reflected a sleepless night and his hair was as messy as an untended garden. He was so upset, he just blurted out, "Dixie Dowling is dead. The sheriff probably thinks I killed her."

"What?!?!" This was serious. Alec *always* took half an hour or so leading up to the problem, blaming the whole world for not adjusting to his needs and whims. He'd stopped coming to his mother with his money problems when he finally realized she wouldn't bail him out. Today he looked like a man who knew he'd been beaten by his own stupidity.

"What happened? Why do they suspect you? When did she die?" Pauline nattered on, then stopped to get a grip on herself. "Maggie, Alec will eat with us." Pauline called out.

Maggie came to the archway between the kitchen and dining room. "Okay."

"Now Alec, tell me what this is all about."

"Well, sometimes I hang out at Guzzler's Bar. Yesterday, Dixie came in and sat next to me. I bought her a few drinks and she seemed to be pretty interested in me. After a while, she said I could make some easy money if I helped her out. I asked her how. She said to wait half an hour and then come out to the old Wormwood cabin, where Jim and Cal wouldn't interrupt us; Jim's her husband and Cal's her son. There she'd tell me all about it. By the look in her eye, I thought I might get more than money. Oh." Evidently he realized he should spare his mother a few of the details. "I waited for half an hour, then left. I was driving on Q, maybe a mile from the trail to the cabin, when I saw Dixie's yellow SUV, coming from the opposite direction and turning onto the trail. I followed her into the woods. I could see by her tracks that she was getting along all right, but the mud nearly buried my car, because of all that rain we had the last four days. Then I saw a car parked at a wide spot in the trail; it looked like Vern Fitzelditz's old heap. So I parked there, too. I figured it was only a mile or so farther.

"When I came to the clearing in front of the cabin, I stopped to catch my breath. I couldn't see Dixie's car. I went up on the bridge over the narrows to look and there was her car, upside down in three feet of water. I rushed down and tried to get her out, but I couldn't open the door and then I realized I was too late anyway. I had only been a minute or two behind her until I walked the last mile.

"I went back to the trail. Suddenly I didn't want anybody to find me there with a dead body so I left, even faster than I arrived. By the time I came to town, I realized my footprints and tire prints were all over there, but I called 911 from the pay phone at the gas station to tell them there was a car crashed off the bridge at the narrows of Blueberry Lake and the driver was dead. I guess they'll think I killed her."

Maggie came to the dining room. "The cornbread will be out of the oven in five minutes. Do you want to eat now?"

"Yes, let's set the problem aside for a bit and come back to it with fresh minds."

Maggie set the table. Since there was company (Pauline liked to treat her family with a little nice fussing) Maggie set out the everyday china rather than the daisied plastic plates. She used the Oneida silver, which had belonged to Pauline's mother, who had bought it with carefully hoarded cash and Betty Crocker coupons. Maggie served Pauline. "Do you want honey or syrup on your cornbread?"

"Syrup on one piece, honey on the other."

When they finished eating, Pauline was ready to talk again. "All right, Alec, we'll have to find out what happened so you don't have to go to jail. I do mean 'we.' I'm going to put you to work and Maggie will help me, won't you Maggie?"

"Sure."

"Mom, I'm sorry. It's about the stupidest thing I've ever done."

"You're right. You'll pay for it, too, although maybe not the way you thought. I'll expect you to cooperate fully in this investigation. No excuses, no failures."

"Okay."

Pauline outlined her plan, "Maggie, you and I should talk to Dixie's husband. Alec, you see her son. We'll do Vern. You check with the barflies and see if they have any tales. But you're not to drink anything alcoholic," Pauline said in her best 'I-say-what-I-mean-and-I-mean-what-I-say voice. "Not until this whole thing is over. If you do, we quit and you'll have to get yourself out of it."

Alec's thoughts flashed through his mind and onto his face. "*I don't want to quit drinking!*" "But if I don't . . ." "I guess I'll have to."

Maggie thought of the old saying, "You have to crack the nuts before you can eat the kernels." Obviously, Alec would much rather not have to work that hard, but Pauline gave him no choice.

Watching him, Pauline almost smiled. "Alec, you must be Hercule Poirot, collecting the psychology of Dixie and the people who knew her. I think I'll make an excellent Jane Marple. Maggie?"

"I'll be Miss Marple's assistant."

"Excellent."


That evening, Alec was as restless as a July thunderstorm. Since he couldn't hang out with the guys at the bar, he decided to hang out with the guys at AA. When his turn came, he gave the password, "Hi. I'm Alec and I'm an alcoholic," but he didn't believe himself. He traded fishing stories with two of the men. He listened half-heartedly to a third man who whined about how alcohol had ruined his life and thought, "I'm glad I'm not that bad." Two men told lewd stories about Dixie, which interested Alec, but he decided the tales were probably wishful thinking. Like everyone else there, Alec drank a lot of coffee.

As they left the meeting, Fred said to Alec, "Let's go over to the cafe and talk." Fred was a *big* man, several inches taller than Alec and many pounds heavier, with black hair and dark eyes; he looked as though he'd seen too much of the wrong side of life during his fifty-odd years.

It was only nine o'clock and Alec was still restless, so he said, "Sure."

They compared fishing holes as they ate apple pie with ice cream and drank more coffee. Then Fred casually asked Alec why he'd gone to the meeting.

"Ma is going to help me out of a jam, but only if I stay sober. I needed something to pass the time."

Fred's laugh was so big, it stole twenty years off his aging face and lit up every other face in the cafe.

Alec was embarrassed by his own honesty and angry at Fred's reaction. He asked Fred, "What's so funny?"

"You're so much like I was a year ago."

"What does that mean?"

Fred sidestepped. "How about if we meet tomorrow night at the grocery store at a quarter to eight and we'll go to another meeting. Tonight's group wasn't really into the program but tomorrow night you can get a better idea what we're all about."

Peeved but curious, Alec agreed.

# 7

When Maggie came into Pauline's bedroom the next morning, she cheerfully announced, "Pauline, I feel Tookish today."

As Maggie moved around the room, readying things before she helped Pauline out of bed, Pauline said, "I'll bite. What's Tookish?"

"You don't know The Hobbit?

"No."

Maggie responded, "Maybe that should be the next book we read. All right, Bilbo Baggins was a hobbit, a little person, smaller than a dwarf. Like all good hobbits, he loved peace, quiet and good food. His mother was a Took, which meant he had some strange blood. The Tooks went off adventuring from time to time, which was not a respectable thing for a hobbit to do. So Tookish means I'm in a mood to try something new."

Pauline liked Bilbo Baggins immediately. She plopped into the wheelchair, then she asked, "Did you have a particular something in mind?"

"Well, Pauline, you liked my blueberry muffins, my zucchini bread and my carrot-raisin-apple bread. Now

I've a mind to try applesauce all-bran bread." The carrot-apple-raisin bread was Maggie's successful experiment to satisfy their sweet teeth without much refined sugar or cooking oil.

"Sounds good to me."

While Pauline watched her quiz show, Maggie started the bread. She muttered, "Eight and a half cups of all-bran in the box. One recipe makes twelve muffins. If I triple that, it ought to make two loaves." She dumped two, four, six cups of all-bran into a bowl. She looked in the box. Only about two cups left. "No sense keeping such a dribble." She fourpled the recipe. She took out another bowl and put half the all-bran in it, added the milk, eggs and a quarter cup of cooking oil. In another two bowls, she put baking soda and unsweetened applesauce, a quarter cup of sugar, salt and graham flour. When she added the first mix to the second, it almost overflowed the large mixing bowls. She had a monster batch on her hands! She looked heavenward and groaned, "Please let this be edible."

"Pauline, come look at this," Maggie cried out.

Pauline wheeled her chair out to the kitchen. She looked at the bowls and at Maggie. "Well, that should keep things moving!" They burst out laughing. They finally quit, but then they looked at each other and started all over again.

"I guess I'll have to put it in a roaster pan so there'll be room enough to mix in the white flour and raisins. Say, since I'm making four times the normal sized batch, do you suppose I need to set the temperature four times higher, at 1400 degrees?" This tickled their funny bones again.

When she sampled the hot bread, Maggie decided, "It's edible, but not quite right. What do you think?"

Pauline took another bite, chewed slowly, thoughtfully. "I think maybe use all white flour. The graham flour seems a little much with the all-bran."

"Okay, I'll try that next time. That is, if we ever finish eating these five loaves." They found that exceedingly funny too.

Pauline answered the phone, still giggling, but she quickly became serious. "Thank you for returning my call, Mr. Dowling. Because my son may be a suspect in your wife's death, I'm doing some inquiring to see what I can find out. Would you talk with me?"

"Well, uh . . ." He didn't hide his surprise at her bluntness. "All right. Do you want to come to my office?"

"That would be fine. When should we come?"

"How about 1:30 this afternoon?"

"All right. Thank you."

Pauline called her gossipy friend Doris Doppler. "How are you today?"

Doris replied, "I don't know what to do. My eyes were bothering me, so I had them checked. The eye doctor fixed me up with new glasses which cost over $300 and my eyes are still bothering me!"

When Doris finally ran down, Pauline asked, "What do you know about Jim Dowling?"

Doris was delighted to help. "Ten years ago, everybody thought he was the best lawyer our county ever had. Then five years ago, he married that baggage with the ten-year-old son. I expect she's spent all his money and is now working on seeing how deeply into debt she can get. He seems so apathetic, I don't know if anybody still hires him. Why?"

"Dixie's been found dead."

"Is that who they found at the Blueberry Lake narrows? My husband heard about it on his CB. Oh, just wait until I tell him! I bet Jim killed her, poor fellow. I'll never understand why he didn't just divorce her."

Pauline asked, "Do you know anything about her?"

"Well, before she married him, she cooked for a while at the cafe in Mackerel until she was caught stealing. Then she waitressed in Lilac. You know, she affected a terrible drawl when she first showed up here six or seven years ago. I was eating there one day when her son came in and asked her for money. She got mad at him for bothering her at work, cussed him out like you wouldn't believe, without one bit of drawl, mind you.

That's when she picked up the nickname 'Owly' because she was so screechy. Then when she married Jim, she was 'Owly' Dowling. She was blowzy, frowzy, Owly Dowling." Doris laughed at her own wit. "Oh, the other waitresses said she was always stealing their tips and that if you asked her the same question six times, she'd give you six different answers. And they fired her for yelling at her son in front of customers."

"What did she spend all the money on? Her house, her car, her clothes?"

Doris was thrilled to show off her knowledge. "The first thing was she wanted Jim to build her a great big fancy house with fancy furniture and all. Then she took up gambling. Every day she's at the casino. Don't know how much longer they'll let her in. Oh, I guess that's not a problem any more, is it?"

"How did such a lowlife ever manage to marry Jim?" Pauline asked.

"I don't know. She was a fat slob, a bottle blond, a shrieking witch. But I guess she could turn a man on and melt his brains and everything else except his you-know-what."

"Thanks, Doris. I've got to go."

"Goodbye."

That afternoon in Jim Dowling's office, piles of books and papers cluttered the floor; chairs and desk had collected dust -- the room looked as bewildered as its owner.

"Mr. Dowling, I'm Pauline Johnson. This is Maggie O'Neill. I'm sorry you have lost your wife," Pauline said.

"Huh? Don't be. It's the best thing that's happened to me since I met her; at least it is if I don't go to jail for murdering her." His bitterness was blatant.

Pauline asked quietly, "Did you murder her?"

"No, but I surely would like to thank the guy who did!" He smiled faintly. "I'd even be his lawyer, pro bono."

"Where were you when she died?"

Jim answered, "Here. I heard the ambulance call on my CB and a while later, they called me to say Dixie

43

was dead."

"Was anyone here with you?"

He shrugged. "No. We're separated, you know. Not legally. But I had an RV; I put it on a piece of land I own out in the woods. I've been living there for about two years now. I just couldn't stand living with her anymore."

Pauline said, "I've heard she was pretty heavily into gambling. Is that true?"

"Yes," he replied. "I don't know if I'll ever be able to pay off all her debts."

"Your office doesn't look as if you're doing much business these days," commented Maggie.

Clearly, life had overwhelmed him. "No, earning good money for her to gamble away seemed foolish. But she's gone now. I suppose I ought to get going again." He didn't sound convinced.

"What can you tell us about your wife, Mr. Dowling?" Pauline asked.

"She was a compulsive liar, a crazed petty thief, and an obsessed gambler. When she was scheming, she could act normal. Like when she met me. This is what I've figured out. She'd heard that I had lost my wife a year earlier and that I was a very good lawyer. So she joined the Lionesses. She came to my house one Saturday, selling raffle tickets for something. I bought all she had. We talked and well, you know. We saw a lot of each other in the next two weeks and suddenly we were married."

He mumbled on despondently, "A few weeks later, Joan Lefair stopped in at my office. She said that at the last Lioness' meeting, they'd collected money from the raffle tickets. The money box just sat there after the meeting was over. The women meandered around, cleaning up and chatting. When Joan counted the money that night, it was about fifty dollars short. Dixie was the only newcomer; all the other women had been members for years with never a problem. They were sure that Dixie stole the money.

"I'd known Joan all my life. She wouldn't lie. I gave her a hundred dollars and asked her please to forget the whole thing.  I didn't even talk to Dixie about it.  I simply pushed the whole thing out of my besotted mind and pretended that she was nuts about me instead of just plain nuts.  I set up a joint checking account for us so she'd have all the money she could want and for a while, that was fine.  Then there were overdrafts, just a week after I'd made a large deposit.  She made out most of her checks to the casino.  After a few months of that, I tried talking to her.  That's when I found out that my little pussycat was a man-eating tiger!  I tried to smooth things over but it was no use.  Eventually, I moved out."

Maggie asked, "Are you fond of Joan?"

He flushed.  "I went with her during high school; I guess we were pretty serious, but when I became absorbed with my law studies, she gave up and married Walt Lefair.  He died a while back, but I'm such a nobody now . . ."

"Do you know anything about Dixie from the time before she came here?"

"I know that every time she opened her mouth, she contradicted something she'd said before.  She was born in Atlanta, in Charlotte, in Austin.  She only had ten years of school, she graduated from college.  Hmm.  There was one name that came up several times.  She claimed she worked at the Dear Hearts Nursing Home for about ten years.  That was in Minneapolis or maybe St. Paul,"

"Thank you, Mr. Dowling.  If you think of anything else that we should know, please call."

Jim Dowling suddenly looked very guilty.  But guilty of what?

In the car, Pauline commented, "I think he is keeping secrets.  What do you think?"

"I agree."

"Let's go talk to Vern at the Guzzler."

Maggie pushed Pauline's wheelchair through the narrow door of the tavern.  (No steps -- they had accommodated some disabilities long ago.)  The dim lighting after the bright sunlight blinded them but didn't blunt the fifty years' worth of smoke fumes.  Maggie had

45

quit smoking; she took a deep breath, for old times sake.

"Push me over to that table," Pauline pointed, "next to the wall where I can see everything that's going on. Then get me a glass of tomato juice and something for yourself." She looked impishly at Maggie. "Please."

Maggie grinned and went to the bar. As she waited for the drinks, a forty-year-old, bushy-bearded, cowboy-booted barfly sleazed over next to Maggie and snaked his arm around her, "How ya' doin', Honey?"

Maggie stretched to her full height, which put her an inch or two taller than the fellow in spite of two-inch heels on his boots, looked him in the eye and calmly delivered a verbal ice cube, "Your arrogant assumption of familiarity is contemptible and obnoxious." The beer-bellied bull looked bewildered. "Your unmitigated impropriety in matters of propinquity is despicable and contumelious." His hand fell to his side. "And your pachydermatous disregard for my perturbation, which is caused by your invidious advances is ignominious and abominable. Why don't you absquatulate?"

He walked back to his buddies. "What did she say?" they asked.

"Damned if I know. I think she was talking some foreign language."

When Pauline saw the arm sneak around Maggie, a picture flashed through her mind. Forty years ago, she had taught Vernon in her eighth-grade class. Several years later, she had seen him at the gas station, insinuating his arm around Patsy Sweet. Patsy had liked Vern's touch, Pauline realized; she had probably liked it too much. A few months later, she was dead, having shot herself with her father's gun. Suddenly Pauline realized why Patsy had killed herself.

In the silence that preceded Maggie's response to the unwanted arm, Pauline barked out an order, "Vernon Fitzelditz, get over here. Right Now." There was no mistaking the Authority in that voice. From the far end of the bar, Vernon got. "Vernon, sit." He squirmed into a chair.

Pauline let him squirm a bit. Then very quietly she

said, "You killed Patsy Sweet, didn't you."

His guilt exploded. "Howd you know? I mean, no, I didn't. We just had a fight. She drove off crying. The next thing I heard she shot herself." Vern was all of the same piece: his clothes were shabby, his movements were shabby, his speech was shabby; he couldn't even drink in good style, because he always ran out of money by the middle of the month and the owner of the bar severely limited his credit.

"She was pregnant, wasn't she? She wanted you to marry her and that's what the fight was about."

Defeated, he nodded.

Maggie brought the drinks and sat down.

Pauline sipped some juice. "Vernon, who was the unsavory character talking to Maggie at the bar?"

"That's Nimrod Clapquist."

"Thank you. Now, what we really want to know is what you were doing at the old Wormwood cabin yesterday."

He blustered, "Howd you know I was there?" But Pauline just gave him That Look.

"Hey, I didn't kill her! I didn't have nothing to do with that. He wanted me to meet him out there. Said he had a job for me that would pay really well. I went and waited in the cabin. But he never came so I left."

Maggie asked, "Who's 'he?'"

"Her husband."

"Did you see her car out there?" Pauline wanted to know.

"Yes, Mrs. Anderson." (To him, she was still Mrs. Anderson, Mr. Johnson having come after Vern's time with her).

"Tell us what you saw."

Vern looked at Mrs. Anderson, Former Teacher, and realized he had no choice. "When I was in the cabin, I heard a car coming. They boarded up the windows but they left big cracks between the boards. I could see out. It was her car. It sure was going crazy. She'd stomp on the gas and then no gas, it looked like. She was going on and off the trail, way too fast. Then the car crashed through the bridge railing. It flew off into the water. I didn't know what to do. I ran outside to see if I could help, but then I heard another car. I got scared. I hid behind some bushes. I waited there until his car drove off. Then I left, too."

Maggie asked, "What were you afraid of?"

Vern was perplexed. "I don't know. I probably wasn't supposed to be there. What would she think if she found me? What would that other guy think? I mean, what if Mr. Dowling wanted me to spy on her and that was her boy friend following her?"

Then Pauline wanted to know, "When did you get there and when did you leave?"

"He said be there at 10:30. I was a little late, but not much. I was sitting in the recliner. I must have dozed off because it was 2:30 when I got back to town."

"Your fingerprints are in the cabin, aren't they?"

"Well, yeah, I suppose so." Then he realized what that meant. He yelped, "But I didn't kill her. Honest, Mrs. Anderson, you've gotta believe me. I didn't do it."

She gave him a long appraising look. "Vern, I suppose the world gets more use out of a hill of beans than it does out of you, but I do believe you didn't kill Dixie."

"Thank you, Ma'am," he said, all meekness.

In the car, Pauline looked at Maggie. "What in the world did you say to that octopus, Nimrod Clapquist? I had to say a few words to Vern, so I missed it."

"He's a real shite," Maggie said and told Pauline what she'd said to Nimrod.

"Good for you!"

"And what did you say to Vern?"

Pauline told Maggie, then Maggie asked, "How about banana bonanza for supper? We could stop at the store and buy some bananas." Banana bonanza was Maggie's quick, almost-banana-cream pie.

On the way home from the store, Maggie told Pauline, "I can't imagine how a person could teach eight different grades in one day. How did you do it?"

Pauline laughed. "Actually it was easier than

teaching a whole class of third graders. The older children graded papers for me and watched the younger ones during recess. They closed the one-room schoolhouses around here in the late fifties and early sixties and then I taught in Lilac. It was much smaller then; I guess the population is almost a thousand now. Anyway, my first year in Lilac was a bad one: on days when I had recess duty, I never even had time to go to the bathroom; Andy was just awful those last few months before the accident; I tried to work on a correspondence course, one of those with endless busywork; and I was pregnant with Mary.

"But you asked me about teaching in a one-room schoolhouse. I started teaching in my second life. I taught at Freya during the war and later at Black Brook. We had mostly fifteen minute periods. Fifteen minutes for first-grade reading and language, fifteen minutes for second-grade reading and language, and so forth. We taught arithmetic, social studies, geography, even some biology, a little art, a little singing. I was a terrible singer; luckily the school had a radio which would lead the children in singing <u>Twinkle</u>, <u>Twinkle</u> <u>Little</u> <u>Star</u>, and Stephen Foster songs and patriotic songs like <u>America</u>.

"The county superintendent of schools used to inspect us lots of times each year, which scared me because I didn't think I had enough education to teach very well and he was stiff and formal when he talked with me. He would always tell me I was doing very well before he told me how I could improve; many of his ideas were helpful. Eventually my stomach stopped complaining when he appeared. Every year, though, he'd list things we ought to have, like new fire extinguishers, globes, shades, books for the library, hot lunches. I found that discouraging: never enough money at home, never enough at school. All in all, I liked teaching, especially when I saw understanding light up a child's face.

"Even at Lilac, we always had a picnic at the end of the school year. At our 1965 picnic, Tom Johnson showed up with an old ice cream maker and all the fixings. It was a nice hot day and my children gobbled up this unexpected treat. He spent most of the day making ice cream. That's how he began our second courtship."

Maggie asked, "How long before you married him?"

"We married in 1966," Pauline said with a smile.

### Maggie's Banana Bonanza (low guilt)

Crumble 4 rectangles of graham crackers, keep separate. Slice 1 large banana into the bowls you'll eat out of.
In a pan:
1/8 t salt
1 T cornstarch
1-2 t honey
1 T butter
1 cup milk
1 egg
Wire whip constantly as you bring it to a boil; boil 1 minute.
Add 1 t vanilla. Mix. Pour pudding on top of banana; pour graham crackers on top. Serve warm. 1-4 servings

# 8

While Pauline and Maggie talked with Vern, Alec waited at the high school. He thanked the girl who had pointed to Cal as he came out of school. Alec looked carefully at the awkward sixteen-year-old shuffling toward him and saw himself at that age, resentful of his father's drinking and early death, resentful of his stepfathers wealth (used only once to get him out of trouble), resentful of the world for not being what he wanted.

"Hi, Cal. I'm Alec Johnson."

Cal just looked at Alec.

"I want to talk to you. You want a pizza?"

"At the drive-in?" Cal sneered.

Alec recognized the tactic. "At the pizza place."

"Okay."

Cal ordered a large Super Pizza and a large Melly Cola. Alec winced. Prices were higher here than at the drive-in and the kid ordered the most expensive pizza on the menu. But he joined the game. "I'll take a small Super and a beer . . . no, make that a medium Melly Cola. But hold the order until we've talked. I'll let you know when."

"All right."

After the waitress had gone, Alec asked, "Did you kill your mother?"

"No, I didn't," Cal yelled.

Alec asked calmly, "But you wanted her dead, right?"

"Yeah, well, maybe you would, too, if your Ma was the butt end of every kid's jokes," Cal spat out defiantly.

"When I was in school, it was my Dad the kids joked about. He was the town drunk and we were very poor."

"So what?" Cal was not quite so vehement.

"So you aren't the first kid in the world to have a lousy parent or to feel sorry for yourself because of it."

Cal asked spitefully, "You have kids?"

"No."

"You ever gonna have any?"

Alec wanted to walk out, but then he saw himself again and tried to answer. "If that doesn't open a can of worms! If I'm not honest with you, how can I expect you to be honest with me." He stared out the window for several minutes. "Cal, I don't know if I'll ever grow up enough to be a decent father. Until then, I hope I don't have any kids." Alec waited for this to sink in, to Cal's thinking and to his own.

"Now, let's get to the point. I had a couple of

51

drinks with your mom the day she died and I went out to Wormwood cabin to meet her. So I'm a suspect."

Cal interrupted, "You mean you had the hots for her, too?"

As a calm, objective interrogator, Alec did poorly. He sputtered, "Well . . . uh . . . I . . . oh @#$%& azbycx &%$#@." Cal grinned. "All right, so I did. Anyway, my mom and I are trying to find out all we can about Dixie's death and Dixie and the people who knew her, so we can figure out what happened. Why did you hate her?"

"I didn't."

"Why did you want her dead?"

Cal shook his head.

"Where were you when she died?"

"In school."

Alec told him, "You know in a case like this, the sheriff usually has the family at the top of the suspect list." Cal groaned and Alec continued, "Somehow, I think that you might have wanted her dead but that you didn't kill her. If that's the case, you and I could work together and clear both our names."

Cal took a deep breath and stared out the window as he talked. "I didn't hate her. Sometimes I tried to hate her, when I was mad at her. I just wanted her to love me. I mean, sometimes she'd be really nice to me, when she wanted something. But other times she'd be so mean, I'd cry. Like why is 'bastard' a bad name for me when it was her that made me one? Most of the time though, she was just too busy lying, stealing and gambling to pay any attention to me."

"What was she doing recently?"

"She was crawling the walls for a while. She couldn't get any credit anywhere for the casino. Then a few days ago, she was talking about all the money your mom has."

"Oh, @#$%&! She wanted me to help her steal from my own mother!"

Cal looked coolly at Alec. "You probably would have done it, too. She had her ways."

"I'm lucky she's dead!"

"Did *you* kill her?" Cal asked.

Alec shuddered. "No, I couldn't see where I was going until after she was dead."

"You know," Cal said, "I used to be jealous of her guys. She always had at least one on a leash. But now . . . poor suckers."

"Give me some names."

"There was Fast Eddie Olnitz and Jake Kleidaker. And Nimrod Clapquist."

"Cal, do you want to help me find out what happened?"

Cal looked dubious. "I suppose so. She was the only mother I'll ever have."

"I want to spend some serious time out at the cabin and around the bridge to see if there might be any clues there. Will you help?"

"Yeah."

"As soon as the sheriff's people are finished, we'll go out there." Then Alec motioned for the waitress. "You can fix our pizza now, please."


"Dick Tagley's Bar." The telephone's voice said.

"This is Alec Johnson. I need a big favor. I'm coming over in a little while and I'll be ordering vodka and tonic only I want you to leave out the booze. Charge me for it, of course. I need to look like I'm drinking but I have to be sober."

Dick laughed. "Whatever you say." They usually called his bar "D.T.'s," because so many serious drinkers imbibed there.

At the bar, Alec sat next to Fast Eddie and bought them both a drink. "Hey Eddie, haven't seen you in a while. What do you think about that Dixie babe getting herself killed?"

"Wasn't she something! Did you know her?"

Alec put a heavy leer into his voice, "Yeah! I almost got myself into big trouble though. How about you? Did you have to do any dirt?"

Eddie looked around furtively, and whispered, "You remember when D.T.s got robbed a coupla months ago? I helped her with that."

"No kidding!" Alec sounded admiring.

"Yeah, I gave her all the inside dope on how D.T. closed up and she had some guy rob him. They caught him, but she got away with the money somehow. Scuttlebutt was, her husband paid back the money and hushed the whole thing up. Lots of good it did him."

Alec bought him another drink and went to the bathroom. When he came out, he joined Jake Kleidaker. Because Jake's jaw wasn't limber enough for talking yet, Alec had to buy him several drinks. Jake's story was about an attempted robbery. It fell through because the bartender recognized Jake in spite of the mask and talked him out of it.

When they arrived back at Pauline's after talking with Vern, Maggie said, "Investigating a murder is hard work, isn't it. You look beat. How about if we get you inside and into your lift chair for a quick snooze? I'll make the banana bonanza in an hour and then wake you up."

"Good idea."

Just as Maggie started getting the ingredients out of cupboard and refrigerator, Alec came in, so Maggie doubled the recipe.

Ten minutes later, she asked, "Pauline, do you want to sit at the table now?" She did. Maggie stood ready to help if needed as Pauline stood up from her lift chair, used the walker to steady herself as she turned backside to the wheelchair and sat down. Pauline wheeled herself to the table while Maggie brought the food from the kitchen. She came up behind Pauline with her milk and looked out the window. "Look, Pauline, Alec isn't the only company tonight. There are six deer out in your field. You have a treat for your mouth and another for your eyes." Pauline smiled when she saw them. Deer-watching was one of her favorite pastimes.

When the deer and the food were gone, Maggie took the dirty dishes to the kitchen and returned. After they shared information, Pauline said, "I don't think Jim Dowling or Vern killed Dixie, do you Maggie?"

54

"Vern, no; Jim, probably not. That's my guess. Alec, what about Cal? And Dixie's accomplices?"

"Cal didn't do it. I don't think either Eddie or Jake has the brains to plan a murder. Besides, I don't think they've seen her for a while."

"Alec," asked Pauline, "what aren't you telling us?"

He studied a spot on the table and muttered, "Cal said she wanted me to help her steal your money."

"Why that nasty little witch!" Pauline exclaimed. She didn't comment on what she thought of her son's possible interest in such a scheme.

Maggie said, "Pauline, you had a little nap but I didn't. Could I get you ready for bed and then go home? Alec can help you to bed later if you two want to talk."

"Yes, in a minute," Pauline replied. "Somebody should go to that nursing home, what was it, Dear Hearts? Alec, I'd rather do that one myself, but it's a long drive and you're younger. Will you go there tomorrow? Maggie, I need my swim and I guess we'd better talk to Nimrod. Are you sure you want to do that, Maggie?"

"Yes. I think we'd better do it and get it over with."

"I wonder what Doris' Doppler radar can tell us about Nimrod," Pauline said as she reached for the telephone.

"Hello, Doris, how are you doing?" Pauline asked, though she knew the answer would probably take twenty minutes.

"I've had the most frightful time lately. The doctor says it's benign positional vertigo and there's no cure for it . . ."

Eventually, Pauline asked her second question. "What do you know about Nimrod Clapquist?"

"I know that if I have nothing to do with him, I can almost feel sorry for him. His father drove his first wife to suicide and his second wife, that's Nimrod's mother, ran away with another man when Nimrod was real little -- she left him behind, too."

"What about Nimrod?"

"I think he got caught in a stolen car once. Seems like he went to reform school or whatever they call it nowadays and he picked up a trade, electrician or TV antennas or something. He's been in jail a few more times, got off a few times, beat up a guy once when he was drunk. Rumor has it that he and his drinking pals are usually up to no good. He seems to do a little honest work, but not enough to support his drinking."

Then Doris changed the subject, "Say, did you hear about . . .?"

When Pauline hung up, she said to Maggie, "Now there's a woman who enjoys poor health and a good bit of gossip and if she had to choose between the two it would break her heart." Maggie knew that Pauline liked Doris and she would keep calling her even if she didn't need information.

As promised, the second AA meeting was completely different.

"I used to blame my wife for my drinking. If the house was too clean or too dirty, I'd get mad and go drinking. If a meal was really good, I'd yell at her for spending too much money and stomp out to the bar. She left me and now I finally see that drinking is *my* problem."

"I nearly lost our farm because I was too busy drinking to take care of it. But I'd blame the bad weather or bad luck or the greedy bank."

"I found out my eleventh grade son was using drugs. I wanted to beat the tar out of him, but he just said he'd quit if I'd quit. He was blaming *me* for *his* problem! Now I go to AA on Wednesdays and he goes on Thursdays."

Alec was very uncomfortable; all this was just too close to home. Fred looked at him several times to see if he wanted to talk. He didn't.

For the next month, Fred made sure that he and Alec went to four or five meetings a week, although Alec was only going through the motions at first. He just couldn't admit to himself that he was an alcoholic. They usually went to the cafe afterward for more talk. Sometimes Fred needled Alec about his problems, but Alec wasn't ready to admit to anything.

# 9

The next day, at the Dear Hearts Nursing Home, Alec sweet-talked his way into the confidence of an older orderly.

"Yes, Dixie used to work here, for a few months. She seemed very nice at first. One of her duties was to find out what the residents needed and go buy it for them. Then the residents started complaining about lost money. You know how it is with old folks. We didn't worry too much, but we watched. That time, the old folks were right. Dixie would find out where they kept their money, then go in at mealtimes to steal it. Of course, that was a long time ago. We try not to let them keep money in their rooms now. Anyway, one little lady, Maude, now there was a character!"

The orderly grinned. "You'd think, when you met her, that there was no one at home, but when push came to shove, she'd be the one to look out for. Apparently, Maude had lost some money and figured out that Dixie took it. One afternoon, Dixie and I were talking in the hall and Maude came down the hall in her electric wheelchair. She had muscular dystrophy so she was too weak for a regular wheelchair. I didn't think anything of it when Maude came barreling along, because we were over to one side and she was in the middle. At the last minute, Maude swerved and banged right into Dixie. Dixie turned on Maude, screeching and cussing; she tried to hit Maude, but she was off balance and besides, Maude was already backing and turning so Dixie missed and fell on her face. I didn't want her hurting anyone, so I sat on her." The orderly weighed about two hundred pounds. "Dixie kept right on cussing and trying to get up. Four other residents saw the whole thing; they started cheering for Maude.

"I guess Dixie finally realized what she was doing. She went quiet. I let her go; she stomped out of the building. Maude wasn't hurt, just sat there looking like the canary that ate the cat. Our director decided that since everyone was all right, we'd write it up but not press charges unless she did. We never saw her again."

Since that first time at the pool, Maggie and Pauline went faithfully, every Tuesday and Friday morning. After a few weeks, Pauline tried swimming on her back. She went in a small circle, because her right arm and leg were so weak, but she could swim. She learned to go easy with her left arm and leg. She would swim a few feet farther each time. Then she tried the side stroke, on her left side, always with Maggie right beside her. Pauline tried all the strokes and practiced them, but the side stroke worked best for her.

On their way to the pool, Maggie asked Pauline, "How did you learn all the strokes, when you grew up in a poor family? Didn't lessons cost money?"

"Yes, but I was good at finding back doors and working my way in. When I was a child, we swam in the lake. That was free. We didn't use fancy strokes, we just paddled around. It wasn't until about 1960, well into my fourth life as a widowed teacher, that I learned the 'right' way to swim. I had a pupil who missed a lot of school because of illness. When she came back to school, I spent a lot of time with her after school, helping her catch up. Her mother had taught swimming before she married. She decided swimming would help her daughter regain her full health, so she offered to teach her daughter and my children how to swim that next summer. I went along and learned, too."

At the pool, Jenine started, "Face the deep end, cross your leg over and push your hips toward the edge."

After their strenuous detecting, the water felt especially relaxing. Pauline had been lazily following directions for twenty minutes, when she said, "I wonder if I could swim the width of the pool yet."

"Why don't you try?"

Very slowly, Pauline paddled her way, first on her side, then on her back, a bit on her front, on her side again. Five feet, ten feet, fifteen,  By then, the exercisers had stopped everything to watch her. She struggled on, twenty, twenty-five, thirty, she made it! As she pulled her head up at the far end, everybody cheered and clapped. Pauline was embarrassed. And pleased.

After lunch and a nap, Pauline was ready to tackle Nimrod. They found him and his five cronies at their usual table. Standing behind the wheelchair, Maggie politely said, "Nimrod Clapquist, Pauline and I would like to talk with you, please."

At the far side of the table, Nimrod scowled as he thought of all the big words Maggie knew. "So, talk."

All sweetness, Maggie replied, "We'd rather talk to you alone."

Nimrod decided he'd rather not be embarrassed in front of his drinking buddies, so he motioned for them to move away. Maggie moved one chair aside, pushed the wheelchair up to the table and sat down herself.

"Watcha want?"

Pauline said, "We're looking into the death of Dixie Dowling. We've heard you might have reason to kill her."

"Me? You're crazy. Watcha saying something like that for?" Nimrod was definitely belligerent. Then he leaned over the table toward Maggie. "I'll bet you just wanted to talk to me some more." He leered.

"Mr. Clapquist, we want some information about you and Dixie. If you'd rather talk to the sheriff, we'll tell him what we know and he can deal with you."

"I know." Nimrod threatened, "You just need a little softening up. Me and my boys could come out to your place tonight . . ."

Maggie exaggerated the patience in her voice. "Mr. Clapquist, you could.  But I grew up with four brothers; one joined the army, one joined the marines, one was in the air force and the other in the navy. Do you really think I don't know how to defend myself?" He scowled; he liked bullying, not fighting.

Maggie continued, "But if you decide to come anyway, watch out for the skunks. I feed them regularly so they don't bother me, but they're not so friendly to intruders." His nose wrinkled. "Besides, if something happened to me, you'd have to shut Pauline up too. Did you know that she taught the sheriff when he was in school? He still thinks the world of her. Of course, she has so many connections that the sheriff might not get to you in time." She paused. "I wonder what the sheriff would find if he followed you around for a while."

Nimrod did not want the sheriff following him. He grabbed the table, looked as though he wanted to dump it over on the women. "Mr. Clapquist," Maggie said calmly, looking him in the eye, "do you think your chums would approve of you hurting a poor helpless old woman in a wheelchair?" When bulldozing didn't work, Nimrod didn't know what to do; he collapsed backwards in his chair.

"How long have you known Dixie?" Pauline asked quietly.

He muttered, "A coupla months."

"Did you kill her?"

He glowered at Pauline, then growled his answer, "No. Why would I do that?"

"Maybe you didn't like to see her flirt with other men." Pauline's soft words stung him like a whole nest of hornets. Her next words were altogether quiet. "I don't think you killed Dixie, but we need information. Would it be easier for you to talk if we met somewhere else?"

Nimrod nodded.

"Suppose we meet in an hour at the Rock River Cafe. We'll leave now; you come later."

He nodded again.

In the car, Maggie asked Pauline, "Why did you let him go? I thought we had him ready to talk."

"Did you see how surprised he was when I said he had reason to kill Dixie?"

"Yes."

Pauline explained, "I stretched that point a bit, but his reaction seemed genuine. I don't think he killed her, so we don't have to trick him into a confession. But we might get some good information about Dixie if he isn't trying to put on a show for his cronies. At the cafe, we're far from them and maybe he'll talk."

Maggie said, "Aren't you the clever one! You're probably right about him, but of all the suspects, I'd much rather find him guilty; he's, well to properly describe him, I think I'd have to use some of my deceased husband's foul language, and I'm so sweet and innocent, I forgot all those words."

"How about 'He's a boil on the nose of humanity?'"

Maggie laughed. "Perfect description!"

At the cafe, which was as cheerful and bright in blue and yellow as the bar had been dark and dreary, they ordered while they waited for Nimrod. The French silk pie turned out to be chocolate pudding in a pie crust; it was very disappointing. Maggie decided to lighten their mood. "Tell me about Tom."

"Ah. My second husband was a good man. He brought me a gentle less worrisome life, my fifth life. He had the good sense to know when and who to help. For instance, he and I quickly agreed not to bail out Alec when he needed money because that would only encourage his irresponsibility. But when Mary was in a bad car accident in 1980, he was a perfect dear."

"What happened?"

Pauline told her, "A drunk driver ran a stop sign and hit her car. She was lucky: her left leg was badly broken and she had a lot of bumps and bruises, but that was all. I told Tom I wanted to move in with them and help until she could manage on her own. That created a problem: I wanted to move in but they had no room. So while she was still in the hospital, Tom arranged with her husband and one of his contractor friends to put an addition on their small house. They built the addition as two bathrooms and a huge bedroom which later they could divide so that each child would have a separate bedroom. It was my room while I was there and sometimes a retreat for Mary or John. Tom spent weekends there.

"It took about six weeks before she could manage everything again and I thoroughly enjoyed all the grandmothering. They only had three children then. We celebrated Anne's seventh birthday while I was there; Jack was five and Jean was two. I read Dr. Seuss to them and played Uno with Anne and Jack; we baked cookies together.

"The night before I left, Mary came to my room. She thanked me for all the help and then she gave me a check. I tore it up, but she just smiled and said, 'Read it.' I put the pieces back together. It was a check for one month and no days of no responsibility for children, signed by Mary and Stuart. Mary said 'Mom, you look like hell. You've taken on a family of five for six weeks and I know you like helping, but you're exhausted. Why don't you and Fuddy Duddy take a nice long trip? Stuart and I will hold the family together while you're gone.'"

"Fuddy Duddy?" repeated Maggie.

"That was my children's nickname for Tom, at least behind his back. It was an honest, affectionate name. He'd never been married before. At age forty-six, the needs and noise of one wife and five children, ages six through eighteen, shattered his quiet existence. It was terribly difficult for him. He had no natural affinity for children, but he was always good to them. So, Fuddy Duddy.

"Now, where was I? Oh yes. After I returned from helping Mary, I was thinking about my children: Dorothy, my youngest, was in college, Mary was doing fine and Alec's wedding four months earlier meant he was settled for the moment; Stuart and Sara were married and busy with young children. Mary was right. Helping her had been good and it had worn me out. Since I had no pressing responsibilities, and we had plenty of money, I said, 'Tom, let's travel.'"

Pauline's face lit up as delightful memories flitted across her mind. "Tom had always wanted to see the west, ever since he'd read Louis L'Amour's cowboy novels as a boy. We booked a week at a dude ranch. It was his dream come true and he relished every moment of it, from sore muscles after our very first horseback ride to the magnificent scenery we saw on the trail rides, from the perfect sunsets to our new friendships. Well, we didn't fight Indians, but we did chase cows around. My dear Fuddy Duddy even laughed when he stepped in some fresh horse droppings."

She slowly let go of those memories and then continued, "I wanted to see Las Vegas. We liked some shows, Andy Williams and Mel Tillis, but gambling bored us. I wanted to do the old Hollywood, but that was long gone. Laurence Welk was gone by then, too. One little tourist town had bicycles for rent. We spent a riotous afternoon learning to ride them in the empty parking lot of a factory. We went to a concert of Tchaikovsky's music in San Francisco which began our addiction to good music. We explored Fishermen's Wharf one afternoon, sampling delicacies until we nearly burst. The Grand Canyon was magnificent beyond description. Do you suppose it's wheelchair-accessible yet?"

They laughed and Maggie asked, "Did you fret about being away from your kids?"

Pauline laughed again. "I called one of them each night for the first two weeks. Then I realized they could survive without me, so I only called every two or three nights."

"Did you travel other places, too?"

"Tom died in 1986, but during those six years, we went to Europe, the Far East, the Holy Land, eastern United States, oh, all over the place."

Maggie looked at her watch. "Nimrod is twenty-five minutes late. Do you want to go?"

"Yes, I think so."

Just as the waitress brought their check, Nimrod walked in. He sat down and asked gruffly, "Watcha wanna know?"

"Tell us about Dixie."

"Her husband was a real drag. When she wanted a real man, she'd come looking for me." Nimrod smirked.

He was about to continue when Pauline rephrased her statement and made it into an order. "Tell us about Dixie, but skip her sex life; skip your sex life, too."

Nimrod protested, "But what else is there?"

63

"Did she get you to help her with any jobs?"

"Jobs? What kind of jobs?"

"Any kind," Pauline said.

Maggie interrupted. "Mr. Clapquist, we asked you to come here to give us information. If you don't intend to help us, why did you come?"

Nimrod, Pauline thought, looked like a second-grader who should have gone to the bathroom during recess and felt plenty guilty about it and felt even worse because he'd soon have to admit it by asking to go during class. Pauline asked him, "Have you been helping her to rob places?"

"How'd you know that?"

"Tell us. We won't talk to the sheriff about it."

"We robbed a coupla cabins, TV's and stuff."

It was a little easier than squeezing blood from a turnip, but not much. Nimrod and Dixie had robbed four cabins but she hadn't paid him his share because she hadn't found buyers yet, or so she said.

Maggie asked, "Did she dump you?"

"That's none of your @#$%& business."

"Right, but tell us anyway."

"Yeah, well, we had a big fight last week."

Maggie thought that Nimrod must really want the sheriff to keep his distance. Otherwise, he would never be telling them so much. She asked, "What did you fight about?"

"I wanted to pull another robbery. I wanted . . . you know. I wanted my money."

"What happened?"

"I tried to hit her, but she ducked. Then she yelled at me and left."

"Were you mad enough to kill her?"

He looked mean. "Yeah, but I didn't. I ain't stupid."

"When did that happen?"

Nimrod muttered, "The day before she died,"

"Do you know of anyone else who wanted her dead? Do you know who might have killed her?"

"Lots of people wanted her dead. She made

64

everybody mad. But not mad enough to kill her."

Afterward, Maggie commented, "I'm sure glad I don't have to interview Nimrods for a living; he's a creep and being with him makes me feel creepy."

Pauline responded, "Just think of it as another challenge, well-met and finished."

When they were back at Pauline's, Maggie said, "You know, Pauline, I think you and I should have a super special treat to help us celebrate when we accomplish something. Like *real* French silk pie. I'll have to get a recipe for that." Maggie consulted Betty Crocker and thought several of her chocolate pies deserved a try. She decided she'd also see if her friend Leona, an excellent cook and baker, had a recipe.

That evening, Pauline told Maggie, "I want to talk to Jim Dowling again and I know where his RV is. Let's go see him."

The trees hid the RV until they neared the end of the driveway. The sun shone on Jim's home, which was tucked into a small clearing. Maggie pushed Pauline's wheelchair forward, but stopped about twenty feet short of the door. "I hear wasps. Look at all of them. I hope he comes out, because I'm not going any closer."

Jim Dowling came out the door and walked over to them. Smiling, he said, "Sorry about the wasps, but they're my best protection against Dixie. Because they drive her crazy, she won't come near the place. No phone here, so she can't even call. What can I do for you?"

"Mr. Dowling, a few things are bothering me," said Pauline. "For instance, I don't understand why you didn't divorce Dixie or at least legally separate."

"Well, it bothers me, too," he quipped.

Pauline just waited.

"I guess it doesn't matter anymore." He seemed to be talking to himself. "She was blackmailing me. She wanted all my money or she would go to the radio stations and newspapers with the story of how a bunch of us kids stole a car when I lived in Minneapolis. When I was an up-and-coming lawyer, I thought that would hurt, but I don't suppose it would have been any worse than what happened."

"Why did you want Vern to meet you at the Wormwood cabin the day Dixie died?" Pauline wanted to know.

He looked at her, the sweet little old lady in her wheelchair -- dragging all these things out wasn't sweet at all. He screamed at her, "I was going to get him to help me kill her, but I couldn't go through with it!" He was nearly in tears, apparently feeling worse about his ineptitude than about his murderous plot. He calmed down and continued, "I'd been making plans for years. A week before she died, I overheard a conversation in the grocery store. It was Dixie's hair stylist telling another woman that Dixie had an appointment the next week. Even I knew what that meant. I told Vern to meet me out there while I was sure she'd be gone. I was there, about half an hour early, but I turned right around and came back, so the sheriff has found my tire tracks and no doubt, he'll be coming for me soon."

"I see." Pauline thought about it. "You have good reason to be glad she's dead. What are you going to do about it?" she asked.

Her response confused Jim Dowling. "What do you mean?"

"Are you going to make a life for yourself? What about Cal? And Joan?"

"I . . . uh . . . I don't know."

"Thank you for your time, Mr. Dowling. Let's go, Maggie."

As they drove away, Maggie said, "She sure had a bull ring in his nose. I wonder if he'll take it out now."

When Pauline, Maggie and Alec shared information that night, Pauline concluded the session with the comment, "If we summed up the IQ's of those three, Nimrod, Jake and Fast Eddie, I doubt if they would add up to one hundred. And if we add in the IQ that Jim is using these days, we still wouldn't have a hundred."

# 10

The next morning, Pauline not only swung her right leg off the bed by herself, she lifted her right foot into the shower by herself. Because Maggie had been lifting less, she knew this was coming, but she made a big fuss anyway. Pauline's swimming was paying off. Maggie proclaimed, "This definitely calls for a celebration. Let's have one of Betty's chocolate pies."

"Let's!"

They had a light lunch because they wanted plenty of room for pie. Betty Crocker's recipe made a good pie, but not spectacular. Maggie commented, "It may take a lot of testing to produce the perfect pie. That means we'll have to find plenty of reasons to celebrate." Pauline agreed.

After lunch, Pauline called Doris. "How are you doing today?"

"Well, my sciatic nerve is bothering me again. The last time that happened, I couldn't sit or stand or lie down or anything. My doctor sent me to a chiropractor and he pushed and pulled and shoved and I nearly screamed the whole time. And I had to go back again and again. Worst of all, I had to *pay* him for bludgeoning me."

Much later, Pauline said, "You know, Doris, I think you ought to come to exercise hour at the swimming pool. It would do your ailments a world of good."

"Do you really think so?"

"Yes, I do. Maggie and I could stop and pick you up; it isn't much out of our way. Say about nine-thirty Friday?"

"But I don't have a swimming suit."

Pauline wasn't about to accept any excuses. "That's all right; you can wear a pair of shorts and a top, old ones, because the chlorine is hard on clothes. Then if you liked it, you could buy a suit"

"Do you really think it would help?"

"Absolutely. We'll pick you up Friday." Then Pauline asked, "What can you tell me about Joan Lefair?"

"Oh, Joan. She was in 4H and in church activities since high school, always collected stray dogs and cats. Her husband Walt worked for the electric company and played guitar or something in one of those little country-western bands they have around here. They never had any kids. He died a few years ago in some weird accident at work, so the insurance benefit was good but she works at the hardware store anyway. Joan's still active in all the clubs. She's one of those do-gooders, but I like her anyway. I always thought she'd be great with a big mob of her own kids. Joan's only about thirty -- she's still young enough if she'd get to it."

When she finally hung up, Pauline said, "Maggie, let's go see Joan Lefair this evening."

"You want to find out more about Jim Dowling?"

Pauline answered, "Yes. Also, I was thinking she is one more person who would be happy to see Dixie dead. With her out of the way, she could have Jim for herself."

"Do you think she killed Dixie?"

"No, but I'd like to meet her before I decide about her guilt or innocence."

Maggie knew there was something Pauline wasn't telling her, but she replied, "Okay."

When Pauline and Maggie got out of the car at Joan's house, which was about a mile from Lilac, they heard a big ruckus in the back yard, so Maggie pushed Pauline's wheelchair around the house. They saw a big lawn, dominated by a dozen old oaks and brightened by a dozen flowerbeds. Because the first freeze was late this year, there were still a lot of flowers blooming. Twenty barking dogs of all sizes and meowing cats of all breeds danced around Joan as she pulled a wagon with large bags of dog and cat food. Joan was a tall woman who stood up to her height. She wore no-nonsense clothes and had a short, no-nonsense haircut. She blew a whistle and ordered them, "Line up." They immediately took positions at their own food bowls which were lined up with about three feet separating each from the next. "Sit," Joan said. They sat.

"Perfect," Pauline whispered.

Joan walked down the line scooping the right amount into each bowl, talking to each one as she went along. She had chained a big black dog to a tree, fifty feet away from the rest of the animals; he growled all the while she fed the others. When she finished filling all the bowls, she walked over to the tree. "Quiet," she ordered. He continued to growl. "When you learn to follow orders, you'll get fed. When you learn some manners, you'll get to eat with the others." She continued talking to the dog until he became quiet. Then she set his food where he could reach it. She turned around and finally saw her visitors

"Oh, hello. I didn't realize you were here."

"Hello. Your friends were in a bigger rush than we were. I'm Pauline Johnson and this is my friend Maggie O'Neill. My son Alec is a possible suspect in the death of Dixie Dowling and we're trying to find out everything we can about her and her husband."

"Your son is a suspect -- was she murdered?" Joan was obviously shocked. The idea of murder was definitely distasteful to her. She picked up a brush from the wagon and sat down in the grass, brushing the coat of the first dog to finish his meal. "I never met anyone as easy to dislike as she was, but murdered . . .?" She shook her head. "From what I've heard, she was cruel to Jim and I guess to anyone she sank her claws into . . ."

"Tell us what you know about her," Pauline said. A long-haired white cat, with its tail pointed straight up, rubbed across Pauline's legs as she sat in her wheelchair, then it jumped onto her lap and curled up comfortably. Maggie sat on the ground and joined the pet petters. A leggy mutt laid down and put her head on Maggie's leg and another snuggled up on the other side.

Joan told them about the stolen money, which they already knew. "He wanted to pay for what she'd stolen and pay to keep it quiet. I wanted to charge her with robbery though the amount was small, because letting her get away with stealing only encouraged her to do it again. He couldn't hear it then. I went to him because I thought I could deal with him more honestly and more gently than any of the others in our club, but it didn't do any good. We got our money back, but he lost another bit of self-respect." While she talked, the dogs took their turns with Joan's brush.

The black dog at the tree started whining and pulling against his chain. Joan said, "He must have had a good home once; he knows what he's missing." She walked over to him and said sternly, "If I let you free, will you behave yourself?" He sat and thumped his long tail on the ground. She unhooked the dog, who jumped happily at her side.

"He's a bully," Joan said. "Three days ago, he showed up at meal time and tried to steal Topper's food. That's why I chained him up. Just once I had a mean dog who refused to learn; I had him put away. All the others are free to come and go. Some are adopted by people looking for a pet. Some wander on after a few days. If they stick around, I take them to the vet for shots and a checkup."

The big dog lay quietly on Joan's right side; she petted him as she talked and brushed a beagle on her left. Some of her strays wandered off for a bit and returned, others lay close waiting to be brushed. Maggie shifted to a new position; the young dog allowed her that, but immediately moved to put her head on her leg again; the other dog moved away.

"Tell us about Jim," Pauline said quietly.

Joan replied, "Jim and I go way back. His folks moved up here when he was in some kind of trouble in the Cities. High school kids around here don't welcome strangers, but I never followed the crowd. He and I were friends all through high school. We dated some, went to Senior Prom together.

"He could be really boring when he blamed everybody else for his troubles, but he found out I wouldn't put up with that, so he quit doing it, around me anyway. When he became interested in something, nothing would do but that he understood it completely. He ended up knowing more about the Revolutionary War than our teacher did. We used to work together on homework sometimes. Since he was great at figuring out how to solve a problem, and I was good at keeping up on the everyday stuff, we worked well together.

"He went off to college and I was dating a few fellows. Jim and I were still friends, but he wasn't my boy friend. After a few years, I married Walt. I heard Jim went on to law school. I saw him a few times over the years. I was horrified when I heard he married Dixie. I knew she'd give him plenty of reasons to blame the world for treating him wrong."

"Do you think Jim killed her?" Pauline asked.

"I want to say he wouldn't even kill a fly, but he would if it bothered him. Hmm. From what I've heard though, I think he's been past the bothering stage and deep into his shell, just like when he first moved up here. When he's like that, I doubt he could figure anything out, much less how to commit a murder. But I would think that a lawyer's way out would be divorce."

Pauline told Joan, "She was blackmailing him; she didn't want a divorce because he was rich. He admitted he planned to kill her but said he couldn't go through with it. What do you think? Was he telling the truth?"

Joan sighed. "I don't know what to think. I doubt if he killed her, but if he did, he also killed the Jim I knew." She was close to tears. She looked at the lowering sun. "I guess I'd better get some work done." She looked at Pauline. "Snowball is usually as nervous as a long-tailed monkey in a room full of rocking chairs; I think she's found a friend." She looked at Maggie. "Spunky, too. Can you give them a home?"

Startled, Pauline and Maggie looked at each other. They hadn't come to get pets. They were trying to solve a murder! They looked at the cat and dog. It seemed that Spunky and Snowball understood; they looked at their new friends, begging silently. "Okay."

Pauline wrote a check to Joan, "For taking care of the next strays." Snowball and Spunky followed them to the car and hopped into the back seat as soon as Maggie opened the door. Maggie helped Pauline in, put the wheelchair in the trunk and got into the car. She looked at Pauline. "What have we done?"

Pauline grinned. "I've adopted a Little Princess."

Maggie looked back at her dog. "I think my little friend is not so blue-blooded as yours. Part spaniel, part Heinz 57. But she does look a bit Irish. Her name is Kathleen." Kathleen smiled.

When they arrived back at Pauline's house, Pauline said, "You'd better bring Kathleen in too. She's new to you and probably shouldn't be left alone for a while. We'll see how she behaves." Kathleen jumped out of the car at Maggie's command and Little Princess gracefully followed.

"Kathleen, you can run around while I get Pauline into her wheelchair." Kathleen bounced away, with her nose to the ground sniffing excitedly, this way and that, then head up as a cow muttered in the next field.

Princess was a well-brought up blue-blood, exhibiting no vulgar curiosity as she sauntered along surveying her new kingdom, except that as her head moved majestically from side to side, her ears flicked eagerly forward, then side to side, on a constant search for excitement. As Maggie wheeled Pauline into the house, Princess followed. The cat wanted to keep her in sight. Maggie called Kathleen, who was very undecided about priorities: which were more important, her new friends or all the fascinating new smells? Her friends were leaving her behind. She raced after them. Maggie petted and praised her, "Good dog, You come when you're called. Good girl, Kathleen." Kathleen's tail wagged her whole body. She was so very happy to have her own human again. Joan had treated them well, but this human was *hers*.

While Maggie took Pauline to the bathroom, Princess and Kathleen explored the house. Maggie set up the litter box they'd bought on the way home and then gently picked up the cat to show her the box. She put bowls of water out for their pets.

Kathleen followed Maggie into the kitchen. "I can't have you underfoot when I'm cooking." She walked to the corner. "Come here, Kathleen." The dog rushed right over. "Stay." She pointed down. Maggie walked to the refrigerator and Kathleen followed. "No. I said stay." After a few more tries, Kathleen decided that Maggie wasn't leaving, so she lay down to watch. "Good girl. Good dog, Kathleen. Stay. Good dog." Kathleen happily wagged her stump of a tail.

They had another piece of chocolate pie for dessert. After supper, Maggie turned on the TV. Princess hopped up on Pauline's lap and soon her motor rumbled her contentment as Pauline gently scratched her back, her head, behind her ears. Maggie said softly, "It's for her own good that a cat purrs." Then Kathleen jumped up on the sofa and rested her head on Maggie's leg. "Hi, pretty girl."

"There's no need for you to leave Kathleen home alone when you come here." Pauline said. "She looks like she's been too long without a friend; she's better being with us."

"Thanks, Pauline."

The next afternoon, while Maggie was gone, Pauline called Alec; she asked him to drop in on Joan, about five thirty in the evening would be a good time. She wanted him to question Joan further about her recent relationship with Jim Dowling. She, too, had reason to be glad Dixie was dead.

# 11

Alec arrived at Joan's in time to see her feed the strays. The black dog had his dish in the line with the others. He was not too happy about behaving, but he did it anyway. Joan finished scooping food and turned toward Alec; she had the quiet glow of enjoying what she was doing. "Can I help you?"

Alec saw a woman he'd like to be with, as opposed to the kind of woman he'd like to be seen with. "I'm Alec Johnson. My mom asked me to come over here and ask you some more questions about Dixie and Jim and you, but now that I see you, I don't believe for a minute that she thinks you killed Dixie."

"What?!" Joan was shocked and angry. The woman who had taken one of her strays thought she was a murderer!

"I'm sorry. I'm really messing this up." He stopped to try to find the right thing to say. "You see, my mother wanted me to come over here, but while I was watching you, I thought you're just like her, loving all her 'kids,' but not about to take nonsense from any of them. She couldn't possibly suspect you of hurting anyone. So why did she tell me to come here?"

That sounded better to Joan. "Did she tell you that she adopted one of my cats?"

"No. Do you think she wants me to take one too?"

"Maybe . . . you don't suppose she's match-making, do you?"

Alec smiled. "I wouldn't mind that, would you?"

"Yes. Well, maybe not. All right. I devote the next hour or two to my four-footed friends. If you'd like to have a seat, you're welcome to join us." They sat on the grass, about six feet apart.

One homely mutt lay down next to Alec; others came and went, but the mutt stayed. "Where did you get all these animals?"

"They just show up." Joan laughed. "I've heard that during the depression, hoboes would get off a train and look for a house with a special sign chalked on it. That meant the owner was good for a handout. I think stray dogs and cats have left their sign on my house."

"How do you take care of them in winter?"

"See the lean-to built onto the garage? I throw in

a lot of loose hay and leave the door open. All kinds of critters take shelter there. Sometimes I find cats and dogs all curled up together. I guess they're house pets and need more warmth."

She finished brushing one dog and started on the next. "I like your mother. When I saw the wheelchair, I was ready to feel sorry for her, but two minutes later, I was talking to her and she was so interested in what I was saying I forgot all about pity."

"She's had several strokes. But life has treated her pretty rough all along and she's never given up yet. It's a shame I'm such a . . . No, never mind about that. Did you grow up around here?"

Joan answered, "Oh, yes. My folks live just down the road; they've lived there ever since they married, which was two years after they graduated from Lilac High School."

"Really? Mom taught at the Lilac grade school for about ten years. She was Mrs. Anderson then. She married Tom Johnson in 1966 and quit teaching."

"Mrs. Anderson. That name sounds familiar. I'll have to ask Mom. Did you go to school in Lilac?"

"No, we lived in the Cranberry school district."

They talked about school days and movies and music. The yard light had been on for over an hour before the chill of the evening penetrated their conversation. Joan stood and reluctantly broke the spell. "Alec, I've enjoyed talking to you, but I have work to do. Come back again, won't you?"

Alec was disappointed; he wanted to keep talking. "Yeah, I will." He looked at her, memorizing her, then left. On the way home, he began to feel very uncomfortable about how comfortable he'd felt with her. He didn't call Joan or go back for a long time. Joan was disappointed but she'd heard he was a bit of a wastrel, so that didn't surprise her.

The next morning, Maggie noticed that Pauline looked very tired and she said so.

"I haven't been sleeping well because I'm too

worried about Alec. I dream about the people we've talked to. They're on a merry-go-round, bobbing and circling around me, grinning because they aren't guilty so Alec must be."

Maggie was shocked. "Pauline, do you think Alec is guilty?"

"Yes, but guilty of foolishness, not murder. All the stories fit together too well. Unless they're all in it, but Jim, Vern and Alec, plotting murder together? I don't think so. We know what happened but not who caused it to happen or how."

Maggie didn't like to see Pauline upset. "Do you think we should let the problem simmer on the back burner for today? We could do something completely different this morning and then come back to work on it with fresh minds. We could go fly a kite or go jump in the lake or go visiting neighbors."

Pauline thought about it. "Yes. Let's go see Pierre O'Hara."

At Pierre's door, Pauline said, "Mr. O'Hara, I'm Pauline Johnson and this is my friend Maggie O'Neill. I'm so happy to meet you. My mother used to talk about you, but I had no idea you were still around, until I saw the article in the paper about your one-hundredth birthday party. Congratulations."

"Thank you. Come in. Who is your mother?" Pierre was a little stooped and a little hard of hearing, but he looked and acted more like a man of seventy than of a hundred. Pauline and Maggie followed him into the kitchen and sat at the table.

"Minnie Wilson. She died some thirty years ago." A shadow of sadness crossed Pauline's face; she still missed her mother. "She went to the Orange school with you."

Pierre replied, "Minnie Wilson. Yes, I remember her. She was one of the few children there that I wasn't related to. Do you know, a few years after I started there, we had forty children? They had to build an addition on the school and hire a second teacher. The early years of the school, before 1900, there weren't so many children;

then they only went to school for three months; in my time, though, we went from September until early June. Most children started school when they were six years old, but I wanted to go when I was only five and they let me. Once it was raining hard as I went to school. My clothes and my moccasins were soaked when I arrived at school. The teacher took my moccasins off and set them and me near the wood stove to dry."

Pauline said, "My mother told me that an Indian midwife delivered her. Do you know who that would have been?"

"Yes, that was my Aunt Lizzie. She was half Indian, my father's sister. They both knew the Chippewa language, as well as English, Norwegian and a little French. At home we spoke mostly Norwegian, but at school we used English."

Maggie wanted to hear more about his Aunt Lizzie.

"Aunt Lizzie was in Chicago when she met Charlie White. He had been a brakeman for the railroad but he lost a leg in an accident so they made him an inspector. They married and had a son who was nearly blind. Charlie spent all his money on drinking, so Lizzie had to earn money to take care of herself and her son. Charlie's spinster sister Adaline taught biology at the University of Chicago; she was a doctor who went on calls in the evenings. Adaline welcomed Lizzie as an assistant on these calls and taught her midwifery and doctoring.

"Lizzie finally left Charlie and came back here, about 1900. She midwifed for Indians and whites for fourteen years. Then she moved to Minnesota, near Cloquet, where she cooked and doctored for a lumber company. She lost a leg to diabetes and saw her son marry. Several years later, in 1918, influenza broke out. Smoke from bog fires added to their misery. They took the sick people out in box cars. Lizzie's son and his wife died, leaving two babies, one and two years old. Lizzie's diabetes was very bad by then so she wrote to her sister-in-law (Charlie was dead by then) and Adaline took in the babies and raised them as her own."

Pierre related fascinating stories about making

maple syrup, harvesting wild rice and picking wild blueberries. He told them all about local lumbering in the early 1900's and described how to build a log cabin. He had experienced the details of pioneer living and, from nearly a hundred years of reading, he had the historian's larger view of where his stories fit.

On their way home, Maggie said, "I wish I had known his Aunt Lizzie. I've heard ugly stories about the way whites have treated the children of interracial marriages, especially women. Lizzie must have been really special; she commanded enough respect that white women wanted her for their midwife. And her sister-in-law, Adaline taught biology at a university and was a doctor. In 1890! His father spoke four languages and could look at a pile or trees, cut and trimmed, and tell you how much lumber would come from it. No wonder Pierre believes that mixed blood produces more intelligent people."

After a moment, Maggie said, "Pauline, I want to show you something special."

"All right."

Ten minutes later, Maggie drove to the top of a small hill, pulled over and stopped the car.

"Ooohhh." Pauline liked what she saw. Straight ahead, a small lake reflected gold and scarlet maples. To the right, a large cluster of sumac blazed bright red against the pine trees. On the left, yellow popple trees gleamed. Everywhere they looked they saw glorious reds, yellows, oranges set off by evergreens. Pauline said, "They're about to die for the winter and they're all dressed up for their last dance."

The next day, Maggie pushed Pauline's wheelchair up the ramp and into the Community Center, for the salad luncheon to honor Local Living Legends. Ten long folding tables had white tablecloths topped with large vases of bright fall leaves. Trophy cases, photographs of veterans, several large mounted fish, a bingo call board and plaques decorated the walls. The table decorations and people's clothes brightened the large room. Maggie's quick eye took in all this before their friends paraded over to see them.

Pasta salads, garden salads, Jell-O salads, fruit salads, potato salad -- the long serving table showcased salads of every kind and color imaginable. Pauline and Maggie found it hard to choose, so they took a bit of everything within easy reach.

Conversation flowed and glowed around the delicious meal. The highlight of the event came after the meal, when a friend of each honoree told the people why that person was a local legend.

Pauline and Maggie were delighted when Pierre was honored for his age, his many years as a barber in Mackerel, his painting and birch bark canoe building. He still lived alone and took care of himself.

Everybody knew Brownie, mother and grandmother, because of her many jobs, at the locker plant, grocery store, library; they knew her from bowling, softball and card games; they worked with her, as she volunteered her help organizing the county fair and other events. Pauline knew Pierre, Brownie, Vi and Edna, but not the other three honorees.

Pauline and Maggie congratulated Maxine and Edna, the organizers of the event, "What a pleasant afternoon: good food, good people to talk with and most of all, people saying good things about their friends in front of God and everybody."

# 12

The mud had mostly dried up, so Alec drove his car to the beginning of the clearing at Wormwood cabin. He and Cal studied the ground from there to the bridge.

The rescue squad and the sheriff had muddled the tracks, but several deep gouges on either side of the trail supported Vern's story.

"It sure looks like she had a bee in her bonnet," said Alec. Then he asked, "Do you know of any drug that would make a person go crazy at the wheel like that?"

"Sure. But she never used drugs. She gave her toadies plenty of booze, but she didn't drink much either."

"Do you think someone might have put something in her food or drink?"

Cal looked at Alec. "You were the last one with her. Did you drug her?"

"No!" Alec was undone again, but he pulled his thoughts together. "How long before those drugs take effect?"

"Oh, could be right away, could be hours later."

Alec thought aloud, "She said she'd just come from having her hair done. I don't know why a woman would pay to have her hair fussed up like another Medusa."

"What's a Medusa?" Cal asked.

"She was a Greek myth. Anyone who looked into her eyes was turned to stone. Snakes grew on her head instead of hair."

"Does that mean that girls who have snaky hairdos are after that kind of power?"

Alec smiled. "I suppose they are. Let's get back to your mom. Did she have her hair fixed that day?"

"Probably. That's what she did when she was out to get a guy to do her dirty work for her."

"We could see if she ate or drank anything there, but why would they drug her? We should also try to find out where she went during the half hour after she left Guzzler's and before she came here."

They stood on the bridge facing the grassy area where the trail circled in front of the cabin. The cabin windows were boarded up, the siding weather worn, the new roofing was noticeably incongruous. As they followed the trail, they saw two clear sets of car tracks in the dried mud. Several chunks of gray dental stone lay

80

next to the tracks. Cal kicked one away. Alec said, "That's the stuff they use to get an impression of the tracks." He paused. "Your principal told me you skipped school the day your mother died. Were you here that day?"

Cal didn't answer.

"Which of these tracks are yours?" Alec waited.

Cal scuffed out the tracks. "Yeah, I was here," he mumbled, "in the morning." Alec felt sorry for Cal, reduced to spying on his mother.

The main color inside was lemon yellow with bits of bordello red for accents. Alec looked anxiously at Cal, who said, "Don't worry about me. I've been in here before. What are we looking for?"

"I don't know. What was she like? What was she planning? Are there any signs of people we don't know about yet?"

Cal replied scornfully, "This was obviously where she did her wheeling and dealing and we both know what her approach was. We know she was planning to rob your mom. So we're looking for signs of other men. Okay?"

As they opened drawers and looked behind pictures and underneath cushions, Alec asked, "Is there anything you like to do, Cal?"

"Nah."

"Nothing you're good at?"

"Well, maybe photography," Cal said.

"What kind of pictures do you like to take?"

"I dunno. Chipmunks."

Alec's tone was admiring. "You mean you can sit still long enough to get their pictures?"

"Sure. And deer, geese, lots of animals."

"I'd like to see your pictures sometime, if you wouldn't mind showing me."

"Yeah. Sometime."

Alec finally said, "I don't think we'll find anything, do you?"

"No, let's go."

After leaving Cal at the big house, Alec stopped at

the government center to pick up copies of plat maps for the area around and between Guzzler's and the cabin. At his trailer home, he filled the sink with the dirty dishes from the table, put peanut butter, jelly, crackers and other food into the cupboard and wiped the table clean. Then he spread the plat maps out and taped them together. He thought out loud, "She had a half hour head start. Although she was infamous for many character defects, speeding wasn't one of them, so she would drive about thirty miles in half an hour."

He tied a piece of string to a pin and stuck the pin into the map at Guzzler's. He measured, according to the map's scale, thirty miles on the string, and tied it there to another pin, which he stuck in the map at the beginning of the trail to the cabin. Then he stretched the middle of the string with a pencil and marked the map; moving the pencil while keeping the string taut, he marked an elliptical shape. He studied all the places included in the area; he knew most of the people who lived there. They simply weren't Dixie's type.

He called his mom on the phone and explained what he'd done. She asked "How long did it take for you get to the trail from Guzzler's? Dixie had half an hour lead, but she also had that half hour or so that it took you to get there."

"Thanks, Mom."

"You know, now you sound like the Alec I named you for." Pauline bragged.

He lengthened the string and drew the new area. "Aha! D.T.'s!" He called D.T.'s.

"Dick Tagley's Bar."

"Hey, Dick, this is Alec Johnson. Was Dixie Dowling there about 12:30 the day she died?"

"Noon or night?"

"Noon, of course. She was dead by night."

Dick said "Lemme think. Yeah, she was. Met some guy here. He looked just like her, a big fat slob. Why?"

"Did she have anything to eat or drink?"

"I dunno, well, yeah, she ordered a drink, but she

got mad at the guy and left; she hardly drank anything."

"Thanks."

Alec called Cal. "Do you know who Dixie met a few hours before her death? It was at Tagley's, a big overweight fellow, looked like your mom. They argued and then she left."

"That could be her brother, Squirrel. His real name is Wiley Wenkel."

"What kind of guy is he?"

"I think he just got out of jail last week. I suppose he came up here to see if he could get some money from her and they argued about it."

Alec asked, "Where would I find him?"

"He's probably gone by now."

"Would Dixie have had a picture of him?"

"I doubt it," Cal said.

"Would you look? And if you can't find one of him, would you get one of her?"

Cal agreed reluctantly.

"Now?"

"Yeah, okay."

Cal found a picture of Dixie for Alec and Alec took it to bars, motels and resorts asking if anyone had seen Wiley. He started close to D.T.'s and worked outward. Alec found out that Wiley had been in several bars, but he couldn't find out where he'd stayed. After searching for many hours, Alec learned where Wiley was. A bartender told him, "I think that's the guy the sheriff picked up for robbing Dixie Dowling's place last night. When the sheriff arrived on the scene, Wiley had his old pick-up half full of things from her house and he was carrying out her stereo speakers."

Alec went to see Wiley in jail; he found a sallow, very nervous, drug-aged young man. "Hi Wiley. I'm Alec Johnson. I'm looking into your sister's death. I under-stand you're the last person to see her alive." The essence of charm is the sensitivity to know what will please another person and the ability to do the pleasing things. Alec had charm but this time he tried to use his sensitivity to manipulate Wiley into talking.

"So?" he snarled.

"So what did you put in her drink?"

"What the @#$%& are you talking about?"

"The sheriff has your record by now. How much time have you spent in jail?"

Wiley growled.

Alec sounded to himself like a bully, but he excused himself because it was important. "You're in here for burglary. Does the sheriff know you're the last person to see Dixie alive? Does he even know she was your sister? Did you kill her because she wouldn't give you any money for drugs?" Alec stood up. "You can talk to me or you can talk to the sheriff. Right now, it's your choice. Tomorrow I'll tell the sheriff what I know and what I guess. Here's my phone number." He gave Wiley a piece of paper and left.

He went to see his mother. "Mom, I went to see Wiley Wenkel; he's in jail for trying to rob the house of his sister last night. I don't think George knows that Dixie was his sister or that Wiley met her at D.T.'s about half an hour before she died. I left Wiley thinking that I wouldn't tell the sheriff if Wiley talked to me. Wiley could have slipped some drug in Dixie's drink; when it took effect, she went out of control, drove the car into the water and drowned. Cal thought Wiley was gone, so I'm thinking he probably would be gone if he hadn't been caught and he will certainly leave if he's free to go and suspected of murder."

Pauline agreed. "He'd be gone faster than a young boy could dirty his Sunday clothes."

"Do you think sheriff George would tell you how long he'll keep Wiley in jail? Knowing what's on Wiley's record might be useful, too, but I don't know if you could find that out."

Pauline said, "I'll see what I can do."

A little while later, George came to see Pauline. "Thank you for coming, George. Help yourself to coffee in the kitchen and there's gingerbread on the table there if you want a piece." His eyes lit up. "There's whipped cream in the refrigerator. Bring me some too, please."

"I haven't had gingerbread since I was a kid and this tastes even better than I remember it," George said.

When they finished, Pauline said, "I asked you here because I have some questions; I don't know if they would be awkward and it seems like taking care of them here would be easier than at your office. My first question is how long will you keep Wiley Wenkel in jail?"

That surprised George. "Why? What do you know about him?"

"This is very difficult. I've made promises . . . I can tell you that I suspect Wiley of another, very serious crime. If he gets out of jail, he'll be gone and you'll probably never see him again."

"We caught him red-handed, he's got a record, and he broke parole. I've been trying to reach his parole officer. If Wenkel may have committed another crime, I'll ask the officer to revoke his parole. Then we can hold him in jail indefinitely, giving us plenty of time to determine if he's guilty of more. If he's charged with burglary, he could get out on bail and disappear; we'll avoid that possibility."

Pauline asked, "How long does it take to get an autopsy report done?"

"The complete report usually comes back in seven to ten days." George was puzzled, then he realized there was only one autopsy report due and that was Dixie Dowling's.

Pauline said sternly, "Forget what you're thinking for a few days." George looked at her. She'd sounded fierce, but immediately she regretted that tactic. "Please."

"All right."

"Can you tell me what is on Wiley's criminal record?"

"Since jail time is a matter of public record, I can tell you that he's been in jail twice for burglary. But I wouldn't tell you that my guess is he's been stealing to get drug money. I could get into trouble for saying things like that."

Pauline said, "Thank you."

George said, "Thank you, too. Now I know what

85

to do next about Wiley Wenkel."

After George left, Pauline called Alec and gave him the information.

"Thanks, Mom."

"You're welcome."

As Alec expected, Wiley wanted to see him the next morning. Alec said to him, "All right, tell me all about it."

"How much are you going to pay me?"

Alec laughed, long and hard. "If I gave you every penny I have, there wouldn't be enough money to get you one dose of your favorite drug. Take a good look at my clothes. Do they look like I paid a lot of money for them or do they look like the kind you get at a second hand store?" Alec didn't volunteer any ideas on his nickels, dimes or dollars. "The reason you want to talk to me is that you can probably avoid a lot of trouble with the sheriff if you do. You already have two convictions for burglary, you're here on a third count and you may be involved in murder. If that isn't reason enough, you wasted your money when you called me."

Wiley didn't like the picture but he didn't see that he had much choice. "What do you want to know?"

"Why were you in jail and for how long?"

Wiley whined, "I stole a car. I was in for a year."

"That's a pretty short sentence for a repeat offender."

Wiley wasn't prepared for that. He muttered, "I ratted on the other guys. There was a big bunch of us."

Alec had guessed as much. An old saying came to his mind "Don't trust your bone to another man's dog." He reworded it. "Don't trust his dog's bone to Wiley because he'd sell it for drug money." Alec asked, "When did you get out?"

"Last week, Monday."

"When did you come up here?"

"Tuesday."

"What did you do all day Monday?"

Wiley sniveled, "I looked up some of my old buddies. I tried to find Dixie."

"Wouldn't any of your buddies advance you some money for drugs? What do you use, anyway?"

"Ecstasy, cocaine, whatever I can get." Wiley realized too late that he'd admitted more than he wanted to. "So what?"

Alec said, "So you came up here Tuesday. Then what?"

"I called Dixie. She didn't want to see me. Finally she agreed to meet me at D.T.'s Wednesday." Wiley looked resentful. "I got there early. There was hardly anybody there, so I talked with the bartender. He told me all about Dixie. She had huge gambling debts and a bad reputation. I didn't expect to hear anything good about her, but her being deep in debt worried me because I needed money. She always helped me before. Sure enough, she told me she couldn't give me any money. I got mad and yelled at her."

"Is that when you put something in her drink?" Alec asked.

"If I'd had any drugs, I would have taken them myself. I wouldn't waste them on her! Besides, she only drank two swallows of her drink. That wouldn't have been enough to hurt her. I didn't want to hurt her anyway. I was mad, but not that mad."

"The autopsy report will be here any day now, so if there's no sign of drugs, I guess you'll be in the clear." Wiley looked relieved. "Unless of course, the sheriff knows something I don't know. And there's still the burglary charge." Wiley frowned again. "You know, Wiley, I think your best bet is to tell the sheriff everything you know about Dixie and her death and your last talk with her. He just might let you off easy on the burglary charge." Alec stood. "Thank you for talking to me."

87

# 13

On their way to exercise hour, Pauline and Maggie picked up Doris who fussed all the way to the pool. Once in the water, Doris followed directions as well as her limited mobility allowed; she held onto the side as Pauline did. After a while she forgot that she didn't really like being in the water because she'd found a goldmine for gossip, even if Jenine kept interrupting at the juiciest moments.

Brownie asked Pauline, "What's new?"

"What's new is what's old. Maggie and I are reading the children's classics again. We've finished Anne of Green Gables, The Cat in the Hat, Wind in the Willows, and Little Women. Now we're reading Pippi Longstocking."

Brownie worked in the library; she loved books, too. "Wonderful books! Have you heard about our First Books for Kids program?"

"It sounds interesting. How does it work?"

"Karen's the expert on it. Karen," she called, "come tell Pauline about First Books for Kids."

Karen came over and said, "It started on Wisconsin public TV and then the Home and Community Education groups took over. Every month, a specially trained volunteer goes to Head Start to read a book to the kids. Some readers make noises that fit the story or act it out or bring stuffed animals that go with the book. Then she gives each child a copy of the book and an activity sheet to take home. The Head Start teachers encourage the parents to read the books with their children and help with the activity sheets. The library has the program, too.

"Right now, the Friends of the Library and the HCE clubs are working on plans to raise the money for next years program"

"Great idea!" Pauline exclaimed.

In the dressing room, Doris told Pauline she hadn't felt so good in ages.

Pauline called her the next Monday to see if she wanted to go again. After Doris explained all her ailments she said, "Of course I want to go to exercise hour again. But I think I should drive by myself. I get talking with people and don't know when to quit and I don't want to keep you waiting. I hope you can understand."

Pauline understood. She didn't argue with Doris, because Doris was a little like liquor, better taken in small doses. When she hung up, Pauline told Maggie, "The water exercise has helped Doris so much that it took her only fifteen minutes to tell me about her infirmities."

"But you like her anyway."

Pauline laughed. "Yes, I do."

Maggie was running out of ideas for meals, so she reached into the cupboard for Pauline's Betty Crocker Cookbook. Hiding next to it was a spiral-bound, yellow paperback, Kitchen Secrets: Trade Lake Zion Lutheran Church, published in 1958.

The cookbook devoted its first hundred pages to breads and sweets; the other fifty pages covered hot dishes, meats and so forth. Maggie took it out to the dining room table. Pauline sat next to the table watching Wheel of Fortune on the TV in the living room.

During a commercial, Maggie exclaimed, "Pauline, I've never seen a cookbook like this." She moved next to Pauline, who turned her wheelchair toward the table. Maggie said, "It starts with grace before and after meals and tells you to think holy thoughts while you fix and eat a meal. The bread section starts with a quotation from the Bible, 'Jesus said unto them, I am the bread of life.' Oh, here's a recipe for Swedish Limpa that makes six loaves of bread. Wow!"

"In those days, we made big batches because we had big families. Swedish Limpa, that's rye bread, a good recipe, but my very American children wouldn't eat it. I had to make white bread. Now the whole world knows what we knew back then; white flour has all the nourishment processed right out of it."

89

"Look, here's a whole page of ads," Maggie exclaimed. "Phone numbers 1, 16, 130! Only one, two or three digits for Carlstown phones. I grew up near Kansas City. In 1958, they had just added a seventh digit to phone numbers. Our number was HEdrick 3406, so it became HEDrick 3406.

"Shorty's Ice and Dray had an ad -- I'll bet that business is long gone. Here's an ad for Ben Franklin -- they're still around. The bank offered 3% on savings and on CD's. Abbie's Beauty Shop -- 'Dry your hair under our new air-conditioned dryers. No roaring in the ears.' Do you suppose that women coming out of a beauty *salon* today look better than those who came out of a beauty *shop* in 1958?"

Pauline said, "Lots of churches put out cookbooks like that. We collected recipes and went to businesses for ads, which paid for the printing. We used the money from selling the books for things in the church kitchen and for projects like sponsoring a home for unwed mothers."

The game show continued and Pauline turned toward the TV. When a contestant asked for "n," the puzzle board showed  _ _ _ _ t _      _ _ nnes_t _. Pauline said, "Duluth, Minnesota." The contestant spun a bankrupt. The next one guessed "m" and solved the puzzle, winning $900. A contestant solved the next one before Pauline or Maggie figured it out. Commercial time.

Maggie said, "Look at this picture; the woman is using a pressure cooker to can something in pint jars. She's wearing a house dress and an apron. My grandma wore house dresses, but my aunt wore slacks around the house. I used to rush home from school so I could change out of my school clothes because I didn't have to worry about dirt and rips in my blue jeans." Maggie turned a few more pages. "Here's a recipe for tomato soup cake. Ugh. That sounds terrible. Mayonnaise cake, I can't imagine it. Pauline, most of the pages have spatters and fingerprints and ragged edges; you've used this book a lot haven't you."

"Oh, yes. Many times I couldn't afford all the ingredients though, so I had to adjust the recipes to fit what I had on hand."

Maggie asked, "What's this, Biblical Cake, 4 cups I Kings 4:22, ½ teaspoon Leviticus 2:13 . . .?" Maggie moved the book over to Pauline.

Pauline laughed. "Let's see. Four cups, that has to be flour. I think it called for a lot of eggs, yes, that would be 6 Isaiah 10:14, and sugar, honey, salt, raisins, . . . I forget what all the ingredients were. But whoever wrote the recipe really knew her Bible. For years they served that cake at every funeral lunch and potluck they had." Pauline turned to the last section. "Here's a recipe I haven't used in a long, long time, lefse."

"What is that?"

"I guess you could call it a potato flatbread; it's Norwegian. Mashed potatoes, flour, salt, and cream or butter, rolled out very thin and then baked on a pancake griddle without grease. It was a lot of work, but fortunately my children didn't like it, so I didn't make it after Andy died. They loved rosettes, though. I had to make rosettes when they were at school if I wanted them to last more than a few minutes."

Pauline pointed to another recipe. "We ate a lot of these potato pancakes in our poor days. We grew our own potatoes and flour was only about $5 for a hundred pounds, so that was a cheap, filling meal. We didn't have enough maple trees right around here to make syrup, but we made blueberry syrup and my children liked that on their potato pancakes."

Maggie asked, "Would you like for me to make lefse?"

Pauline laughed. "You have no idea what a tedious messy, difficult job it is to make lefse. Besides, you need a pastry cloth, a grooved rolling pin, and a lefse stick for turning it over; mine are long gone. But how about making potato pancakes?"

"I'd be glad to. For lunch tomorrow, with ham?"

Pauline agreed enthusiastically.

Then Alec came in and it was again time to share what they'd discovered and see if they could reach any new conclusions. Alec told them what Wiley had said.

Sitting at the table, sipping coffee, Alec scratched his head to see if that would help him to think better.

"We know," said Pauline, "That Vern, Alec, Cal and Jim were there the day Dixie died. Cal, Jim, Nimrod and Squirrel had reason to want her dead. Alec had reason, but he didn't realize it yet. We don't know what killed her. Alec, do you think she was shot or stabbed or anything like that?"

"I didn't hear a gun and I didn't see blood, but I wasn't looking for anything like that. The autopsy will show what happened for sure, but I think she was driving crazy, went off the bridge and either she broke her neck when the car landed or else she drowned."

Pauline said, "So the murderer was whoever made her drive crazy, unless the autopsy shows us differently. Was she drugged, Alec?"

"According to Cal, Dixie didn't use drugs. If drugs were the cause, let's suppose someone put them in her food or drink. If everybody told the truth, Dixie saw her hair stylist in the morning, ate at the cafe at noon, went home, met me at Guzzler's, met Wiley at D. T.'s, then went to Wormwood where she died. She could have been with someone else after Cal left and before her hair appointment or else after lunch and before she met me."

"Then we know four people," Pauline said, "who could have drugged her: the hair stylist, the waitress, you and Wiley. Maggie and I talked to the beautician, Clara. Clara owns the place; although Dixie never tips her, she gets plenty of money from her because Dixie goes for anything fancy. We also talked to the waitress, Madelyn. Madelyn caught Dixie stealing tips when they used to waitress together. Madelyn told her off, in front of all the waitresses. Dixie walked out and never went back. If Madelyn were dead, I'd suspect Dixie. But Madelyn would use her tongue, not drugs, to get back at someone."

Alec said quietly, "Neither of them had any motive that we know of for giving her drugs. I didn't give her any and I doubt if Wiley did. I don't think drugs caused her death."

"What would make her drive crazy, if not drugs?"

"What would drive her crazy?" Maggie muttered.

After a long moment of concentration, they all shouted, "Wasps!"

Pauline was excited. "Alec, were there wasps around the Guzzler that day? Did she have her car window open so one could fly in?"

"That's it! When I turned off my engine, I heard wasps and I closed my windows. But she parked farther down, so she probably didn't see them; if she had, she probably would have driven away."

Pauline called the sheriff at home. "George, this is Pauline Johnson. My son, my friend and I believe a wasp stung Dixie Dowling, which drove her crazy and she went off the bridge and drowned."

"So, you have figured it all out, have you?" The sheriff admired his former teacher, but this was amazing.

"Yes, we have," answered Pauline.

"Well, the pathologist's report came late this afternoon. He checked for venom because of swelling and several small holes in her neck. It was a wasp all right. How did you figure it out?"

"We used our heads for something besides hat racks. I guess Wiley Wenkel didn't kill her, so you can charge him with his latest burglary or whatever it is that you do." She hung up and said to Alec and Maggie, "We were right!" Pauline grinned. "That means even wasps are occasionally useful."

With Dixie's considerable weight off their backs, Alec, Pauline and Maggie nearly floated up to the ceiling. Even the old house laughed with them.

After Alec left, Pauline commented, "You know, the more I've thought about it, the more I think, judging from all our interviews, that Dixie made a lot of promises but I think as soon as one man said he'd had her, all the others had to say so, too. I don't think she knew how to give anybody what they wanted from her."

"I think you're right."

Pauline suggested, "We should celebrate our cerebral expertise with a special treat. How about trying French silk pie tomorrow?"

"Pauline, you're absolutely right." Kathleen's tail was thumping against the floor. "Pauline, do you think Kathleen understands what you're saying? You said 'treat' and she looks at you as if you'd just said the magic word. What do you think? Should our little friends get special something, too?"

"Of course. I have a can of tuna in the cupboard. I'm sure Princess would like that."

"There are those ham bones in the freezer." When Maggie bought a ham for Pauline, she had the meat man slice it into four fat slices so it was easier to debone. Then she could cut it up and freeze it in one-meal packages. "Could you contribute a bone to the cause? There would still be enough for soup."

"Yes, Kathleen is welcome to a bone. "

The next day, Maggie tried another of Betty Crocker's chocolate pie recipes. It was good, but not fantastic. She would keep trying until she found the perfect recipe.

Princess nibbled daintily at her tuna fish. She seemed to eat even more slowly than usual, to savor every bite. Maggie gave Kathleen her bone outside. When Princess finished her treat, she wanted to go outside, too.

A little later, Maggie looked out at them. "Pauline, come look at our friends." Pauline wheeled herself over to the door. Kathleen was lying down on the slightly overgrown lawn, bone between her paws, totally focused on chewing it down to nothing. She ignored Princess who was curled up next to her, enjoying the warm sun.

Kathy and Dave's big brown dog came walking over, lured by the smell of the bone and the dog and cat. They'd met before, warily, and accepted each other. Princess raised her head. The big dog growled, wanting the bone. That got Kathleen's attention. She stood up to face the intruder, who was twice as big as she was, and growled fiercely.

Maggie was all ready to run out and break up a fight, but Pauline said, "Wait." The big dog, twenty feet from Kathleen, took another step forward, growling.

Princess leaped up next to Kathleen and hissed viciously at the interloper. He looked at the two of them, backed up a few steps and lay down.

"Well I'll be darned," Maggie said.

"Me, too," Pauline agreed. "I guess it's a good thing you bring your dog with you. Even animals can never have too many friends."

They moved away from the door. Twenty minutes later, Maggie looked out again. The neighbors' dog had the bone; Kathleen and Princess lay nearby watching him calmly. Maggie told Pauline, who said, "Females are good at sharing."

Jim asked Cal if he wanted to move in with him until they settled on what to do. Cal took a few of his things from the big house and moved to the RV.

It was Wednesday. At the AA meeting that night, Alec told the group that he and his Mom had figured out how Dixie had died, so he wasn't a murder suspect anymore. As he told them how good it felt to do something right for a change, he finally recognized how wrong his life had been. A little later he said, "You know, I really am an alcoholic."

Fred said, "You have taken the first step to solving your problems. We'll help you through the other steps."

### Pauline's Favorite Potato Pancakes
(From the Trade Lake Cookbook)

2 cups raw potatoes
1/4 cup milk
1 egg, slightly beaten
2 T flour
1 t salt
Grate the potato and immediately add to the milk. Add egg, flour and salt. Drop from tablespoon onto greased skillet. Fry until well-browned and crisp on both sides

# 14

Alec was at the drive-in, supposedly to talk to Fred, who owned it. When Alec saw Cal ride up on his bicycle, Alec left quickly and went over to Grandma Marion's (her real grandchildren lived far away, but all the locals had adopted her). At his knock, Marion appeared at her back door. She smiled. "Go ahead." Alec walked into the back yard and took a brown fuzzy puppy out of a pen where it had been playing with its litter mates. Marion had asked Fred if he knew anyone who wanted a springer spaniel and Fred had told Alec. The puppies were old enough to wean; it was time to find homes for them.

Alec sauntered over to the table where Cal sat eating a hot dog. His normally sullen look brightened a bit when he saw the puppy, but quickly returned. Alec said, "I'm thinking of getting a puppy. What . . ."

"Alec, telephone," Janet called out the window of the drive-in.

"Here, Cal, watch her for a minute, will you?" Alec handed the puppy to Cal and hurried in to answer the phone.

"Alec Johnson speaking."

"This is Marion." She laughed. "Do you think it will work?"

"Thanks, Marion. You are the perfect conspirator. I'm going to hang up now, because you can see him from where you are, but I can't. Thanks."

Cal had the spaniel on his lap, feeding her the last tiny bites of his hot dog. Then he set her down. Nose to the ground, she sniffed excitedly, rushing this way and that and the other way, too. All those new smells! Cal followed her, grinning most uncharacteristically, as she led out to the graveled area where the cars drove up.

A junk heap came in, driven by Patty, one of Cal's classmates. Patty wasn't the sort of person anyone noticed in a crowd, until she smiled. Her smile lit up a room like sunshine after a spring rain. "Hi, Cal. Whatcha got there?"

Cal was embarrassed. She'd never spoken to him before, at least not more than "Hi." He didn't know how to talk to girls. That was why he didn't do sports or clubs or anything like that. "That's Alec's new puppy, I guess. I'm just watching her." And he turned to see what the puppy was doing. She was chasing a butterfly, heading right for the road and a car was coming. Cal raced across the thirty feet of gravel; the oncoming driver hit the horn and the brakes, which scared the puppy; she stopped right in the path of the car. Cal grabbed the puppy and kept going. The car stopped, several feet past where the puppy had been. When Cal reached the far side of the road, his legs decided to sit him down. The driver pulled into the drive-in and joined Alec and Patty and the waitresses who went to see if Cal was all right.

His body was fine. The spaniel had buried her head between his arm and his side where she whimpered her fear, but otherwise she was fine, too. Alec chased everybody away and sat down next to Cal, who immediately started blubbering, "I can't do anything right, not even take care of a puppy for five minutes!" Alec listened for a while, then asked, "What's the puppy's name?"

"Sunrise," Cal answered, without thinking.

Alec checked for traffic, then he took Sunrise from Cal and set her down, five feet from Cal. She ran right back to him and nudged his arm until he picked her up again.

"Seems to me Sunrise likes you better than me," Alec said. "I'd better pick one of her litter-mates. Why don't you take Sunrise back to Grandma Marion's and see if she'll let you have her? She can tell you how to take care of her and train her."

Sunrise was already asleep as she lay between Cal's arm and his stomach. He looked at her, amazed; she liked him and trusted him! Quietly he said, "Okay."

Marion told Cal, "The first thing you need to know

about your springer spaniel is that she will do anything to please you, so that she will be easy to train if you do it by praising her. Scold her only when you catch her in the act of doing something wrong. She can be a real pest if you spoil her so you must be firm when you tell her 'No.'"

Then Marion gave detailed directions about feeding and house-training. Cal had questions, so it was over an hour before he left. He held Sunrise with one hand and arm and steered his bicycle with the other as he practiced his speech to his stepfather.

At Jim's RV that night, Jim stared curiously at his excited stepson. Cal had avoided him from the beginning, had never talked him to when they were together; now Cal just kept talking about how he'd take care of the puppy. But lethargic Jim didn't respond. Finally Cal set Sunrise on Jim's lap and walked out, saying, "I have to get her some water." Cal came back in five minutes with a bowl of water. Jim was on the floor and Sunrise was trying to crawl up inside the leg of his pants.

Jim and Cal smiled at each other.

The next day, Jim said to Cal, "We have a lot of decisions to make and if you're going to have a puppy to take care of, I guess we'd better start deciding. First, should we find your father?"

"My birth certificate says he's John Doe," Cal said bitterly.

"Well, I'd like for you to stay with me, but we could probably find him if you wanted to."

"You want me to stay?" That surprised Cal.

"If you want to, yes. I've been thinking I'd sell the big house and build a house here. I'd have plenty of room for you and Sunny. I suppose we'd have to get another puppy, so Sunny wouldn't be lonesome while you're in school and I'm at work. Yes, I'm really going to start working again. It'll be slow for a while, but I hope to build up a good clientele again. I think it's high time I came out of hibernation, don't you?"

Cal nodded.

"I plan to sell the fancy furniture and things as well

as the house, but if you want anything other than your own things, it's yours, whether you stay or not.  Also, we have to set up some rules.  Your mother refused to set limits on you.  I can't do that.  If you stay, we'll have to work out some basic rules; we'll have to decide on consequences for you if you break the rules.  Think about these things for a few days and let me know."

Cal thought.  School wasn't great; he didn't think much of Jim; it might be quite an adventure to live with his real father.  But much of his thinking time was spent with a small puppy curled up on his lap.  Jim was as honest as his mother had been devious and he had offered his home to Cal and Sunny.

"Jim, I'd like to stay with you." They shared a timid smile.

They designed the new house together; they agreed on some rules and chores for Cal.  Jim bought another spaniel and named him King.  He cleaned up his office; he sent out letters to former clients, apologizing for his unprofessional behavior and telling them that he was back in business.  He worked hard on the few small cases he picked up.  He arranged for the sale of the big house.  In preparing the furnishings for auction, he discovered dozens of TV's and other suspicious things in the basement.   Sheriff George checked them out; sure enough, some of them had been reported stolen.  George took them so he could return them to their owners, as many of them as he could find.

Doris called Pauline.  "I know you were interested in the Dixie Dowling thing.  Did you hear the latest?"

"What is that?"

"Well, you wouldn't believe what they found at Dixie's house!  All kinds of TV's and stuff.  The sheriff figures they're stolen, but he doesn't know all the owners.  And did you know . . .?"

Pauline called the sheriff and told him that some of the unknown owners might be Mike Callahan, Virgil Smith, Jacob Jorgensen, and Toby Torment.

George asked, "And how do you know that?"

"I was hoping you wouldn't ask. I guess I can tell you that I was looking for information about Dixie and promised not to tell you what I heard about other matters."

George was very curious, but he respected Pauline too much to demand an answer.

"I don't think my source got anything out of the robberies except promises and besides, I feel sure you'll catch him on something sooner or later. He's so crooked, he could hide behind a corkscrew. Of course, if you found his fingerprints on the stolen things, when you catch him for one thing, you'd have him for two."

"All right. Thanks for the tip." Of course, her tip was correct, thanks to Nimrod.

Pauline picked up the ringing phone. "Pauline, this is Marion. You'll never in a million years guess what your Alec has done."

Pauline couldn't imagine anyone calling with good news about Alec, but Marion sounded quite cheerful, so she asked, "What now?" When Marion finished telling Pauline about the puppy plot, Pauline laughed. "Oh, Marion, you are such a dear to tell me about that. I've had plenty of 'friends' give me bad news about him, but this is the first time anyone has called to tell me he's done something fine. Thank you! Say, it's been far too long since we had a good long chat. How about if Maggie drives me over to see you tomorrow afternoon?"

"Yes, I'd like that. About two?"

"Fine."

At Marion's, they sat at the kitchen table, with fresh coffee and a plate of Marion's delicious cookies.

After catching up on recent events, Pauline asked, "Marion, didn't you go to Europe when you were young?"

The question surprised Marion; then she laughed. "When I was in high school in the late 1920's, I had long hair, a funny name, Marion Vavrina, and I milked cows. Boys didn't look at me. In college at Grand Forks, North Dakota, I was heartbroken at first because no sorority wanted me. But I got involved in student YWCA and even became president in my senior year and traveled to conferences. I was big stuff after all. I graduated from

100

the U and taught phy ed there for $85 a month."

Marion enjoyed telling stories; Pauline listened and nodded and Maggie followed her lead.

"After a year of teaching, I had a grand opportunity. For $491, I could go from New York to Europe and back. I'd be in a group of students earning graduate credits for studying phy ed in Europe. I had always worked and saved, so I had a little over $500. I had to work for two weeks in a summer camp to earn train fare to and from New York and some spending money. My mother was dead set against my going; maybe it was all that money (in 1936, we were still in the Depression) or maybe she was afraid I'd never come back, I don't know. At the last minute though, she gave me $25 of her carefully hoarded money.

"My roommates at the New York hotel busied themselves spending money to fill their trunks. Their wealth almost drowned me: I had only two suitcases and $85 spending money for the whole trip. I wanted to see the Statue of Liberty, but didn't quite dare. I wandered the streets and lost myself among the millions of little stories that were unfolding there. On the boat trip to Europe, thirty-two of us, mostly young phy ed teachers, traveled third class, down with the fish smell. We'd tip the steward and sneak up to first class to listen to the orchestra and watch all the bored rich people. My new friends wanted to treat me to cigarettes; I tried one, but it didn't taste good, so I didn't smoke. I didn't drink. I didn't chase men. We got along anyway."

Marion told about her studies, "I studied the gymnastics programs -- we'd call them calisthenics today. The schools that specialized might have two or three thousand students in line doing a twenty- or thirty-minute, complicated routine, all in perfect unison.

"We slept in gyms for little or nothing. While the other women hunted men and bargains, I admired the beautiful glass windows and glassware in Sweden, the magnificent fjords of Norway, the beautiful children who were not ashamed to be naked. My hungry eyes gorged at the Louvre, my spirit soared at Notre Dame, I waltzed to Strauss' music in Vienna and climbed the Austrian Alps. I even met my cousins in Czechoslovakia and translated for my friends while we were there.

"We went to the 1936 Olympics in Berlin. Hitler was in power; the Nazis surrounded the games with impressive spectacle, impressive but uncomfortable. The crowd cheered for Hitler, who opened the Olympics with an ugly speech about white supremacy. But they also cheered enthusiastically when Jesse Owens, an American Negro, won his four gold medals in track events and broke all records. My biggest thrill, though, came from seeing Fritz Pollard."

"Who was Fritz Pollard?"

"He was a Negro athlete who went to the university. I taught him and other phy ed majors a six-week course in folk dancing. Anyway, we arrived at the stadium in the morning in time to watch the Olympic athletes practice. I saw Fritz Pollard jumping hurdles, so I ran down to the fence and yelled, 'Hi, Fritz!' He came over and I hugged him."

"You hugged a young Black man in 1936?"

"I know, that was considered horrendously improper for a white women back then, but I never paid any attention to things like that. That afternoon, Fritz won third place and I was thrilled for him and for myself, because I knew an Olympic medal-winner."

"On the way home, I had nothing to declare, so the other women asked me to take their things. I wore a velour hat, Italian gloves, an English herringbone jacket; I had some of their perfume and jewelry in my suitcase, less than the amount for which duty would be collected. We thought we were very clever."

Marion paused. "It was a great adventure and it has stayed with me; that trip began my lifelong love of adventure and love of all things beautiful."

"Marion, that's a great story. I enjoyed hearing it. But we've eaten all your cookies and we have errands to run. Come over to see me some time. Maggie makes excellent bran muffins."

"Pauline," Maggie groaned, "you wouldn't tell her

about that, would you?" She couldn't quite suppress a grin.

Pauline didn't even try to hide her grin. "Yes, Marion, come on over and you'll hear the bran muffin story."

Cal rigged up a basket on his bike, carpet lined so it was easy on Sunny and King's feet, and strapped them in so they couldn't jump out. "Go for a ride?" were magic words that set the dogs' feet dancing and their tails wagging all the way up to their noses. They rode to the drive-in, while it was still open; Cal saw Patty there sometimes and they talked. They rode out to the wildlife refuge at Crex Meadows, one of Cal's favorite places for photography. Sometimes he let them run behind the bike on leashes. As soon as they learned to be quiet and not chase after bugs and birds, they became excellent companions and their noses led them to birds and animals he would have missed by himself.

Once Sunny spotted a bear and growled softly. When Cal saw it, he patted her. "Good girl. Now be quiet. Stay." He stood a few hundred feet from the bear, with nothing to keep it from attacking him, but he was more in awe than in fear. He and the bear stared at each other for a long moment, then Cal raised his camera, telephoto lens already in place, and took pictures. The bear turned and walked away.

Cal forgot how to look sullen.

Before Cal left for school, he put the puppies in the basement, with food and water; Jim came home for lunch to let them outside so they wouldn't mess in the basement. Cal came home from school one day and King rushed right up to him. Cal sat on the floor, petting King but Sunny sat back a few feet and howled, telling Cal how lonesome she'd been without him. Cal howled back. She howled again, and Cal harmonized with her. She howled so hard, her front paws rose off the ground. King just looked at one, then the other; he was happy with the attention he was getting. After a while, she walked over to Cal and put her chin on his knee. He petted her and talked to both of them until they were all three contented.

"Want to go for a run?" Of course they did. So off they went.

# 15

After months of practice, Pauline could swim forty-five feet non-stop. She usually carried the lightweight walker at home to have it just in case; she used the wheelchair only for long trips. She insisted that she still needed Maggie and raised her wages, befitting an assistant detective and perfect companion.

Pauline bought a ball for Princess. Princess swatted it with her paw and it rolled across the room. Kathleen jumped up after it, picked it up in her mouth and stood looking at Princess. She meowed so piteously that Kathleen took it over to her. That became their favorite game.

"Maggie, the snow has put me in a mood to watch ice skating." The first snowfall of the season, about two inches worth, brightened the world for those who could stay inside; careful drivers groaned; kids tested it to see if it made good snowballs.

"Is there skating on TV tonight?"

"For us, yes. I have some videos in the cabinet under the TV."

Pauline picked a video she'd made from several skating shows that had been on TV, with all the commercials cut out. Maggie served up large bowls of lightly buttered and salted popcorn.

Pauline clapped again for the spinning leaps, "oohed" and "aahed" at the balletic grace and the beautiful music. She cried a little when Ekaterina Gordeeva and Sergei Grinkov danced their sweet love; she remembered her shock at his death, knew how Katia had felt. She grinned back at a young Scott Hamilton, though she knew that cancer had dulled his exuberant joy; she and Tom had known Scott, even helped him once. Kristi Yamaguchi reminded Pauline of Sonja Henie, not in her style, but in the captivating charm of her smile. Maggie enjoyed it almost as much as Pauline did. A smiling Pauline went to bed much later than usual that night.

The next day, Maggie said, "Pauline, you should build a skating rink out there on your field. Then while you're waiting for me to bring your lunch, you could be watching the birds in your feeder and skaters, too."

Pauline laughed.

"Or maybe you could light up the whole field with Christmas lights so you'd have something to look at after dark."

Pauline mused, "You know, before I had those strokes, I might have done something like that. Now, I have no energy for foolishness."

"Okay. Let's plan an imaginary park then. Would you want a skating rink?"

"Oh, yes."

"How about putting in animals, lighted up?'

"I'd like that."

"What animals should we have?"

"Lots of deer, cows and lions, wolves, skunks and giraffes, bears . . ." All day, off and on, they planned a grandiose park for the quarter mile by quarter mile field just north of Pauline's house.

The next day, Pauline was preoccupied. She'd been wondering what to do about several requests she'd had for money, from her old HCE group (which they called Homemakers Club when she was a member), from the Friends of the Library for their First Books for Kids program, from her friends in the Lioness' Club and so on. They were worthy causes. Her first impulse had been to write each group a big check that would cover the whole

105

thing. She hesitated and then realized the flaw: she could finance all their projects but that would end the clubs; they existed only to raise money for projects that needed doing. If she started a park, volunteers could collect donations instead of an admission fee, say $5 for a family.

The warming house would have glass sides so people could look out. The center of it could have an office and a small kitchen, so the volunteers could sell cocoa and cookies and popcorn . . . She knew she was being ridiculous. She was 75 years old, too old for such nonsense. It was way too much work and responsibility. Watching it would be fun, though, and Jamie Campbell would be just the man to do it. He could figure out the electrical needs, plumbing, parking and all. From his Irish mother, he had a fine sense of beauty, so it would be done right. But Jamie was 65 and retired -- he wouldn't get involved in such a wild scheme -- not true -- it was only a harebrained idea that *would* attract him.

When Maggie left for her afternoon break, Pauline called Karen, who was active in all the clubs. Karen agreed that the idea was grandiose and preposterous and she loved it completely.

When Maggie came back that evening, she found Jamie Campbell and Pauline arguing vigorously at the table, which was buried in large sheets of white paper. "Maggie, this is Jamie Campbell. He's going to build our park."

"Saints preserve us!" Maggie was flabbergasted. She collapsed into a chair at the table and stared at Pauline and Jamie.

"Alec may be acting like his namesake, but if there's going to be an adventurous mouse in the family, it'll have to be me. Just call me Stuart Little." Pauline grinned. She gave a sheet of paper to Maggie. "See, here are the rink, the warming house, the animals, the walkways. I'll call it the Icy DeLights Park."

Maggie's grin was huge. "Can I help?"

"Of course. You might start by fixing us some supper."

Maggie grilled ham, chicken and cheddar sandwiches, a huge one for Jamie, a small one for herself and a tiny one for Pauline, to suit their different appetites; cranberry juice washed down the sandwiches. For dessert, they polished off the apple pie that Pauline and Maggie had made that morning.

During the next week, outbursts from her children interrupted the excited planning. Sara called first and berated her mother for carelessly throwing away her grandchildren's inheritance. Pauline listened for a minute, then asked her, "If you are so concerned that your children inherit lots of money, why don't you go out and earn it for them? What I give you and your children as a monetary inheritance is a gift, not your birthright." After Pauline hung up, she cried.

Stuart was puzzled. For him, the tried and true was always best, so when his mother took a notion like this, he couldn't understand, couldn't really approve; he never argued with her, he just wondered why. Dorothy didn't understand the park, but she knew about pursuing a dream.

After the week of protests and puzzlement, all her children except Sara pitched in to help Pauline and Jamie. Mary was the one who knew this side of her mother. She had only the youngest of her four children at home; Carl was a senior in high school. She left him with her husband, and stayed with her mother for a week to help design the park.

Alec, who was jobless at the moment, showed up when the work started; he stood off to the side and glowered. His mother could happily spend tons of money, but it all came back to her. Every time he started something, he lost, but she never bailed him out. Sometimes it really bugged him. This park was ridiculous: a 200' x 200' outdoor rink in northern Wisconsin? Today's kids wanted to skate indoors and even the indoor rink at Little Fork could barely make a go of it. She actually expected that people would pay to see all those lit-up animals? With her luck, they probably would. No, there just weren't enough people around here to support the park.

Then Alec thought of how he and his mother had puzzled out Dixie Dowling's death. He smiled. They had worked together and he had liked that. At AA meetings, he was beginning to learn to put aside his childish thinking and take responsibility for himself. Then Jamie Campbell came over to Alec and asked for his help pounding nails. "Sure." He showed up for work every day after that. He even looked beyond himself for a change to see his mother's zest for making things happen.

Stuart brought his two sons up every weekend and they helped. Bewildered he was, but generous. Dorothy pitched in whenever she could.

Jamie found a whole zoo of plastic, life-sized animals. Pauline rented an empty shop where they could repaint them. Mary came again; this time she brought her two sons and two daughters; her two grandchildren stayed with their other grandma. Mary gathered a crew of high school and other aspiring artists and their teachers. They set up an assembly line: clean the animals, mark them for painting, paint them. Mary spent Saturday, Sunday and Monday starting the project, then left the teachers in charge. She came back the next weekend to help finish it.

Pauline offered Alec the job of managing the park when it opened. He liked the idea, but not the responsibility. He declined. Five minutes later he accepted, which delighted Pauline and made her wonder if her forty-three-year-old son might be ready to start growing up. "I'll start you at a modest wage; as you prove yourself, I'll give you sizeable increases."

"Okay." Alec grinned.

At the park, they laid out the rink, built the warming-house, put in walkways, and constructed bleachers. When the paint dried, they brought the animals to the park, placed them carefully and draped them artistically with Christmas lights. They put up a seven-foot fence at the same time, but that failed to deter the long slow line of gawkers who drove by. Reporters and photographers gave the park a big write-up in local papers and the sheer grandiosity of the park spread the story.

Because Pauline wanted a new outfit for the park's opening, Maggie took her shopping. She found a light blue (her favorite color) pants suit. "I guess this could be my last dance -- God willing, it will be a long one -- I guess I'll dress my best for it." She also bought four pairs of slacks, two pairs of warm-up pants, six blouses, four sweaters and three zip-up sweatshirts (one with flowers, one with hummingbirds, one with deer on it). Her new wardrobe was almost as colorful as the fall scene Maggie had shown her a month earlier.

The Icy DeLights Park was set to open at 9:00 a.m. Saturday; it was a cold, sunny day, ideal for drawing a big crowd to a winter park. A hundred cars were there by 8:30. Alec called for more help and opened early. Pauline and Maggie sat in the warming house; Pauline wore her new light-blue pants suit; Maggie wore her favorite clothes, jeans and a new sweatshirt, bright red with three bears on the front. They greeted a constant flow of friends and strangers. Because of the crowds, they couldn't see much, but Pauline noticed Alec, in and out, playing the charming host, helping a little girl with a bloody nose, arranging for breaks and meals for all the workers. Alec's very large nose and huge ears were diminished by the sparkle in his eyes and the charm of his smile.

Starting at ten o'clock, the intercom wafted a variety of lively music from the warming house across the park. A dozen of Pauline's children, grandchildren and great grandchildren, joined by another dozen people who couldn't resist the fun, sang Christmas carols. Then a local jazz band entertained. After lunch a high school chorus performed. At four o'clock, Mary's daughters, Anne and Jeanne, who were professional musicians, played harp and flute duets.

Stuart directed the traffic directors. Pauline's friend Karen was in charge of the concessions and Mary was her gopher. At eleven, Karen sent Mary to buy out all the grocery stores' supplies of cocoa and popcorn; Karen also called a dozen of her club members: "We need cookies." Doctor Dorothy took charge of the monster kettle of chili and the cold cuts for sandwiches; the workers would have plenty to eat. Dorothy's nieces, Anne and Jeanne helped her.

Most families wandered around for an hour or two, came in for cocoa and cookies, then left. After lunch, a few skaters showed up. The huge rink dwarfed them, so Pauline sent Dorothy and some of her grandkids out to join them. It would be good medicine for Dorothy who never got much fresh air because she was too busy doctoring.

By three that afternoon, supplies were plentiful, there were dozens of skaters and Pauline was nodding. Maggie asked, "Pauline, why don't I wheel you home for a nap? Then you'll be fresh for this evening when they turn on the lights and whatever else Alec has planned." Reluctantly Pauline agreed.

The nap and a bite to eat put the sparkle back in Pauline's eye. Then Sara drove in, so Maggie went to do dishes. Sara was miserable. "Mom, I'm sorry."

Pauline knew Sara, knew her greed was a lifetime habit, but Sara was her daughter. "It's all right. I'm glad you're here."

"Is there anything I can do?" Sara asked.

Pauline called out, "Maggie, there's a charter bus pulling in my driveway. Will you tell them they're not supposed to be there?"

"Sure." By the time Maggie dried her hands and went to the back door, Pauline's daughter Mary came prancing in, followed by a dozen people. "Come in Mary. What's all this?"

Right behind Mary, a young man removed his stocking cap and grinned. Maggie recognized the grin. Her mouth opened, but no sound came out. Scott Hamilton walked past her and knelt by Pauline's wheelchair. "Hi Pauline. How are you doing?"

"Just fine. How are you?" Then it hit her: *Scott Hamilton* was here! "What are you doing here?" she blurted out.

Scott answered, "Mary called, said she was your daughter and told me about your park. She said you helped me out once and could I please return the favor and send a note congratulating you. I still remember your kindness, so I thought we'd come and do a little show here to make sure your park gets off to a good start."

Pauline's thoughts raced, "After all these years, so sweet of him, oh, my, this is too much." Pauline burst into tears.

Scott understood. He introduced the others and chattered on while Pauline pulled herself together.

"What goes around comes around," Pauline said. "Scott and all of you, thank you for coming. Welcome. Have you eaten? Would you like coffee?" Her grin was as big as Scott's.

Scott laughed. "We're fine." He looked at his watch. "Right now, we'd better get you over there. It's almost time for the show."

"Sara, come into the other room with me, please." In the bedroom, Pauline asked her to get a snack ready for the skaters. "There are plenty of cold cuts left; make up three dozen sandwiches, big fat ones. Take the chocolate loaf cake out of the freezer; it's one of Maggie's delicious concoctions that's low in sugar and fat. Mix up a big bowl of frosting for it. Fill one of the coffee warmers with cocoa and one with coffee. Just before they leave, put it all on the bus." Sara was glad to do it because it made up a little for the awful things she had said.

Maggie helped Pauline put on her heavy coat, furry hat and warm boots; she wrapped a small blanket around her legs. Scott pushed the wheelchair down the ramp and into the park, followed by Maggie, Mary and the skaters. Dusk was deepening as they entered the park. Alec turned the animals' lights on; hundreds of thousands of tiny white lights outlined the animals. The people in the bleachers breathed out a unanimous sigh of approval.

Earlier, it had become obvious that the bleachers, which were made to seat two thousand people, would not hold everybody. All small children moved to laps; still not enough room. The crowd detoured then, to the woodpile, built up for the warming house fireplaces. Each adult carried chunks of wood to use as seats along the edge of the ice.

Alec turned the lights on for the rink as Scott pushed Pauline out on the ice; Alec announced, "Friends and soon-to-be friends, may I present my mother, Pauline Johnson, who does outrageous things, like making this park." Thousands of people stood, stomped, clapped and cheered. Scott turned the wheelchair to face each section of the audience and Pauline waved her embarrassed, pleased thanks for their cheers. "Let's also give a warm welcome to Scott Hamilton and his group of skaters who came here tonight because he likes Pauline Johnson, too." The cheering was almost as enthusiastic as it had been for Pauline.

The skaters had planned a half hour show, but their great talents, crowned by Scott's exuberant performance, electrified the audience; with their delighted cheering, the crowd magnified the skaters' joy and reflected it back to them. After an hour, Scott invited all skaters in the audience to join them. Word had spread for kids to bring their skates, so hundreds of them joined the snake: Scott led, pushing Pauline, a girl held Scott's waist, a boy held hers and so on as they skated in a snaky pattern around the rink. Then for a while, they played "follow the leader": anyone who couldn't do what the leader did, had to drop out.

Finally Scott announced that they had to leave or they would miss their plane. The audience stood and cheered until the bus took the skaters out of sight.

At the end of the evening, Pauline looked at Alec. He looked like the little barefoot girl who had just won the spelling bee. He had done a great job and he knew it, but he wasn't nearly as proud of himself as his mother was.

Several days later, Maggie looked out at the fence around the park. "Pauline, when we first talked about a park, it was so you would have more to watch. But the fence that keeps people out until they pay also keeps you from looking in."

Pauline laughed. "Instead of looking on from a

distance, I go over there and talk to all those people. If I just want to watch, I can always turn on the TV."

"Then you like it this way?"

"I do." Pauline seemed amused by Maggie's concern.

"Okay." Then Maggie suggested, "Pauline, now that we have recuperated from the grand Grand Opening, we should celebrate its success. Should I try again for the perfect French silk pie?"

"Good Idea!"

The third attempt was also good, but not superb. Maggie had one more recipe she wanted to try. She decided that if she didn't get what she wanted out of that one, she'd make up her own recipe, using ideas from the ones she had tried.

A week after the grand opening, the UPS truck delivered a large box to Pauline; the coffee warmers and cake pan had returned, with a note from each of the skaters expressing their appreciation for the snack and for the wonderful audience. The notes went on the wall of the warming house.

### Maggie's Chocolate-Apple-Zucchini Cake (Low guilt)

1/4 cup vegetable oil
½ cup brown sugar
4 eggs
2 t vanilla
1 t cinnamon
1 t salt
2 cups grated zucchini
2 squares melted unsweetened chocolate
1 ½ cups whole wheat flour
Mix the above
2 t baking soda  in
1/8 cup sour milk (1 t vinegar in unsoured milk)
Grate 2 apples
1 ½ cups white flour

1 cup pecans
Mix everything together. Use loaf cake pan, 350, 45 minutes? (Stick a toothpick in; if it comes out clean, cake is done) Serve warm. Or cool and add frosting.

# 16

Pauline showed Maggie an ad in the newspaper. "Maggie," she said wistfully, "they're going to have a lutefisk dinner at Lakeside Lutheran Church."

Maggie thought, "Lutefisk -- is that one of those Norwegian things my Norwegian husband hated?" She asked Pauline, "What's lutefisk?"

Pauline smiled sweetly, "A specially prepared cod."

It sounded innocuous, but was it? "How is it prepared?"

"Norwegians catch the fish off their northern coast and dry it, then ship it all over the world. To reconstitute it, you soak it in water, then in lye, then in water again."

"Lye."

"Yes."

Maggie groaned. "I remember now. My Arland wouldn't even go into the house if his sister was fixing lutefisk. He used to fish a lot though, and freeze what he caught. Whenever he wanted fish, I'd fix something else for myself, because I don't even like ordinary fish."

"They serve Swedish meatballs, too."

"Not even my husband could get me to like fish, but you want me to take you to church to eat stinky fish?" Maggie asked.

Another sweet smile from Pauline. "Yes, please."

Maggie gave up. "Okay."

Maggie pushed Pauline's wheelchair into the crowded church vestibule, where strangers smiled their welcome and acquaintances greeted them warmly; many of them congratulated Pauline on the successful opening of her park. Past exiting eaters smiling widely, they wove their way to coat hangers, then to the ticket table, where they received numbers. While they waited for seats, they examined the tables of baked goods, which included rosettes, krumkakke, and spritz cookies, as well as the more usual treats like zucchini bread and chocolate chip cookies. Pauline bought krumkakke and rosettes.

Maggie helped Pauline to a chair at the long table and pushed the wheelchair off to the side. White-haired waitresses with small red caps and bright red vests over ruffled blouses served plates with lutefisk or meatballs, whole boiled potatoes and rutabagas. Baskets of rolls, plates of lefse, bowls of cranberry sauce and of cream sauce were on the table, with cream and water pitchers and butter plates.

A huge laugh erupted from the next table as their plates were served. Next to Maggie, Karen explained, "Juan is a member of our church; he said he would come to the lutefisk dinner only if his lutefisk was served with jalapeno peppers. So that's what he got."

As their table was served, Colleen quipped, "Wherever two or three Norwegian Lutherans are gathered in My Name, there is food."

Irish Maggie reluctantly tried one bite of Pauline's lutefisk with butter and another with cream sauce. She told Pauline, "Okay, I've tried it, now. It isn't terrible, but I'd rather have Irish stew."

"So would I," whispered Pauline, "but they aren't serving it here."

"Do you want to try a meatball?" At Pauline's nod, Maggie put one on her plate and they both settled down to serious eating, occasionally interrupted by passing cranberries or lefse, until they reached the point where their stomachs said, "Enough" but their tongues still said "More." Their plates weren't nearly empty yet, so they started chatting, to give the food time to settle between bites.

Maggie told about her husband's aversion to lutefisk and added, "It doesn't smell too bad here, even though they've cooked a lot of lutefisk."

Seated across from Maggie, Karen stopped eating meatballs long enough to tell her, "I've heard that they get more of the lye out now. When I was growing up, I suppose about 1950, my mother's friend boiled some lutefisk and it boiled over and ruined the enamel finish on her brand-new stove."

"I grew up in the '30's," Pauline said. "By 1938, my father found carpentering jobs in the winter to supplement his meager farm income. That's the first time I remember having lutefisk. On Christmas Eve, my mother served up a huge meal, much like this one except we had pudding instead of pie for dessert. Mother was so proud to be able to serve us this traditional Norwegian meal, she could hardly eat any herself. We finished eating, my parents sat back and told us stories about the 'Old Country,' then, as their parents had told them." Maggie heard a faint trace of Norwegian accent slip into Pauline's speech as she relived the old days: "jobs" sounded like "yobs," "his" became "hiss"; she lengthened some sounds and strengthened accents.

Pauline continued, "I used to go into the woods with my father to cut our Christmas tree. We would string popcorn and cranberries and drape them across the branches. We put cookies and candies on the tree, then. After we were in bed, my parents would put our presents on the tree: mittens, wool caps, hair bows, stockings, shirts, all homemade things. In 1938, we had store-bought presents. My new dress thrilled me, but I couldn't understand why my mother was crying. Now I realize how hard it must have been for her to see her children without nice presents for all those horrid years of the depression."

Colleen's Aunt Bernice said, "We had all our relatives, about fifty of them, for our Christmas Eve dinner and everyone had a candle by the plate. That was in the twenties. After dinner, the men did the dishes in wash tubs in the basement."

"In case you hadn't guessed," Uncle Clifford informed everyone, "Colleen's father was Irish. But he loved lutefisk anyway. Every year he ate too much and was sick the next day."

"We always went to Grandma's for Christmas; we had to recite our part in the Christmas program for her," Colleen recalled. "I liked showing off for her. But a few years later, I had another recitation that I *dreaded*; that was the Public Questioning for Confirmation."

"What was that?" asked Maggie, as the others nodded their heads in agreement.

"Before we could be confirmed, we went to Confirmation classes on Saturday mornings, besides Sunday School, vacation Bible school and Bible camp. After two years of classes, we had to prove we were ready for Confirmation: at the Public Questioning, the minister asked us the catechism questions in front of our parents and anyone else who wanted to be there."

Maggie responded, "That sounds awful."

"It was."

Evelyn said, "Confirmation was a rite of passage when I grew up out in western Minnesota. After that, girls could wear lipstick and nylons and could even go on dates."

"How old were you when you were confirmed?" asked Maggie.

"We had just finished eighth grade."

Colleen commented, "I grew up in Richfield, Minnesota. So near the big city, I suppose we took religion less seriously. Confirmation for me was a big deal, but not as important as a rite of passage."

After a moment, Maggie said, "When I agreed to bring Pauline here to the lutefisk dinner, I borrowed several books from my friend Carol, books about Norwegians and Lutherans and I'm really curious. My impression from the books is that for Lutherans, 'tried and true is best,' anything out of the ordinary is bad and Norwegians are hardworking people who keep everything to themselves."

"Hardworking, yes!"

"All men of our generation keep everything to themselves. They don't talk about their feelings or their philosophy of life or anything."

"My parents had a horror of anything out of the ordinary but my kids have a horror of anything that *is* ordinary."

"My mother was a woman who suffered in silence, but not me!"

Retired pastor Richard said, "Pietism was probably the main cause of the attitude that everyone should be alike. Pietism was a powerful movement across all religions in Europe in about the middle of the 1600's. The emphasis had been on pomp and ceremony in the liturgy and they practically worshiped pastors. The printing press made the Bible available to everyone and that started the pietist movement, which de-emphasized the clergy, decreased the pomp and ceremony and let the community, rather than the minister, judge people's behavior. So, owning too much land became bad, unwed mothers were very bad; thus, the 'lowest common denominator' rules for conduct."

"And yet," Maggie commented, "the Lutheran Church isn't as conservative as the Catholic Church. The Pope still won't allow women priests, but the Lutherans have women ministers."

Evelyn spoke, "Many things have changed, some for the better. I grew up in rural Minnesota. One of my mother's sisters married a German, which was not good in those days, even though he was a Lutheran. Her other sister married an Irish Catholic, which was a terrible thing. My mother, good girl that she was, married a Norwegian Lutheran, who lost everything in the Depression, while her two sisters' husbands prospered. She questioned that for her whole life. Now mixed marriages are so common nobody even notices them." Evelyn thought of another change. "My mother told us that when she was a child, they all had to wear the shoes her father brought home for them, whether they fit or not. I think that kind of absolute authority is gone now and good riddance."

Colleen said, "My kids didn't have to memorize the catechism like I did. They learned to understand it and they discussed life's problems, like loneliness."

"Some things I hope never change," Aunt Bernice said. "I like hearing the choir sing the four-part hymns. I like singing, too, but without a good choir, I hardly feel like I've been to Church."

Everyone had long since finished eating and the cleanup crew was clearing tables. Aunt Bernice noticed that they were practically the only ones left, so she said, "It looks like we're holding things up here. As much fun as this has been, I think we'd better go."

As she drove Pauline home, Maggie said, "Pauline, all those things about Norwegians, hardworking, stuck on the ordinary, unemotional, . . . I know you've been hardworking, but you seem to delight in the unusual and you're about the least emotionally repressed person I ever met. How did you escape from the stereotype?"

Pauline laughed. "If my mother had been Irish, I'm sure she would have thought me a changeling. When Mother caught me doing mischief, she would say, 'I don't understand why you do such things.' I would be punished for fighting and the next day I would be spanked for throwing snowballs at the minister's fussy wife. I wasn't mean; mischief was my way of saying 'tried and true is *dull.*' I don't know. Maybe I named Stuart after an adventurous mouse because I'm an adventurer."

Suddenly a deer leaped out from the side of the road and before Maggie could even hit the brakes, it passed within inches of the front of the car. She gasped, and as it ran out of sight, she said quietly, "Thanks, Ma." Pauline exclaimed, " Oof da!"

Just ahead was the town hall and volunteer fire department. Maggie pulled into the parking area. "I need to stop a minute so my knees can quit knocking."

"That was close, wasn't it!" Pauline exclaimed. "Why 'Thanks, Ma?'"

Maggie looked at Pauline and said slowly, "You know, there isn't a living soul who knows about this, but I'd like to tell you." A little of the Irish brogue and a bit of a southern drawl crept into her speech as she talked about the past. "Ma was very sick when I was little. I spent many hours by her bedside, reading to her. Sure and she always said it took her pain away. She died when I was eight, don't you know. My three older brothers stayed with Da, but he took me to live with Aunt Irene, Ma's older sister. She lived nearby, in Kansas City. My cousins were grown up and had moved away from home, so I had a big bedroom all to myself. My aunt was a kind woman, but my first night there, without Ma, I nearly drowned in my own tears. When at last I quit crying, Glory be to God! There was my mother! She was so radiantly, gloriously happy I started crying all over again. Sure and I knew that she would always be with me when I needed her. When I told Aunt Irene about it the next day, she hugged me close and said that sounded just like what Ma would do, but don't go tellin' anyone else, because some people would think badly of me for talkin' that way."

"Has your mother always been there for you?"

"Oh, yes." Maggie smiled and started up the car.

Pauline asked, "How did you get up here, then?"

"Just before I graduated from high school, my brother's wife died in a car accident, so after graduation I moved in with him in Minneapolis to help him with his kids who were one, three and four years old."

"Wasn't that hard for you, I mean you didn't meet many nice young men there, did you?"

Maggie replied thoughtfully, "I didn't really want to get married. Partly it was because of two old ladies who visited my sick mother. As they left, one of them pontificated, 'It's having all those children that's killing her, four living and all those miscarriages!'"

Pauline exclaimed, "What a horrid thing to say in front of an impressionable child!"

"Sure and it was," Maggie agreed quietly. "And later, Joe's wife died, too. But probably those things weren't the causes, they only reinforced my disinterest in marriage. If Joe had been my husband instead of my brother, I doubt if I would have been brave enough to insist on going to college when his kids were all in school.

"What a campaign I waged! It lasted for months. I started with 'Joe, I want to go to college,' stepped up to 'Joe, I'm going to college,' followed by 'If you want me to stay here and help you, I'll go part-time.' The last statement shattered his resistance, but when I told him that if he wanted me to help him, he'd have to pay me four hundred dollars a year toward my college expenses, he was a man defeated. Many years later he told me he was glad I'd stood up for myself, that I deserved to go to college and I certainly deserved his help."

"Did you get a degree then?"

"That I did, though it took me eight years. After that, I worked part-time as a social worker in Minneapolis until the kids were out of high school and then I worked full-time."

Pauline asked, "What brought you up here?"

"I liked my work; I liked helping the people, but the frustrations piled up. I had a boss who was obsessed with every letter of every law, good or bad; she fixated on every letter of every scrap of paperwork. And the apathy of the poor people I worked with wore me down. 'Give me enough for today. I don't want to build a better tomorrow.' So I studied accounting and came up here." She turned the car into Pauline's driveway. "And here we are, home again."


That same evening Alec showed up at Joan's at feeding time. After Joan fed the dogs and cats, Alec said, "I see Gregory is still here. I thought I might like to take him home with me." Gregory finished eating and bounced over to Alec. He leaned over to pet the dog and stood up again. Joan just looked at him. She wasn't going to make it easy for him. He'd been afraid of that.

"I was going to call, but I got really busy helping Mom start the Icy DeLights Park. Now I'm managing the park" he said proudly.

Joan just looked at him, waiting. He thought that if his mother were here, she would say something like "Your excuses are as thin as soup made from the shadow of a starving chicken." He wanted to give it up, but he'd been thinking about Joan for months. So with a shudder, he blurted out the truth, "When I was here in September, I liked being with you, but I was a loser. I had only been sober for a few days; I didn't have a job; I didn't deserve to be with you. But I've decided I don't have to be a loser all my life. I'm not a winner yet, but I'm working on it." He took a deep breath. "So, can I come see you sometimes?"

Joan's four-footed friends had listened quietly. She was overwhelmed; her mushy legs sat her down on the cold ground and her pets swarmed over her, nudging, licking her face, trying to decide if she was all right. She petted this one and that. "Well, Alec, I don't know what to say. I was disappointed and mad when I didn't hear from you. We made a good connection that night and I value that. But it's hard for me to deal with someone who doesn't have the same values."

Alec interrupted, "If I didn't value that night, I wouldn't have been thinking of you constantly ever since." He smiled sadly. "And I wouldn't be here now."

"Okay, fellas, that's all for now," Joan said as she gently pushed a dog and a cat off her lap and scrambled up. She looked at Alec, "Why did you name him Gregory?"

"After Gregory Peck. My sisters always said he was the handsomest man in the world. Every creature should have something fine, even if it's only a name."

"I think you'll find that Gregory has enough personality for ten Gregory Pecks." She hesitated then said, "Come on in."

He didn't leave until much later.

The next day, Alec stopped in to see his mom, at her request. After a bit of nothings, Alec asked, "What's up, Mom?"

"Alec, I just don't know what to do."

"Can I help with something?"

She mumbled, "Oh, dear."

"Mom, you always tell me to just spit it out."

"That's the problem, don't you see?"

"What, you don't have any spit?"

"Alec, don't be disrespectful!" She took a deep breath. "You have always been so good at messing things up and now you managed the grand opening of my park with such style and efficiency and having Scott here and the whole thing was so wonderful, I can hardly believe it now, weeks later, and the problem is how do I thank you properly without getting your head so blown up that you decide you've done enough good to last for the rest of your life because the park opening was spectacularly successful and I loved it completely but it doesn't begin to match what you have done with yourself." At that, Pauline had to blow her nose and wipe her eyes out a bit.

While she was busy with that, Alec wiped his eyes on his shirt sleeves. After a moment, he said, "You promised me a big fat raise if I earned it. How about if you give it to me when the season is over. That way, I won't have to run out and spend it and forget my duties." He put his hand over hers and squeezed gently. She smiled her agreement.

Alec took their cups out to the kitchen for more coffee. When he returned, Pauline asked, "Why don't you try to get Vern to AA?" Everybody knows that AA is strictly confidential about who is there and what they say. But in small towns, everybody seemed to know anyway, so Alec wasn't surprised that his mother knew he was going.

He took a medallion out of his pocket to show her. It commemorated his first month of sobriety. "I didn't tell you about it because I wasn't sure I'd make it. I didn't want you to get your hopes up and then disappoint you."

"Congratulations." After a moment, she added, "I suppose now you'll really get a big head."

"Probably." Neither of them seemed too worried about it though.

Alec did take Vern to AA. Vern went to church that Sunday; he wore an old, clean suit with a tie; he had a neat haircut and shave. He received Communion, which meant that he'd been to Confession. When Vern received his medallion for a month of sobriety, he celebrated at Guzzler's Bar. That was the end of AA for him. He told Alec, "There's nothing to do when you're sober."

# 17

In spite of the two brown and white fur-balls chasing each other, their new house was big enough to feel empty because of its sparse furnishings. After Cal went to his room one night, Jim made a phone call. "Joan, this is Jim Dowling. How are you doing?"

"Jim, what a surprise! I'm fine and how are you?"

"Well, that's just it, you see. I've been hiding out for years now, worse than when I was in school. You remember how I was?"

"Yes."

He hemmed and hawed for a while and finally he managed to say, "What I mean is, I'm finally putting my life together again and I'm hoping we can be friends again."

She didn't answer right away so Jim was sure she'd turn him down. But she said, "Yes, we could be friends, but I want you to understand that I'm seeing someone else and he stays in my life until I decide otherwise."

"Oh." He was disappointed and thrilled. "Are you serious about each other?"

"Serious as in do we plan to marry? No. But you know I always take my friends seriously. Enough about him. Tell me what you've been doing."

Half an hour later, Joan said, "Jim, it has been great talking to you, but I have to get some work done. Call me again or come over and see me. All right?"

"Yes. Fine. Joan, it's good to have you for a friend. I've missed that all these years. Good night."

As Joan hung up, she thought of the men who had approached her since her husband had died. She hadn't been the least bit interested in men, at any level. Now there were two men in her life. She smiled. She was glad she'd told Alec she just wanted to be his friend for the time being. What a look on his face when she'd said that. Apparently he thought he could charm the pants off any woman, given five minutes or so. Joan wondered if either of the men would grow up enough to become more than friends.

When Maggie arrived at Pauline's a few days later, Pauline said, "Maggie, my good friend Olga died and I'd like to go to her funeral, Saturday morning. Will you please take me?"

"Sure."

On the way to church, Pauline told Maggie about Olga. "She and I went to Karlsburg school together, back during my first life. When Miss Swanson read <u>Anne of Green Gables</u> to us, Olga and I decided we were kindred spirits. We didn't get into as much trouble as Anne and Diane did, but we certainly tried."

Pauline laughed at her memories. "We had a new teacher every year or two because they would marry and then they couldn't teach any more. Olga and I liked school, but some of our teachers weren't very good. When we had a teacher we didn't like, we'd catch a snake or a frog and put it with her things. The teacher always blamed the boys. Once, ratty Robert told on us, but the teacher didn't believe him. She punished him for the mischief and for lying.

"Dear Olga. She had a dozen children. We didn't see each other much while we raised our families. She lived in Little Fork and we had no time or money to spare for visiting. When I moved back here eleven years ago,

I called her up and we became best friends all over again.

"Olga was poor all her life and suffered from bad health for many years, but she never complained. She was the kindest person I ever met, but she didn't put up with foolish or bad people. I wish Adele Pinch had tried to sell tickets to Olga while I was a fly on the wall watching them."

Maggie asked, "What would happen?"

"Adele would come barging in, demanding that Olga buy tickets. Olga would say, 'Of course, dear, but first you must ask me properly. You must *ask* me, not *order* me. You must show respect and consideration for me by saying please.' Olga would be so gentle and humorous about it that Adele would give in and Olga would buy a ticket, which was one more ticket than she could afford."

Hundreds of people came to the funeral to honor their beloved Olga. The minister based his sermon on the text, "It is easier for a camel to pass through the eye of a needle than it is for a rich man to go to heaven." Pauline looked around, No furs or diamonds; there had been no fancy cars in the parking lot. As far as she could tell, she was the only rich person there. Was the minister sermonizing just for her?

After a few minutes of sermon, Olga's eighty-seven-year-old sister started crying loudly. Her daughter sat next to her, put her arm around her mother's shoulder, made quiet soothing sounds. The old woman cried out, "Olga, you weren't supposed to die before me!" Her daughter led her out and down to the church basement.

The minister ignored the disturbance.

Then in the middle of the church, a teenaged girl hiccupped noisily. After the fifth hiccup, the embarrassed girl went out. An old man off to the side had a sneezing fit, which wouldn't quit. Pauline started coughing violently. A baby bawled. A three-year-old yelled out, "I want my Gramma Ol." Two more people coughed vigorously.

Maggie wanted to take Pauline out, but she was afraid Pauline would cough herself right out of the wheelchair, so she stood behind the chair with her hands on Pauline's shoulders, ready to pull back if necessary.

The minister looked around, scowling at the noise. Suddenly all the little children were wailing and half the adults were either coughing or sneezing. The disgusted minister kept talking, but he skipped to the last paragraph of his sermon and finished quickly. He was very upset as he sat down.

Olga's oldest son went to the microphone and talked about his beloved mother. Not a sound interrupted his happy-sad reminiscence. Several more relatives and friends spoke. Pauline pushed her wheelchair up the aisle. When the woman at the microphone finished, Maggie helped Pauline to stand and take her place.

Pauline said, "To know Olga was to love her and to know she loved us. She was a blessing in our lives. We'll miss her, but we know she's in heaven enjoying the reward she has earned." Pauline paused as if she were listening, then she said, "Let's all of us who believe she's in heaven clap our hands."

Pauline clapped, and Maggie; the oldest son joined in and then the whole crowd stood and clapped with great gusto. The minister was bewildered. He clapped half-heartedly.

On the way home, Maggie asked Pauline, "What happened back there?"

"Apparently Olga had her differences with this young minister ever since he came to her church several years ago. Olga wouldn't speak unkind words about anyone, but from what I heard this morning, I'd say he's much more concerned with pushing his ideas of the truth at others than he is with Olga's death or with the sorrow of her family."

Pauline thought a moment before continuing. "What happened? I'd say Olga played one last trick, tried one last time to break through his self-righteousness. And he'll never know who did it. Well done, Olga!"

"Amen."

Rumors told that the minister lost his self-confidence, retired from the ministry for several years, but eventually returned, as a somewhat *human* human being.

# 18

Jim called Joan again. "I'd really appreciate your help. I've cleaned up my office so it looks quite respectable now. Nevertheless, it looks, I don't know, stuffy or something. I wonder if you could give me some ideas."

"Sure. How about if I come over there Saturday morning? About ten?"

"Great. Thanks. See you then."

Once there, Joan looked around. "I see what you mean. Floor to ceiling books on two walls, dark burgundy carpeting, dark burgundy drapes, metal desk and filing cabinets. How much do you want to spend?"

"Not much." Jim replied.

"Hmm. I wonder if we couldn't bleach this carpet, brighten it up a bit. We could try the piece under the desk, so if it doesn't work, we could hide it. The drapes are too heavy; get some new lightweight ones in a lighter burgundy -- no wait a minute; they have a nice backing. We could try washing them in really hot water. Maybe the color would leach out of the burgundy and onto the white backing if we washed them in really hot water. Or we could just buy some dye and dye the backing and hope we match the carpet, if the carpet bleaches all right. We could try the carpet first and if that works, do something about the curtains. A few plants would be good -- get some life in here. Are there any decent paintings in your old house for those walls?"

"Almost everything Dixie bought was too garish or hectic for my tastes, but she accidentally bought a few things I like. I saved a few things. They're at our new house."

A week later, it still looked like a law office, but it was far less formidable. The curtains were much lighter, the plants and paintings added interest and color and the carpet now had random spots of lighter burgundy, the lighter color predominating. It turned out that men didn't even notice the unusual effect, but the women loved it.

Jim closed up early and went home. As he entered the living room, he heard a girl's voice coming from Cal's bedroom. "I really like that!" Jim froze. "Isn't she adorable? How do you get Sunny to hold still long enough to take these pictures?" Jim started breathing again. After he calmed down, he went to Cal's door.

"Hi, Cal. Who is your friend?" He thought he sounded quite genial in spite of his scare.

"Uh, this is Patty, from school. That's Jim. He, uh, he was married to my mother."

"Glad to meet you, Patty." He shook her hand and then she handed him the pictures of Sunny and King. Jim knew Cal used his camera a lot, but Cal had never shown him any of the results. What Jim saw in the pictures was patience, timing, storytelling, and a lot of talent. "These are incredibly good, Cal."

Patty grabbed a school newspaper from the desk. "This just came out today."

Jim looked at the pictures first. Every page had photographs of school activities, each with the notation, "Photograph by Cal Dowling." There were also several of his wildlife pictures.

Cal was embarrassed and proud and hardly knew what to do with himself. "Well, see, Patty saw some of my stuff and talked me into working on the paper. Pretty cool, seeing my pictures all over the paper."

"Good for you both!" He stopped, not sure what to do next. "Say, Cal, I brought home a pizza for supper. Would you like to ask Patty to stay and help us eat it?"

Cal grinned. "Want to, Patty?"

"Sure. Can I call my folks and check with them?"

"Of course. Phone's in the living room."

Jim and Cal were a little uncomfortable about being friendly, but Patty was so delighted with herself and with Cal that she had them laughing all through supper. The dogs were puzzled because they'd never heard Cal and Jim laugh before, but not too puzzled to snap up any tidbits thrown to them from the table.

After Patty left, Jim said, "I like Patty. She's good company."

"Yeah."

"Could I see your paper again? I'd like to look at it more thoroughly."

Cal went to his room and brought it back.

After a while, Jim said, "Cal, you have a great talent for photography. Do you think you'd like to make it your life's work?"

"Maybe. I guess."

"Have you looked into where you might study after high school?"

"A little."

"Is your guidance counselor at school any good? Can he help you look for places and funding?"

"He's all right, I guess."

As with all Jim's attempts at conversation with Cal, this one was stiff and stilted. "I doubt if I'll be able to help much in paying for it. I have to pay off your mother's debts and pay for this house and I'm barely working again. But I'll do what I can."

"How come you're paying her debts?"

"It's the law, for one thing. And I feel responsible in a way. She ran up the debts, but I let her. I thought I could hold on to her with my purse strings. I was very foolish."

They were quiet for a while and then Jim said, "Joan Lefair helped me fix up my office; it looks a lot better now. Would you like to come see it?"

"Yeah, sure," Cal's response lacked enthusiasm.

"I've been trying to think of a way to thank her. What would you think of having her here for dinner Saturday night? We'd have something kind of special but not so fancy that we can't cook it?"

Cal sounded mildly interested when he spoke, "Yeah. Can I invite Patty, too?"

"Good idea. What should we have?"

"Your pork chops are pretty good. And I can make mashed potatoes."

"And applesauce and green beans and salad. What about dessert?"

"How about make-your-own banana splits? We put out all the makings and everybody piles on whatever they want." Jim thought that Cal's pile might get quite large.

"Sounds good to me."

Joan and Patty happily accepted their invitations, but Joan was very curious about a meal prepared by a man and a teenager. Jim had politely refused her offer to bring something. "Just bring your lovely self."

When Joan arrived, Cal and Jim wore white chef's aprons which sported the slogan "Eat at your own risk," but the smells from the kitchen were promising. A few minutes later, Patty came to the door.

The men seated the women at the candle-lit table, then went to the kitchen. They returned, with suit jackets and ties replacing the aprons and they brought in corsages of small red and white roses. The men presented the flowers saying "Thanks for your help." Then they brought in the food.

Joan asked Jim, "Did you really cook all this? It's absolutely delicious." The women were pretty quiet because they were busy eating but the men had already sampled frequently, to insure that everything was perfect, so they kept up a conversation. Jim told Joan that Cal was photographer for his school paper and Cal told Patty how nice Jim's office looked.

Joan was delighted with the food and with the company, most of the company, that is. She was quite opinionated, she knew, but pets did *not* belong at the table begging for scraps. When Sunny gently pawed her leg (and her brand-new pantihose), she pointed down and said "No," quietly. Sunny left her alone after that and so did King. The bad moment passed and she enjoyed herself again.

Jim told stories about some ridiculous cases that had come to court. Joan recounted tales of her strays, Patty was excited about college possibilities; Cal was charmingly silly, which was a delightful change from his old self.

When it came time to leave, Joan said to Jim, "This has been a totally elegant and delicious evening. May we have many more like it."

Before she left, Patty told Cal, "I like being treated so special."

A few nights later, Cal hesitantly started a conversation with Jim. "I talked to Mr. Mortenson, our guidance counselor. He thinks I could do it."

"Do what?"

"Go to college and study journalism with a focus in photography. He told me a bunch of places have good programs and gave me some stuff about them."

"How about your grades?"

"He figured if I earned all A's the next year and a half, I'd probably be in the top half of my class, which I'd need to get into a four-year college. But I'd have to take English, physics, math and all tough courses next year plus I'd have to study like crazy to get ready for the ACT test."

Jim was amazed. He stood up, walked around the living room, looked out the windows. Finally he turned to Cal. "Do *you* think you can do it? Do you *want* to do it?"

"Yes," Cal said with a new assurance.

Jim dug deep inside himself for the right response. "I'm proud of you. If there's anything I can do to help, let me know. Do you need tutors? Are you especially poor in any area?"

"I'm not very good in math."

Jim thought. "Mrs. Koenig down the road used to teach math. She might help you in exchange for doing odd jobs. She used to do everything for herself, but she's getting old now and needs help. I'll give her a call." Mrs. Koenig agreed and asked Cal to bring an algebra book to their first meeting.

"What about money, Cal?" Jim asked.

"Mr. Mortenson says that federal and state funding will pay for everything if I qualify for the aid." Cal grinned. "You get to fill out all kinds of paperwork to prove you can't afford to pay for my education."

"Thanks a lot." Then he frowned. "But I'm not legally responsible for you. That could be a problem. Well, all right. I was going to wait with this, but here it is. I want to adopt you. Would you like that?"

"You'd do that for me?"

"Yes. I couldn't help your mother, but maybe I can help you. Besides, I kind of like the Cal I've seen lately."

"Oh."

"Think about it."

Mrs. Koenig had Cal start with the first set of problems and work the first, the middle and the last problem in each set until he got stuck. He reached page thirty-five before he stopped. She explained what to do and had him work the whole set of problems, which he did quickly. By the end of the hour, he was on page forty-five.

Mrs. Koenig said, "Alec, from what you've told me, it seems to me that you need to review your algebra and geometry courses before school starts next fall. You'll need to *know* them before you start more math and besides, if you're going to take a lot of hard courses and earn A's, you won't have time for going over old courses. It would also be a good idea if you worked your way through an ACT study guide before next fall. Fortunately you have an excellent mind, even if is quite rusty from lack of use."

Cal thought about being adopted by Jim. It scared him a little because it would mean Jim had control over him, and he was used to doing whatever he wanted to do. But it would be more secure than what he was used to and that appealed to Cal. He couldn't have explained why, but he liked watching Jim with King. Jim taught King to behave and he petted him and praised him and played with him and liked him. He knew he'd say yes to adoption, but he'd let the commitment wait a while.

More pressing decisions confronted Cal. He figured out that he'd better talk to his teachers to see what he could do to bring his grades up for this period. If he concentrated in school, he could probably ace all his next semester classes without much homework, because he had an easy schedule. Then he could really focus on the algebra review, doing as much as possible between weekly sessions with Mrs. Koenig. As soon as he finished that, he'd start on geometry and on getting ready for the ACT test. Maybe Patty would work on that with him. His English wasn't bad because he'd always linked words with pictures, but history? Maybe he could ask Mrs. Johanson for names of some books to help him out. He was really good in shop. Mr. Kofal always pulled the best out of his students. But shop wouldn't help him get into college.

Once he had it all figured out, he opened the algebra book and worked through four more pages. They had new algebra books this year, so the teacher had given him a teacher's edition of the old book, with answers in the back. That was a big help.


Pauline called a meeting of all the presidents of clubs and organizations which had offered to help staff the park in return for money for their projects. Twelve women and men came, one for each weekend they planned to be open.

"First," Pauline said, "Karen, here is the check for the First Books for Kids program." Everybody clapped enthusiastically.

"Now, I'll get right to the point of this meeting." Pauline said. "We have a serious money problem."

Vigorous protests erupted. Pauline smiled sweetly, as though she hadn't intended the misunderstanding. "I didn't mean not enough money, I meant too much. Our opening weekend was a fantastic success. We took in enough money to fund all your projects in our first weekend." Pauline paused to let that sink in and she passed out sheets of paper. "In the first column are the figures we estimated for our first year's income. If we raise the estimated income to better reflect our incredible opening, we get the second column. What we can reasonably hope for is enough to pay all operational expenses, give each of your clubs the money you want for your projects and have lots of money left over."

When Pauline saw that they understood, she continued, "Our plan was that each group would specify how much money it needed for its project. That would be paid out of the weekend's proceeds and the rest of the money would go toward maintenance and salaries for a small staff. I would pay if the income fell short, due to a blizzard or just a slow weekend. Well, it looks as though my purse can stay closed." Pauline grinned.

"So why did I ask you to come today? To let you know that there is money to play with. If you want to plan some extra attractions for your weekend, go right ahead. Plan well and as early as you can. Be specific when you ask for money. Alec and I will both need to know your plans as soon as possible. Remember, I set this up as family entertainment, which means keep it sober and keep it clean. If all goes as well as I think it will, we could get really grandiose next year."

They discussed possibilities for another half an hour and then went happily on their ways. After everybody except Maggie had gone, Pauline said, "I wonder if we'll get any camels."

"What?"

"A camel is a horse put together by a committee."

# 19

Late one snowy January afternoon, Alec and Gregory Peck drove up Pauline's driveway. Maggie's dog, Kathleen, barked twice; she just wanted to make sure Maggie and Pauline knew they had company. That bark was the established signal for Princess to leap to the top of the China closet. From there she could observe the company; she usually stayed there until they left because she didn't care much for people, except for Pauline. Occasionally she let Maggie pet her but that was about it. Kathleen was just the opposite; she expected everyone to love and pet her.

Alec was just in time for supper. "Hi, Ma, how are you doing?" Kathleen wiggled over to Alec, sure of a good petting and then nosed up to Gregory.

Pauline smiled. "Judging from the look on your face, not nearly as well as you. What's up?"

"You'll never guess!" He waited for her response, but she waited longer. "Monday I start my new job." He wanted her reaction, but she just grinned back at him. "I'm going to be a janitor at the high school."

"You're what???" Pauline didn't know whether to be thrilled that he was taking on more work or worried that he was going to quit managing the park. Ever since his divorce, twenty years ago, he had worked only long enough to loaf around until his money ran out. Was he running from one job to another or was he settling down?

"I figure I can do that and run your park, too. I'm thinking of saving up money to buy myself a house." The ancient trailer home he rented was so awful, Pauline had only been there once. So much good news!

"I heard at my AA meeting that the janitor has to quit because he found out he has a really bad heart, so they're looking for someone. I went over to the superintendent's office this morning and he hired me! I start tomorrow if the blizzard doesn't keep me home."

Pauline had never expected great results from Alec's many grandiose schemes, but this sounded down-to-earth and possible.

"Hey, I met Cal at the store the other day. He desperately wanted me to go over to the new house to see his puppy. You should see him with that dog! Jim even bought another puppy so Sunny has somebody to play with while Jim and Cal are gone. Cal's doing much better in school too. With his mother gone, he's completely different. Oh, Jim Dowling is going to legally adopt him."

Pauline wondered when she'd last seen Alec so

enthusiastic. Several years, at least. But sober and enthusiastic? It hurt to realize she couldn't remember when it had been.

"Ma, what's wrong?"

Pauline wiped away a tear. "I'm just proud of you, that's all."

"Oh." Alec didn't know what to do with that, so he went to the kitchen and fumbled around getting a cup of coffee. When he came back, they chatted about less important matters as they ate.

Suddenly Alec realized that the blizzard could wreck his plans. He had asked Joan to meet him at the park Saturday at closing time; they would skate under the full moon with soft music on the intercom and it would be so romantic, how could she resist? He was sure that her insistence on friendship only was just a front.

He anxiously asked, "Mom, do you think this blizzard will close the park Saturday?"

"Alec, it's only Monday. Why so worried?"

"Well, the Cranberry Town pep band will be playing in the afternoon and those ice skaters from Eau Claire are coming up to give their show in the evening. It could be a big weekend."

Pauline gave him her famous tell-me-the-whole-truth look, tempered somehow by if-you-want-to. Alec wanted to. "I've asked Joan to meet me here at closing time for some romantic skating by moonlight."

"Joan?"

"Joan Lefair."

"You've been seeing a lot of her then?"

"Kind of." They went out once or twice a week, to a movie, or dancing, to a restaurant or to her house.

"Good." Pauline thought. She said, "We'll be snowed in for a few days and then everybody will want to get out over the weekend. The park will be open and packed."

"But we have to clear the snow out of the park." The monumental size of that task weighed heavily on him. "I've talked to the high school principals. If we get a foot or more of snow as predicted, they'll announce, when school resumes, that we need help after school. That would probably be Thursday and Friday." Alec hesitated, He thought his next request would be too much, even for his Supermom. "Do you think you and Maggie could fix supper for an unknown number of starving teenagers?"

Pauline looked at Maggie with a question on her face. Maggie nodded. "It would best be something we could fix ahead of time, some kind of casserole would be easiest, but who knows what fussy eaters we'd get."

"Spaghetti. Everybody likes spaghetti. We could cook up the sauce with the meat right in it and cook up the spaghetti at the last minute."

"Do you have any idea how many there would be?"

Alec replied, "Their bands have played here and a lot of them have been hanging out here. I promised they'd be well paid. I'm hoping for at least thirty, maybe forty. Most of them should be here by 4:30 or five o'clock. If they had a snack when they arrived, they could probably last until 6:30. That gives you time to adjust."

"We can take care of the food and you can take care of the snow. Don't worry."

"You're probably right."

Pauline replied, "Of course I am. Now go on home before the driving gets bad."

Right after he left, Kathleen, barked again as another car came up and Princess leaped to the top of the china closet again.

In came Dorothy. "Hi, Mom, how are you? Are you ready for the big storm?" Kathleen bounded over to greet Dorothy.

"Of course. Coffee's on. Bring us all a cup, if you please." To Pauline, Dorothy had the look of a child who is going to try to persuade her mother how very useful she could be if only she had a bicycle.

When Dorothy brought the coffee, the cookie jar made its way from its permanent place on the dining room table to each of the women.

"Do you have enough groceries if you're snowed

in for a few days?" Dorothy asked.

"Maggie and I went shopping today. The propane tank is full and Alec brought in a good supply of wood in case the electricity goes off and the blower for the gas furnace won't work. Maggie is staying here to keep me company. We have water for washing dishes and for flushing the toilet. We have a dozen candles and fresh flashlight batteries."

Dorothy laughed. "All right. You're ready for the storm. I knew you would be, but you know I like to fuss. There's something else I'd like to talk to you about."

Pauline thought, "Here it comes." She said, "Yes?"

"I've been thinking it's been a long time since you had a birthday party. You haven't been feeling up to it for years and now you're doing so well, I'm wondering if you wouldn't like a party this year."

"A small one?" Pauline asked.

"How about a really big one?"

"Oh." This *was* a surprise! "Who did you have in mind?"

"All your relatives. Your sisters and brothers and all their kids and grandkids; there are even a couple of great grandkids, aren't there?"

"That's a lot of people!" Pauline paused. "I like your idea. What brought it on?"

"I was thinking the other day about when I was little; you and Fuddy Duddy used to pack us kids in the car every summer and we'd visit famous places and relatives. Those trips were really special. We learned history, we got to know our family and we tried all kinds of fun and food."

Pauline smiled. "I enjoyed planning them almost as much as I enjoyed the trips; Tom was reluctant, but noble; he had to force himself to have fun in those days."

"Stuart and I would do all the work for the party. We should start right away so everybody has time to plan. If you'll let us. I'd really like to do this, for you and for me, too. I'm lonesome for those cousins I haven't seen for all these years."

"I'd like that." Pauline smiled again. "I'd like it very much."

By the time Dorothy left, the snow was coming down hard, but there was only about an inch of snow on the road so driving wasn't too bad.

Pauline said to Maggie, "The weather has certainly cooperated for our benefit. Even with all the snow we've had this winter, it hasn't interfered with our concerts. Do you suppose your mother has been helping us out?"

Maggie *knew* her mother had been taking care of the weather for them, but she just smiled. Maggie figured her mother knew how important the concerts were to Pauline. Two weeks ago they had been to a Rachmaninoff concert; the music crushed and exalted them, touched their hearts in a thousand places.

Pauline said, "I hate to miss swimming; now that I can swim the length of the pool, I want to do two lengths."

"You're never satisfied, are you." Maggie laughed. "You just like to hear everybody cheering for you when you reach another goal."

"I like accomplishing things; yes, I enjoy the applause even if it is embarrassing." Pauline laughed, too.

In the morning, there were eight inches of snow on the ground and more coming. Pauline and Maggie liked looking at the snow and were quite pleased that they didn't have to go out in it. They ate, played cards, watched Oklahoma with Gordon MacRae on TV. They made split pea soup and cornbread for lunch; they watched the snow come down.

The phone rang often; Dorothy and Stuart called to make sure Pauline was all right; Alec called to check on the park and Pauline; other housebound friends called to pass the time of day.

Then the electricity went off. Maggie had already made sandwiches for supper and set them between the screen and the window; they could heat them up on the gas stove because Pauline's was on old one with gas pilot lights; that way Maggie wouldn't have to open the refrigerator. When the electricity went off, she started a good fire in the wood-coal furnace in the basement. She packed the food from the freezer into garbage bags and put them on the front porch. If the electricity stayed off for a long time, she would empty the refrigerator, too.

"Well, Pauline, I think everything is set. Should we build a snowman or play cards? Would you like for me to read more of <u>Mrs. 'Arris Goes to Paris</u> or go fly a kite?"

"Let's read while there's light. We can play cards by candlelight."

After a while, Pauline dozed off in her electric recliner lift chair. The thickly falling snow had silenced all man's busy noises, cars, refrigerators, televisions. Maggie stretched out on the sofa and accepted the quiet.

At dusk, the furnace blower came on and woke them up. The snow had ended. Maggie bundled up and took the yardstick out. When she came back in, she announced, "Twelve to fourteen inches of new snow on the road. There's well over two feet in the back yard. The wind is picking up and the temperature's going down." She went to the basement to put more wood on the fire. The wind howled through every crack in the house -- the remodelers had missed quite a few cracks.

"This wind means that the plows will be busy trying to keep the main roads open and they'll clear the roads for the school buses. We probably won't get plowed out tomorrow. Can we stand each other for that long?" Pauline asked.

Maggie just grinned. Then she realized the blowing snow had another effect. The path she'd shoveled for Kathleen and Princess would fill in quickly, so every time they needed to go out, she'd have to shovel it again. The weather forecast predicted twenty below, fifty below with the wind chill factor, for the next morning. Maybe she'd shorten the path.

"Pauline, I think the time has come to try the recipe I put together for French silk pie. We could celebrate our friendship. What do you think?"

"What do you think I think? Of course!"

Maggie's recipe called for whipped cream, egg

whites and gelatin in the filling with a graham cracker and pecan crust. It should have cooled in the refrigerator for three hours, but neither Pauline nor Maggie could wait past an hour and a half. It was "supermelagorgeous beyond which there isn't any whicher," even better than what the big city pie restaurants served.

Pauline said, "My daughter Mary would love to have your recipe."

"It tastes spectacular, but before I start giving out the recipe, I'd have to get rid of the speckles and I'd want to be sure it would set firmly."

Thursday the township plow opened Pauline's road; Dave used the plow on his tractor to clear his driveway and then he plowed out Pauline's driveway. He couldn't get too close to Maggie's car for fear of scratching it, so she had more shoveling to do.

Dorothy stayed at the hospital during the blizzard; she spent some time writing a letter to a hundred relatives, omitting only those who were still living at home. On her way home after the storm, she dropped them off at the post office.

Thursday after school, the mob came: sixty-five high-school students with snow shovels, six snow-blowers, four bobcats, and nine pickups. The kids demolished all six batches of cookies Pauline and Maggie had made for them. Then they went to work. At first they used all the snow-blowers around the outer edge of the park to blow the snow over the fence. The bobcats loaded snow from the walkways onto the pickups. After the bobcat moved on, the kids shoveled away from the animal displays onto the walkways; the bobcats then loaded that onto the pickups. Five of the pickups were loaded directly by shovelers. Other kids used their hands to pull snow off the animals. Then the shovelers moved that snow onto the walkways. Twenty of the kids shoveled the snow off the pickups into the field behind the parking lot. For the first hour, Alec ran from one group to another, choreographing the ballet of the snow removal.

When Pauline and Maggie heard there were sixty-five for supper, they put plan B into operation. Maggie went to the store; she bought fifteen dozen wieners and buns and everything to go with them, including paper plates. She went to the bakery to buy whatever they had left, sweet rolls, cookies, cakes. She followed Dorothy's car for the last few miles on her way back to Pauline's.

Pauline welcomed Dorothy. "I'm so glad you came! Would you please take charge of the hot dog supper in the warming house? Alec can get some of the shovelers to help you or I'll send help if more people show up here. We'll serve spaghetti here."

Dorothy liked being in charge and being useful. "Okay."

Then Marion, Betty Ann, Maxine and Doris showed up. Betty Ann stayed with the house crew while the others went to help Dorothy.

Pauline, Maggie and Betty Ann served a boisterous crowd. The kids ate in shifts; their high spirits were contagious, but all three of the women were glad when the noise level decreased to the grumbling of all the engines in the park.

By seven o'clock, the next influx of helpers began: more pickups arrived with men who had gone home after work, eaten supper and then brought a bobcat or snow-blower. Cars came bringing men with shovels and women with coffee urns and brownies, which they took into the warming house. Kathy stopped at Pauline's. "It looks to me like the crowd is just beginning to show up and they are nowhere near finished. I'll go home and aggravate some sandwich makers." She returned later with sandwiches and a shovel. Mary and Pat from the water exercise group brought food. Dave came and plowed the snow away from the outside of the fence; he did this three more times before the park was all cleared.

At nine o'clock, cars and trucks were still coming with workers, sandwiches and coffee. Men and women who had volunteered to help their clubs raise money at the park, parents of ice skaters, one principal and some teachers and many cheerful strangers pitched in. Cal was

143

there taking pictures; some of them showed up in the school newspaper. As soon as he finished taking pictures, Cal started shoveling. Jim and Patty had come with Cal. Joan showed up, which pleased Alec immensely. Fred and some of his other AA friends came. None of his drinking buddies offered to help.

While Maggie and Betty Ann were doing dishes, sheriff George stopped in.

"Mrs. Johnson, you and Alec have a good thing here. I came to help, but I wanted you to know that I'm here because I appreciate your park."

"George, thank you. How kind of you to tell me. I think you should sit down though. You look as though your whole world just caved in."

"I'm sorry. I don't want to bother you with my troubles."

"George, sit down." Pauline spoke gently. "What is it?"

"Sylvester Blottom was driving home last night from D. T.'s. He crashed headlong into a car. It was Smitty and his wife coming home from her Dad's funeral. They're both dead and they leave three kids behind, ages six to twelve."

Pauline shuddered. It could have been Alec driving drunk. Thank God he had quit drinking! They sat in silence until Maggie brought them coffee.

Everybody knew about Blottom. He'd been drinking and driving before he was twenty and he was at least forty. Something should be done! Drunk drivers should be *forced* to see the consequences *before* they killed someone.

Pauline told George how she would deal with drunk drivers. "Double the jail time and the fines. The added time would be in community service, helping the victims of drunken behavior, like Martha Bjornfeld, whose husband was killed by a drunk driver and Ann Tiddly, whose husband is a useless drunk. The drunk driver could personally give half the larger fine to pay part of little John Smith's hospital bills. He could visit John in the hospital when they're doing another surgery to try to make a normal child out of a baby born to an alcoholic mother. Have them visit hospital patients whose injuries were caused by drunk drivers. In other words, bring them into frequent, face-to-face contact with the consequences of drunken behavior."

By the time George left, Maggie and Betty Ann had finished cleaning the kitchen. Betty Ann left. It was after nine, Pauline's bedtime so Maggie helped her to bed. Then she went out and shoveled.

At the park, Alec announced over the intercom, "I want to pay you all for your generous help. Please sign your name and address in the notebook by the main entrance to the warming house so I can send you a check."

Alec could hardly believe his eyes. The more people came, the faster they all seemed to work. The newcomers watched for the work pattern and joined right in. Alec found that nobody needed supervision, so he grabbed a shovel and sent the snow flying.

At eleven, he took a break and walked around the park to see how much still needed to be done. The animal areas were all cleared or nearly so. The rink was about half finished. He directed two bobcats away from the walkways to the rink. He announced again that he would pay everybody.

Alec picked up a sandwich and a cup of coffee. "I don't know where everybody came from, but I sure do appreciate all the help."

Maxine, who gave him the coffee, smiled. "We like what you're doing here."

They finished the whole park and the last pickup left about one o'clock. Alec sat by the window and looked at the notebook. "John Doe, John Doe II, Ann Onimous, Faith Hill, Superman, Tim McGraw, Wonder Woman, Santa Claus, Brittany Spears, Paul Simon, Superman . . ." Pages and pages of names, not one that belonged on the list. "We like what you're doing here," Maxine had said. He looked out at his park. He knew just what to do with the names. He'd get Mary to make a big sign to hang in the warming house; it would say, "Thanks for the snow job." Under that he would hang the framed signatures.

He could never have imagined such an exhausting generosity as he had seen. Some of the kindness was for his mother, some for the park and very definitely some of it was for him, because he was the park manager and because they liked him. That threatened to awaken some long-dormant sensitivities, so Alec suddenly remembered the early start required by his janitor's job and stood up to leave.

# 20

The first day back to school, Cal met Patty at her locker. "Two days off for a blizzard -- pretty cool," Cal said.

Patty smiled, then frowned. "Cal, there's something I've got to tell you.

He saw that she was upset. Suddenly he was afraid of what she was going to say. What if she didn't want to be his friend any longer?

"The reason I've never asked you to my house is that my brother Rickie is autistic."

"Oh, well that's okay." What a relief! "What's autistic?"

"He can't talk. Well, he did when he was small, but not anymore. It's like, . . . Did you ever have a lamp with a bad cord? Sometimes it works, sometimes it doesn't. It seems like his wiring is bad so sometimes he understands what you say and sometimes not; he can act normal or he can go crazy because he can't tell us what he wants; I think sometimes he goes crazy because he's just a brat."

"You have to live with that?  That must be really bad."

Patty replied, "It is.  No, it's not all bad.  He can be really sweet, too.  Anyway, Mom said I could ask you to come to our house Monday after school.  You can meet Rickie and my sister Eileen and my folks.  I can drive you home after supper.  What do you think?  Do you want to come?"

He thought maybe she was scared of losing him, but this was important to her.  He wasn't used to being trusted with people's problems, but Sunny trusted him so maybe he'd be all right with Patty too.  He didn't know exactly how to explain all that to Patty though; he nodded his head and said, "Yeah."

As Pauline predicted, the park was very busy Saturday; it was also very hectic.  An elderly man brought his grandchildren to the park and became ill.  Alec saw he was in trouble.  He looked as if he were in a lot of pain; he held his hand to his chest.  Alec looked around until he spotted a familiar face.  "Amy, will you please look after these kids until their parents come for them?  Their grandpa isn't feeling well."

"Sure.  Be glad to."  Amy aimed them out the door saying, "Let's go see all the animals."

Alec took the old man into the office where he made him comfortable.  "What's your name?"

"Angus McIntire."

"What's the phone number where I can reach the kids' parents, Angus?"

Alec wrote down the number Angus gave him.  "Tell me what's wrong."  The old man told him about the chest pains; Alec noticed that his lips were blue.  "Angus, I think you're having a heart attack.  I want to call the ambulance for you."

Angus wanted to protest, but the pain told him he needed help.  "All right."

Alec called the ambulance and the children's parents and his mother so she wouldn't fret when the ambulance came.  He told Angus, "If there's anything you

147

want while we're waiting, let me know." Then he talked quietly to Angus until the ambulance arrived. By then, the old man looked as though he could pass out any minute.

When the paramedics wheeled Angus out the office door, Alec stayed. He sat down because he was shaking too badly to stand. Ten minutes later Maggie came to the office. "Your mom wonders if you would go tell her what happened. I could take over here for a while."

"Thanks."

Pauline said quietly, "Tell me about it."

He did and finished by saying, "I did everything right and the minute they walked out the door, I turned to mush. I don't know which was more amazing, doing right or mushing out."

"Alec Johnson, you're made of good stuff. Just because you took longer to realize it than most people take, doesn't make it less true. Now," she said softly, "why don't you lie down on the couch for a while. If you fall asleep, I'll call you in half an hour."

He kissed her cheek on his way to the couch.

When he went back to the park, Alec found that he had forgotten to check supplies; they ran out of cocoa. Someone dropped a stocking cap into a toilet and plugged it up. The ice skaters lost their way, so the good-sized crowd had to wait for half an hour. Alec offered them free refreshments while they waited.

Joan came for the show. That cheered him up. At closing time, she waited in the warming house while he checked that everyone was gone and then locked up. She heard a noise coming from the women's bathroom. She went in and found a teenaged girl crying angrily.

"What's wrong?"

The girl was surprised to see Joan. She thought everyone was gone. "I had a fight with my boy friend."

"What did you fight about?"

She muttered, "He was flirting with another girl and I didn't like it. He left with her. I *don't* want to call my folks to get a ride because Mom's been telling me all along that he's no good; I *don't* want to walk home because it's ten miles, but I guess I'll have to."

Joan thought the girl was a bit too stubborn for her own good and more than a bit unpleasant, but she asked, "How about if I take you home?"

"Would you?"

"Yes. I'm Joan Lefair. What's your name and where do you live?"

"Cora Denton. I live just east of Lilac."

"Let's go then." Joan told Alec what she was doing and that she'd be back in about half an hour.

When she returned, she honked her car horn to alert Alec to unlock the gate, but he didn't come. Because of the fence, she couldn't see in, but it looked as though there were lights on, not the big lights for the rink, but probably the ones for the animals. She went over to Pauline's driveway. His car was there and Pauline's lights were out. She went back and honked again. No response. Why wouldn't he come out? The only reason she could think of was that he was hurt. If he was hurt and couldn't get out, he could freeze to death unless she helped him.

Pauline should have keys to let her into the park, but could she get out of bed and come to the door without help? Maggie must know how to get in. Joan called information on her cell phone to get Maggie's number, then dialed it.

"Hello."

"I'm so glad you're home. This is Joan Lefair." Joan explained the situation. She wasn't about to panic, but she was a lot more upset than she wanted to recognize.

Maggie thought quickly. "I'm only about ten minutes away. I have a key to Pauline's house and she has keys to the park. Hang on, I'll be right there."

When Maggie opened Pauline's door, she said, "It's me, Maggie." She went to her bedroom and told her what happened.

"Take the keys and be sure to let me know what's going on."

"Of course."

149

Maggie and Joan went in the side gate, near the house. They looked around; the warming house lights were on, so they ran to it. They found Alec, sound asleep in a chair by the fireplace.

"Alec Johnson," Joan cried, "what are you doing?"

He woke up fuzzily. "What? Joan. Hi, Maggie. What are you two doing here?"

Maggie was relieved and a little mad at Alec for upsetting everybody. She told Joan, "I'll take the keys back."

Joan was more angry than relieved. "I thought you were hurt; I was afraid you'd freeze to death if you were left here all night. I was looking forward to tonight and you went to *sleep*."

Alec's sleep-muddled brain couldn't find an answer to her anger. "I'm sorry." He was sorry, but he didn't know why.

Joan left.

It was cool by the dying fire and that helped wake him up. Alec thought about his rotten day and became very thirsty. The more he thought about it, the thirstier he became. A six-pack or two . . . No, beer wouldn't be fast enough. Straight whiskey. That would settle things down.

Alec went into the office to make a phone call. "Fred, I'm at Mom's park. I'm desperate for a bottle of whiskey."

"I'll be right there."

Alec built up the fire. He hadn't felt so rotten since he couldn't remember when. Good thing Fred was coming.

Instead of a bottle of whiskey, Fred brought a quart of maple nut ice cream. He served up a big dish for Alec and when that was gone, he filled the bowl again until all the ice cream was gone. Alec ate and ranted about his horrible day.

A long time later, Fred said, "I guess what you've been saying is that today you saved a man's life and your girl friend got mad at you."

"She's not my girl friend!" Alec yelled.

"Oh?"

150

"Well, I want her to be my girl friend, but she wants to be 'just friends,'" Alec whined on the last two words.

"She won't have sex with you? Now there's a problem worth getting drunk over!"

Alec growled, "After all that ice cream, I couldn't even *look* at a shot of whiskey!" Then Alec realized that Fred had been very sneaky. They laughed.

"Fred, you're a good friend. I'll go home now and sleep it off. I'll figure out what to do about Joan tomorrow. Thanks."

"Anytime."

Sundays, the park closed at six. Alec called the hospital and found that Angus was doing well, thanks to getting help quickly. Then Alec went to the grocery store and bought a bouquet of flowers.

When Joan came to the door, he offered her the flowers and apologized. "Joan, I was looking forward to last night too. I wanted to skate with you under the full moon and it would have been wonderfully romantic and I was as excited as a kid before Christmas. But yesterday everything went wrong. An old man had a heart attack, there was a scuffle in the parking lot between a couple of rowdy teenagers, a toilet plugged; I no sooner had one problem worked out when another one popped up. When I sat down to wait for you, the day caught up with me and I fell asleep. Please don't stay mad at me."

"Come on in." They went into her kitchen, where Joan poured a cup of coffee for each of them. "I'm sorry, too. I was really worried about you. I didn't want to realize how much I care about your friendship, so I got mad at you instead of thinking about that."

"Still just friends then?"

"Never *'just'* friends. *'Just'* belittles our relationship. *Still good friends.*"

Alec said, "All right," but then he changed his mind. "No, it's not all right. Why won't you be my girl friend?"

"What do you mean by girl friend? Do you mean have a sexual relationship?"

"Well, yes."

"Leading to marriage?"

Alec didn't like that question *at all.* "Oh, uh, . . . I suppose, . . . no, I don't think so, . . . but maybe, . . . I don't know!"

"That's why," Joan said.

"What?"

"If I have sex with you, I'm making a commitment. Marriage would be a commitment for you and right now commitment just isn't in your vocabulary."

Alec admitted sadly, "I'm just beginning to take responsibility for my own life. I'm not ready for responsibility for someone else."

Joan said, "I like being with you. I like being your friend. Can we continue as before or is it too frustrating for you?"

"Whew. Nothing shy about you. Of course I want to keep seeing you!"

Later, after Alec left, Joan wondered about her own frustration. She knew she was right; she wouldn't be doing either of them a favor by having sex with him, but being right sometimes carried a very high price tag.


# 21


When Patty and Cal arrived at her house Monday after school, her mother was folding up a load of clean clothes. Cal thought she looked very old and tired but pleasant enough.

"Nice to meet you, Cal," she said. "Patty, you can help yourselves to a can of pop if you want to."

When they sat down on the couch, five-year-old Eileen came up to Cal. "See what I drew in school today?" She told Cal all about her teacher and started on her friends when Patty interrupted, "Go do your homework now, Eileen. You can tell Cal more during supper."

Eileen wanted to argue, but Patty suddenly looked very stern, so Eileen went to the bedroom she shared with Patty and opened a book.

"I'm pretty much her boss," Patty explained, "because Mom is always busy with Rickie or else busy catching up on all the housework she neglected when she was busy with Rickie. He's taking a nap now but he'll be up soon."

Cal thought Patty seemed nervous. He wanted to reassure her but he didn't know how so he reached out and put his hand on hers. In the car, she had said, "Just pretend he's a scared little puppy. Then you'll treat him just fine."

Eight-year-old Rickie peeked into the living room and saw the stranger. He caught Cal's eye. Cal smiled and Rickie withdrew. Cal looked at Patty. He murmured, "Now we'll see." He proceeded to tell Patty a silly story about one of his teachers. Cal knew Rickie was coming but he kept his eyes on Patty and continued the story. Rickie stopped two feet from Cal and stared at him. Cal stopped talking and looked at Rickie. Rickie's eyes told Cal many things, but he didn't know quite what they were.

"Hi Rickie. I'm Cal. I go to school with Patty. She's my friend." He talked quietly, as he would to a stray dog. "I have two puppies at home. They're about this big." He held his hand a foot above the floor. "Their names are Sunny and King. They're brown with white legs and noses. I got a big ham bone for them. Sunny grabbed one end and King grabbed the other end and they pulled and growled and squealed." Cal growled and acted out a tug of war with his hands. "As long as they fought over the bone neither one of them could chew on it. Finally they plopped down right there and started chewing. I don't think there's anything a dog loves more than a bone, not petting, not going for a run or for a ride in a car, nothing. They found out they could enjoy a bone together and I discovered that having the meat man cut the bone in half would be simpler."

Then Cal asked, "Would you like to sit with us?" Rickie squeezed between Cal and Patty.

Mrs. Brown looked in on the three of them as Patty told Rickie about Cal's wonderful pictures. She smiled weakly, then went on with her work.

Eileen came out again and claimed, "I'm all finished." Patty knew she was fibbing, but she didn't want to fuss in front of Cal, so she let it pass. Eileen sat on Cal's other side and said, "My teacher says I'm the best drawer in the whole class."

Cal sensed a little stretching but said in an admiring tone of voice, "Is that right?"

"She says I'm really good in reading, too."

"That's good."

"I always get good grades."

"Good for you." Cal knew she was exaggerating and Eileen knew he knew and they were both having fun, when suddenly Rickie started making loud noises of protest and hitting Cal as hard as he could, which was harder than an eight-year-old should be able to hit.

Cal was so surprised he didn't know what to do but Patty grabbed Rickie's wrists, stood him up and dragged him to his room. She came back to the living room and said to Cal, "Let's go." She was furious and ashamed and crying. She yelled, "Mom, we're leaving."

Her mother's anxious face appeared in the doorway. "What's wrong?"

Patty didn't answer. She jerked on her boots and coat. Cal followed. Patty didn't say a word as she drove. Cal didn't know what to say so he didn't talk either.

At his house, Cal said, "Come on in; we'll get a pizza out of the freezer or something."

"Okay."

After they ate, Cal said, "Back when I lived in the Cities, I used to prowl the malls. I saw a book in a window 1001 Ways to Be Mad or something like that. It sounded really cool, all full of nasty stuff, so I stole one." Patty was too upset even to be shocked.

"The book wasn't nasty -- it described ways to get

rid of your anger without hurting people or getting in trouble. I read a little of it because it seemed so weird. It said the Jews used to have a scapegoat at the beginning of the year. Each Jew put his hands on the goat and put all his sins on it. Then they chased the goat into the desert and it took their sins with it so the Jews could start the year all cleaned up. We could pretend we have a goat and put all our rotten stuff on it and chase it out into the woods. Want to?"

"Sure."

"We'll have to have some noisemakers, something to bang on."

Patty asked, "Do you have any cookie sheets? And big metal stirring spoons? That's Rickie's favorite."

Cal found a cookie sheet and spoon for each of them and set them down on the coffee table. He put his hands on the back of the imaginary goat and said, "You first."

"Okay." Patty took a deep breath and said, "I hate when Rickie acts like such a brat and Mom lets him get away with it." Her voice grew louder with each word. "I hate it when I bring home a good report card and Mom doesn't even notice it because she's too busy cleaning up the dishes that Rickie broke having one of his tantrums. I hate having you be so nice to him and then he hits you because you pay attention to Eileen too." By the time she finished she was crying as well as yelling.

Cal shouted, "I hate when Jim is always so nice and I want to yell and scream but how can I when he's here? I want to scream that I hated my mother because she was rotten and I hate her for dying on me and leaving me all alone."

Cal opened the door and bellowed, "Go away, goat, and take all our garbage with you!" He and Patty growled and screeched and banged their cookie sheets. The dogs barked and growled right along. The four of them chased the goat into the woods.

Suddenly car lights swept in at the end of the long driveway. Cal and Patty shut up and so did the dogs. Cal looked at Patty. "Do you suppose he heard us?"

155

"I think the whole county probably heard us," she replied solemnly.

Jim pulled up and jumped out of his car. "What the hell is going on? I heard screaming half a mile down the road!" He wasn't sure if he was supposed to be angry or relieved or what.

"We're sorry," Cal said, but he didn't sound a bit sorry because the giggles gobbled him up. Since his giggle was highly contagious and Patty liked that infection, she joined in. Every time Cal tried to stop and explain things, Patty reinfected him. Pretty soon, Jim gave up and laughed too.

Finally they all went inside. Patty looked at Cal and said, "I think it worked."

In bed that night, Cal relived the scapegoat incident repeatedly, laughing every time. Patty's anger amazed him; he didn't think nice people ever got mad.

Several days later, Jim saw the sheriff when he stopped for gas. "George, you're just the man I'm looking for."

George knew Jim from high school and from the years of his successful law career. "What's up?"

"I want to work on the drunk driving problem around here and I don't know where to start."

"How about if we meet at the cafe at a quarter to five?"

"Great. See you then."

George ordered his supper, because he was divorced and didn't care much for his own cooking and Jim ordered just apple pie and coffee because he would eat later with Cal.

"George, you probably know I flushed my life down the drain when I was with Dixie. Now I'm building a new life. Because I don't have enough clients to keep me busy, I have plenty of time to think. I realize that I don't want to be 'the successful lawyer' again. This lifetime, I want to make a difference. It seems to me that the biggest problem we have around here is drunk driving -- that horrible accident with Blottom should never have happened. I want to do something. Do you have any ideas?"

"Around here, separating a drunk from his pickup is about as easy as separating a mother bear from her cubs," George said. "But I was talking with Pauline Johnson a few days ago and she had some very interesting thoughts on the subject." George told Jim what Pauline had proposed.

Jim asked, "Do you think Judge Jeffries would go for that?"

"Why don't you ask him?"

"I will," Jim replied.

Judge Jeffries agreed with Jim completely, but he claimed he was too old to make such changes. "Son, I have one foot in the grave and the other on a banana peel."

Jim finally talked him into considering one case at a time.

Three days later, Jim had a phone call. One of the young men on the construction crew which had built his house, Don, was in jail for drunk driving. Don wanted Jim to be his lawyer.

Jim went to see Don. "I'll be your lawyer if you still want me after I explain my plan. As your lawyer, I feel I must serve your best interests. I don't think that getting away with drunk driving would help you. I won't try to get you off. I believe it would be good for you to admit your guilt to Judge Jeffries and ask him for a community service sentence, rather than jail. Your service would be to help Mrs. Green, whose husband was killed by a drunk driver. She's very poor, thanks to her husband's killer, so your fine would pay for the new roofing and other repairs her house needs. What I'm proposing is this: you admit your guilt and face the consequences of another person's drunk driving. I don't know whether the judge will accept this. You'd have to convince him. If you decide to help her, I'd supervise you."

Getting out of jail sounded good to Don, but spending all that time helping some old lady -- that sounded downright disgusting.

"Well?"

"I guess."

Jim said, "You have to convince Judge Jeffries that this is a good idea. If you don't really want to do it, you're wasting my time. You might as well get another lawyer."

"I'll do it."

Don talked the Judge into it, which pleased Jim. Don was in his early twenties. He already had one drunk driving charge on his record. If helping Mrs. Green kept him from a lifetime of drunk driving, it would be a great accomplishment.

Jim phoned Joan that night to tell her about his achievement. He liked bragging to her because she always bragged right back to him.

Don told Jim when he would work for Mrs. Green and Jim checked to see that he was putting in the hours he claimed and doing a good job. He also talked to Mrs. Green when Don wasn't there to make sure she felt Don was doing well. At first, Don and Mrs. Green were very uncomfortable with each other, but Don was a good worker and gradually won her approval. He slowly began to realize what her husband's death meant to her. As he began to like her, he came to resent her husband's killer.

# 22

By mid-March, they had put Pauline's plastic animals in storage and they had dismantled the rink, so that Pauline could again enjoy the real animals. The deer would graze in the field after the snow was gone. Pauline's determined efforts had her swimming an eighth of a mile, besides the exercise hour.

Maggie put on her best Irish brogue for the occasion: "Pauline, if it's Irish stew you're wantin' on St. Patrick's Day, you'll have to get Stuart to bring some lamb or mutton from the Cities. The only time we can get lamb around here is at Easter, more's the pity."

"I always thought beef, potatoes, carrots and onions made Irish stew."

"Sure and you're right, except for the beef. The beef would make it Irish-*American* stew; over here, beef is readily available, but not mutton, just the opposite of Ireland."

Stuart brought them some ground lamb, some lamb for stew and some lamb chops, too.

The stew was very good. While eating, they listened to Irish music, some by Michael O'Day and some by James Galway. Then they watched The Fighting O'Flynn, which was quite unhistorical in some respects, but absolutely delightful for two fans of Douglas Fairbanks, Jr.

A few days later they tried the lamb chops, using Italian spices. Excellent.

After a few more days, Pauline proclaimed, "Maggie, I feel Stuartish today! Let's make moussaka!"

Maggie grinned back at Pauline. "Sure. But what's Stuartish and what's moussaka?"

"Stuartish means like Stuart, as in Stuart Little, the great adventurous mouse. In his name, we'll make moussaka, a Greek dish with lamb and eggplant. Get those cookbooks down from the cupboard above the kitchen table, top shelf, please. One of them should have a recipe."

Ten minutes later, Maggie found a recipe. "It calls for mutton hash, demi-glace sauce with tomato, aubergines, seasoning, flour, oil, parsley, and tomatoes."

"Demi-glace sauce? Aubergines? That's getting too fussy. Let's keep looking."

Then Pauline found one. "This one calls for ground lamb, ground chuck, onion, eggplant, . . . yes, this will do, . . . but I remember potatoes in it, too, and topped with tomato sauce and cheese. Hm. That would make a lot of food. We'd better get help eating it. Who shall we invite?"

Maggie grinned. "You invite friends if you're sure it will be good. If you're in doubt, ask relatives -- they can't quit being related just because you served them something awful."

Pauline protested, "The two of us could never cook up something awful! We'll invite Alec and Joan, Dorothy and . . . I wonder if Dorothy and George would get along?"

"Are you matchmaking again?"

"Alec and Joan are getting along, aren't they?" Pauline asked. "And how about a date for you?"

"I'll ask Douglas Fairbanks, Jr. If he can't come, I'll do without a date."

Pauline replied, "Fine. I'll invite Bing Crosby. How about next Sunday evening?"

"Sounds good to me."

Sunday afternoon, Maggie cleaned, cut up, peeled and grated; Pauline browned all the ingredients, layered and spiced them in two casserole dishes and put them in the oven. Then they prepared Waldorf salad and garlic bread. Pauline set the table while Maggie measured, crumbled and chopped the ingredients for her ice cream topping; after they ate, she would melt them together and serve the topping while it was warm.

Pauline had told the guests, "Dress up or dress down, but don't be late or we'll start without you." They took the former schoolteacher seriously and the four arrived together, dressed in their best casuals. Douglas and Bing weren't on time, so they started without them.

Dorothy and Maggie brought the food to the table. The first bite ended all chitchat. Pauline watched Joan and George as they tried the moussaka. Joan liked it immediately. George's expression of surprise changed to interest and then to enjoyment. Full mouths managed an

160

occasional, admiring "Mmmm." Pauline and Maggie looked at each other; both of them winked and kept on eating.

By the time they were ready to slow down and talk, Dorothy was too full of good food to remember that she was a little annoyed with her mother for inviting a date for her. "Mom," she said, "this is the best meal I ever had!"

"Me, too!" Everybody else agreed enthusiastically.

Nobody wanted dessert, but since it was only ice cream, "Just a little." However, they liked the topping so much they all had seconds.

Unfortunately, it had been snowing heavily for several hours, so the guests quickly did the dishes and left early. None of them had far to go, but ever since the big January blizzard, they'd had two- to six-inch snowfalls several times a week. They were all tired of winter driving. It was the end of March. They were all tired of winter!

Pauline was worn out because of all the excitement of having a dinner party so Maggie helped her get ready for bed. Pauline said, "When you first came here, you told me that it was fun cooking for people who enjoy eating. You were right." They smiled.

Pauline enjoyed showing off her refound swimming prowess and she was immensely pleased by the side-effects: she got up, washed and dressed herself except on Tuesdays and Fridays; then she waited for Maggie to be there when she stepped in and out of the shower. Maggie still washed her back and her hair because Pauline liked for her to do it.

That Tuesday, as Pauline showered, she asked, "Maggie, would you help me with a garden this summer?"

"Glory be! Aunt Irene would say you're full of notions! But she'd love you for them and so do I, don't you know. Will you be able to work in it?"

"I've been thinking about that. We'd make the rows far enough apart that I could sit on the ground to weed and pick or I may work on my hands and knees. We could put the garden back where the old cow pen

161

was, by the barn. That will have good soil from all the manure. Otherwise, it's just sand around here. Besides, if the fence hasn't rotted, I could use it to pull myself up. I'll have to get the water going again in the barn because we'll have to water the garden when it doesn't rain. I'll ask Dave to plow it up when he's plowing his field."

"The stores already have seeds. We could pick some up next time we go shopping."

"That's what set me to thinking about it."

Later, Maggie was outside hanging up Pauline's freshly washed blankets when she saw a bear lumbering across the far end of the field. She quickly walked inside and pointed it out to Pauline. After it moved on, Maggie said, "Well, we've seen dozens of kinds of birds, lots of deer, a fox or two, chipmunks, squirrels, but that's the first bear. What will be next?"

Several days later, Pauline said wistfully, "I used to have flowers all around the house. The tiger lilies in front of the house, the spirea along the wheelchair ramp and the lilacs between my yard and Dave's field are all that's left."

Maggie asked, "Is that a hint?"

"Of course. But the problem is, the more I think about it, the bigger the job gets. I don't know how much we can plant and maintain."

"Just how grandiose would you like to get?"

"Grandiose is the right word, Maggie; you know me well." Then Pauline told her what she wanted. "Along the south side of the house is about fifty feet. I'm thinking a two-and-a- half-foot wide flower bed with a row of red and white gladioli, red and white roses, red and white tulips, pink asters and white alyssum. In the front, up to the wheelchair ramp, the tiger lilies, mums, hyacinths, sweet peas, and nasturtiums. That's a lot of work every year.

"But my really grand flower bed would be right across the driveway, fifty feet long and five feet wide. All perennials, so once it gets going, it wouldn't need much work. We'd plant creeping phlox, lily of the valley, daffodils, day lilies, butterfly weed, irises, lupine, four o'clocks, wild sunflowers, and other wildflower seeds."

Pauline hesitated. "I would need a lot of help from you. But I'm feeling so good these days that my mind is planning more than I could possibly do alone. What do you think?"

"I think it sounds great. I love gardening. You can admire the flowers every time you sit at your table. But we'd better buy a good supply of bug repellent. I'd rather not smear dirty hands across my face trying to kill a mosquito or a deer fly."

Dave plowed a fifteen- by twenty-five-foot garden in the old cow pen. He dug up about three inches of grass, weeds and sand to make the flower bed along the driveway. He replaced it with dirt from the cow pen, topped it with some fresh manure and plowed it together. His son spread some manure along the south side of the house and the bit in front and then rototilled all of it.

"Maggie, I've been so busy planning the garden, I've forgotten my birthday party. When I thought about it, I realized that this house badly needs a spring cleaning before all those people come. I asked Sandy if she'd help me with the big cleaning. She said she didn't think I needed her much anymore and she wanted to take another job starting next week. She was right. I don't need her. But I want to clean now because if I don't, Dorothy or Mary will come in before my birthday party and clean. They couldn't possibly clean it the way I want it done. If we do it before they have a chance, then it's done right. Will you help?"

Maggie groaned. "I have to tell you that housecleaning is not my favorite occupation, but," she said with a big grin, "housecleaning with my favorite friend would be just barely bearable."

"The new broom sweeps clean but the old broom knows the dusty corners best," Pauline said. "You're new to this house and I'm old, so between the two of us, the dirt doesn't have a chance. Let's start on the kitchen cupboards right after breakfast."

Since Pauline still couldn't stand for long without

tiring, Maggie emptied the cupboards onto the kitchen table where Pauline sat and cleaned boxes and bags and threw out ancient bottles. Maggie washed the shelves and drawers and every dish, pan and utensil. When they had dripped dry, Pauline and Maggie put them away.

Pauline washed the outside of cupboards, refrigerator and stove as far up as she could reach and Maggie did the rest, because she didn't want Pauline standing on the step-stool.

They cleaned windows the same way. Maggie finished first and stopped to watch Pauline. Pauline concentrated happily on the job, reclaiming her house by caring for it and celebrating her health by using it.

The weeks sped by as Pauline and Maggie steam-cleaned the furniture and carpets, washed curtains and throw rugs, polished wood and cleaned every surface. Pauline even managed the stairs so they could clean the bedrooms upstairs together.

Huge piles of garbage bags awaited the garbage truck each week, because Pauline sorted through everything and found a lot of things she'd never use again. Maggie commented, "You're really getting your money's worth on garbage pickups now! Myself, I just take my garbage to the dump. After I recycle everything I can, I only have about one bag a month."

Finally Pauline announced, "Now the house is ready for my party and we've time to spare. I'm looking forward to seeing all my relatives but I wish Dorothy would let me help."

"You're not allowed to help with your own birthday party! Besides, you've put in far more hours cleaning your house than she will in organizing the party."

Pauline looked around, admiring the invisible windows, the soft glow of the maple table, and the dust-free knickknacks. "Maggie, you may think this strange, but I feel better about being on the business end of a really clean house than I've felt about anything else for a long, long time."

"Good."

Two weeks later, Mary came up for the weekend

with her daughters Anne and Jean; they brought a full supply of rags, mops and various cleaners. "Hi Mom. We came to clean your house before the big party."

Pauline said, "It's no use boiling the potatoes twice."

"What?" Pauline's answer made no sense to Mary.

"If you can find any dirt, you're welcome to it."

"What?"

Pauline said, "I've already cleaned, for weeks on end. Go ahead. See if you can find any dirt," Pauline dared her daughter.

Mary ran a finger along the top of a door, looked in the silverware drawer, checked the knickknacks.

"Mom, did you do all this yourself?" Mary was amazed.

"Maggie helped a little."

They all laughed and settled in for a good visit instead of hard work.

Pauline and Maggie planted potatoes, peas and onion sets on Good Friday, which was in mid-April that year. Maggie shoveled aside the dirt and Pauline dropped in potatoes. They knelt to plant the peas and onions. They were slow and cold, but they both liked gardening, even if it was only a fifteen- by twenty-five-foot garden.

Three days later, the April sun shone its warmest so far, 71, but the bugs hadn't realized how nice it was. Pauline and Maggie ate lunch at the picnic table in Pauline's back yard.

Pauline said, "Today is the day."

"For what?"

"You keep asking me if I want to go fly a kite. Today is the day."

Maggie responded, "All right! Do you know how?"

"No, do you?"

"I have no idea. I'll call Teresa. She has two sons. They probably know how."

Maggie called her friend. "Pauline and I want to fly kites but we don't know anything about it, so could you

165

and your kids join us and help us if we need help?"

"Sure. Now?"

"We have to buy kites. We'll be ready in an hour."

"See you then."

An hour later, Pauline and Maggie were at the south edge of the field, which had recently been a winter park. The melting snow had immediately soaked into the sandy soil; a few bits of green offered the deer some fresh food. Maggie had the crosspieces in place on the new kites. She looked at the assembly diagram but couldn't figure out where to tie the string.

Pauline suggested, "The back of the kite has a flap with a hole in it."

"Aha!"

The wind gusted strongly. Maggie held up a kite and off it flew. It rose about twenty feet and spiraled to the ground. Pauline had the same luck. They tried a few more times and then Teresa drove in with her sons, Nate and Nick.

Teresa watched Pauline and Maggie. "Your kites need tails."

"We can use that old flowered sheet for tails," Pauline offered.

Thirteen-year-old Nate went down the field and ran across-wind to launch his short-tailed kite, then continued running to keep it up. Eleven-year-old Nick followed him. Their kites stayed up as long as they ran, then spiraled down.

Pauline's neighbor, Kathy drove by and then came back. Her two granddaughters were in the car. She told Pauline, "Shelby and Emily want to fly kites, too. Can we join you?" The girls were both ten years old.

"Of course. Do you have kites?"

"In the garage. We'll be back."

Maggie brought out the sheet and scissors. "Teresa, how long should I make the tails?"

"Oh, I don't know, five feet?"

Pauline held up her tailed kite. A big gust blew it up, but it spiraled back down. It needed a longer tail. Finally, with an eight-foot tail, it took off; Pauline let the string unwind; when the wind slowed, Pauline pulled the string in, letting it pile up next to her chair, but she didn't pull in fast enough. It crashed. Maggie's kite was down, too, so she brought Pauline's kite to her as she rewound the string. Then Pauline sent her kite up again, twenty-five feet, fifty feet, a hundred feet, and all the way to the end of the string.

Three of the kids' kites tangled with each other. Teresa and Kathy untangled them. Teresa's kite caught in a tree at the edge of the field, but blew free. Maggie let her string out too fast and it ate a hole in her finger.

Then all eight kites danced in the sky, red, blue, orange, yellow and green kites. High above them, an eagle sailed the wind. Nate pointed and said, "Look, there's an eagle! That means good luck." They all watched the sky, decorated with colorful kites, blessed by the eagle. It was a good moment.

### Pauline's Moussaka

3/4 lb. ground lamb
3/4 lb. ground chuck
1 egg plant
1 onion
3 grated potatoes
1 t Garlic
1 t Italian seasoning
Brown everything, layer in casserole dish or dishes, bake 40 minutes, 300.
Top with a can of tomato sauce and cheese. Bake until cheese melts.

### Maggie's Very Guilty Ice Cream Topping

1/4 cup graham cracker crumbs
1/4 cup pecans, chopped
1 T butter
Heat very slowly, stirring constantly, until butter is melted; add

1/4 cup chocolate chips
1/4 cup butterscotch chips
Heat very slowly, stirring constantly, until chips are melted.  Put topping *next* to ice cream so chips don't harden -- it crunches better

# 23

A few weeks later, Pauline was watching the birds at her feeder: the purple finches darted about in their courtship colors of bright red and brown; the bright yellow and black goldfinches flitted around; three bluebirds checked out the nesting possibilities.  Then she saw the sheriff's car drive up her driveway.  As Sheriff George Dogoodly stepped out of the car, Pauline said, "It's a good thing we made that lemon meringue pie; we may have to buy ourselves out of trouble."  She didn't sound a bit worried.

By the time George and Pauline had finished the "How are you" chitchat, Maggie brought in a tray with three cups of coffee and three large pieces of pie.

George took a bite and grinned.  "This is the best pie I've ever eaten."

"Pauline made the pie crust, I made the lemon pudding, from scratch of course, and she beat up the meringue," Maggie bragged.  "We make a good team."

When the pie plates were empty, Pauline asked, "Well, George, what can we do for you today?"

"Mrs. Johnson, you have been a very clever crime-solver several times already, so I'd like your help again."  He hesitated.

Pauline said, "Most crime around here is stealing

and drunk driving. Which one is on your mind today?"

George replied, "I'd like your help in catching some thieves. It seems we have a very efficient, well-organized gang getting past burglar alarms, quickly taking what they want and getting out. They take TV's, DVD players, power tools, lawn mowers, computers.

"We've heard from three other counties where this pattern has appeared. After the leader leaves, the locals, knowing themselves to be excellent thieves, continue to rob and soon get caught. They've told us a lot about their operation. The leader, a man of many names, recruits about ten locals. In three groups, they practice for a solid week: break in, decide what to take, put the things into the van and go, all in less than fifteen minutes. After the burglaries, they meet with the leader in a secluded spot ten or fifteen minutes from there and transfer everything to a semi. They all leave. It's less than an hour from start to finish.

"They invade an area, rob several homes and cabins a day for about four weeks and then disappear. They may be here now, and I'd like to end their careers! I've called a special meeting of the citizens patrol -- they'll be a great help, but there aren't enough of them for this kind of operation. I want to double the numbers on patrol. And I want ideas."

"Exactly what does the citizen's patrol do?" asked Pauline.

"They drive around in their specified area, at random times, looking for anything unusual, vehicles that don't belong, tire tracks where there should be none, open doors or broken windows."

"You want to double the number of patrollers?"

George said, "Yes, but not with marked cars. If we double the cars with citizen's patrol signs, we might scare them off. I want to catch them. I want to find their hiding places. Most of all I want to arrest the mastermind; it looks as though there's one man who moves in, recruits and trains locals and then moves on after a few weeks."

"If I can gather a group of people together, will you tell us what you want us to do?"

George looked pleased. "Absolutely!"

Pauline called Alec and asked, "I wonder if you have time to help me with my crime-solving?"

Alec laughed. "Are you at it again?"

"This time the sheriff came to me for help." Pauline told Alec all about it. "Could you let me know if you hear anything about kids missing a lot of school or any other suspicious information? The sheriff wants us to keep all this quiet; he knows how easily word gets to the wrong people around here. And I absolutely don't want any talk about it at my party! And I don't want people talking about that scrape we dug you out of either, you hear?"

"Sure. I'll check with Cal and some of the other kids. Whoever would have thought that I'd be an undercover agent when I took on this janitor's job? Yes, I'll be a true undercover operator; *nobody* will know what I'm up to." He didn't bother telling her that he was so ashamed of the Dixie Dowling affair that he wasn't about to talk about it.

Alec asked, "You know my friend Fred, who runs the drive-in? He says he's running out of steam. He wants me to manage his drive-in this summer. I think I'd like that."

"Good for you."


Tuesday morning, Pauline and Maggie borrowed Dave's pickup and drove to the nursery where they picked up their order: nine rosebushes, 100 gladiolus bulbs, ten chrysanthemums (bronze and yellow ones), five flats of phlox, four flats of lily of the valley, five day lilies, a dozen butterfly weeds, and a dozen very nice tomato plants plus about twenty packages of flower seeds. They put the plants on the front porch, which was enclosed. There the plants would be safe from a light frost and they could get plenty of sun. If a severe freeze threatened, they could put the space heater on the porch.

On hands and knees, they planted a package of bean seeds and half a package of corn; the other half they would plant in two weeks; they wanted a long season of fresh corn on the cob. The peas and onions were already up. Then they took the gladiolus bulbs to the south of the house. Maggie spaded a hole open, Pauline placed a bulb in the hole and Maggie filled the hole, fifty times that day and fifty times the next day.

Two days later, Pauline and Maggie met Pauline's neighbor, Kathy, and Maggie's friend, Teresa, in front of the government center. Kathy and Teresa carried in the coffee and cookies, while Maggie wheeled Pauline into the building. Pauline could have walked but she wanted to save her energy. They set up the snacks in the meeting room; soon it was packed with eighty-five people, who brightened the drab room with their colorful clothes and their excitement. Sugar cookies and oatmeal raisin cookies strengthened them for the vigorous chatting which preceded the meeting. Pauline carried her walker around as she moved from group to group, enjoying her friends and meeting their friends.

"Pauline, these sugar cookies are marvelous. Nobody makes them better than you do." Betty Ann declared.

"It isn't easy any more, but Maggie helped. Because of all my swimming, I have much better use of my right arm and leg, but still I find it works better to roll cookie dough using just my left hand to press and roll at the center of the rolling pin, rather than using unequal pressure from both hands at the ends."

"You always find a way, don't you!" Betty Ann exclaimed. They laughed.

Beatrice came up to Pauline. "Are those Oneida spoons you have by the coffee urn? Did you get them with Betty Crocker coupons as I did?"

"My mother started buying them back in the forties." Pauline smiled. "My sisters and I saved our coupons and our pennies, even after we married, and gave her more for Christmas and birthdays. Mother gave them to me before she died. I also have half a dozen of the milk-green cups and saucers that came in the large cans of oatmeal back then." Then she told Maggie,

"Beatrice taught school at the Pansy School. We drove to summer classes together at Superior."

Beatrice remembered, "My mother taught school after six weeks of training, in 1906 for a dollar a month per pupil. She taught for three years and saved enough money to buy a sewing machine. Now, more than ninety years later, that sewing machine still works.

"I taught at the Pansy school, north of Thomasville, from 1937 to 1943, starting at $80 a month after two years of teachers' training. One of my most memorable days of teaching was Monday, November 11, 1940; it was rainy and windy, a nasty day. The children were fidgety, but I kept to the schedule for classes, until noon, when the head of our school board came and closed school. He had heard on the radio that there was a terrible storm in Minnesota and it was headed our way. He had a big car so he drove some of the children home, the ones who lived more than two miles away. All the children reached home safely.

"The weather didn't look all that bad, so I decided to give the school a good cleaning and catch up on my paper work; I only had to drive five miles to get home. I finished a few hours later and found several inches of wet snow on the ground and terrible winds bringing more. By the time I reached the road, I realized that the windshield wiper was useless; it just smeared the wet snow around. I had to stick my head out the window to see where I was going. I drove with one hand and wiped the snow and ice off my face with the other. I thought of staying with the Atkinsons, who lived right next to school, but I was young . . . I made it, but that was the longest five miles I ever drove!

"Later, I found out that 'The Armistice Day Blizzard' left behind as much as twenty-six inches of snow in Minnesota which was blown into ten- and twenty-foot drifts by sixty-mile-an-hour winds. Because the storm caught everyone unprepared, fifty-nine people died in Minnesota. Around here, we only had about eight inches of snow; no one died, but schools were closed Tuesday and Wednesday."

Ruth, one of their swimming buddies, had a story to tell, too. "One of my memories from the 'good old days' when I taught school, is about earning college credits to keep my certification. I'd been avoiding a summer school art class because I couldn't stand the teacher, so when they offered it in Muscoda, I took it there. It was forty-five miles from Prairie du Chien, where I lived; the roads wound up and down and around so I'd get car sick. Classes were on Wednesday nights after long days that included recess duty.

"One night, the teacher gave us a test which included the question, 'What is the recipe for finger paint?' I wrote that I didn't clutter my mind with memorized recipes; I kept all my recipes in a recipe file. During the next class, the teacher told me to read my answer out loud. My hair was very red and I had the temper to go with it. I thought the teacher was going to ridicule me, but I held my temper and read. Mr. Hanson thought about it. 'I think Ruth is right. I'll give her 10 points for her answer.' Nobody knew the recipe, so I was the only one who received any points on that question."

"I was a teacher, too," Mary, from water exercise, told them. "We did weeds, seeds and breeds; that's what my children called the agriculture unit where we studied common weeds, hybrid corn and wheat seeds, and breeds of livestock. My students especially liked tramping around in an empty pasture, gathering samples of weeds."

Maggie's friend, Jo, had a tale not about teaching, but like the others, it was about making do and doing it well. "During World War II, my husband was in the service in New Caledonia in the Pacific and I was living in St. Paul with my parents and our newborn daughter, Joanne. My father went to San Francisco in 1943 to work for the Navy, repairing ships at Hunter's Point. When Joanne was six weeks old, my mother, Joanne and I took the train to join my father. The railroad employees were tired and overworked (as everyone seemed to be during the war) but the train was filled with young servicemen who treated Joanne royally; they took turns walking her up and down the aisle whenever she fussed. The train trip lasted six days.

"We lived in the new Navy housing in a small two-bedroom apartment. It even had a new electric agitator washing machine with the attached wringer; of course we had to hang the clothes on outside lines to dry. My cousin Verna, with her Army husband in Texas, worked as a secretary for the Army; she had to wear dresses to work and she had only a wash board for doing laundry.

"The newspapers had big ads, begging for workers to help with war production, so I found a job with Douglas Aircraft while my mother took care of Joanne. I hated to leave my baby, but duty called. We had a few weeks of training before going to work on the real thing. We earned ninety cents an hour and everyone thought that was really high pay. In teams of two, we worked on pieces of wings; one woman held the pieces together while the other riveted them. It was clumsy work, not hard, but I was plenty tired at quitting time. We all wore slacks, because it was safer and more modest. I made a lot of friends; many of us were in the same boat, husband in the service. Some women worked half a day and did their housework in the mornings.

"After a year and a half of that, my husband thought the war was ending so he told me to return to St. Paul and find us a place to live. I looked for an apartment but no one wanted to rent to someone with a child. I looked for a house, since I had a down payment with the money I had saved while working in California. Then I was very shocked: I always thought I could do anything I wanted to do, but I found out banks wouldn't loan money to a woman for buying a house, even when she had the down payment. My father-in-law bought the house, with my money down, and sold it to my husband for a dollar."

Incredulously, Maggie asked, "Are you saying that you worked for a year and a half for ninety cents an hour and saved enough money for a down payment on a house?"

Jo grinned. "That's right."

"Wow!"

174

Betty, from swimming, told how war affected her cousin. "My Dad's cousin Benji fought in World War II. He suffered from shell shock, which meant the cruelty of war drove him crazy; he was in and out of the VA hospital for the rest of his life, nearly fifty years.

"Dad never told me about Benji until ten years ago. I went to see him at the hospital, a huge, cold, depressing stone and brick building. I waited in a dreary little visiting room for five minutes. Then a skinny, stooped little man shuffled in; his soul was bent so low, it didn't reach his eyes; he looked ancient, but I knew he wasn't even seventy."

Betty continued, "I introduced myself, told him my grandma's name was Helen Balke, the sister of his mother, Marie. He nodded politely. Then I showed him a picture of Grandma Helen.

"Aunt Helen!." His beautiful smile nearly broke my heart. I showed him pictures of Dad and his brothers when they were young. Looking at the pictures, he talked coherently and happily. When I put them away, he withdrew into his shell again, a sad painful place if his face showed true. Benji had twenty years of life and fifty years in his shell. The people who start wars don't look at the Benjis." Betty sighed, "I visited him a few more times and then he died."

A moment later, Pat said, "I remember prices. For instance, in the mid-fifties, I had $25 a week for groceries to feed my family of four. I'd shop very carefully, buy five pounds of hamburger for a dollar, fifty pounds of flour for $2.99, a dozen eggs for nineteen cents, twelve jars of baby food for a dollar. We used a lot of Spam. For a quick meal, I'd grind up a can of Spam, add onion, cheese and mayonnaise, put it on a bun and warm it in the oven. I'd shop the specials and use coupons because I could save the extra money for a new blouse or splurge on a dozen sweet rolls for a dollar at the bakery. It doesn't seem possible that was almost fifty years ago."

Then, having had a suitable interval of feeding faces and ears, the women and men took their places on the folding chairs and the sheriff faced them across the long table. He said, "I see that Pauline Johnson still has her powers of persuasion. I think with your help, we can do it." He explained the problem to them. "There have already been robberies at Sand Lake, Trade Lake, Pickle Lake, Cadotte Lake; they have robbed the homes of farmers, business people and retired folks.

"I'd like some of you to patrol the areas where there is no citizen's patrol, for instance along River Road and in Zook township; those are state and county forest areas, where there aren't many people; they are likely places for them to transfer their stolen goods to larger trucks. I want some of you to help the citizen's patrol where they are low in numbers or where there are a lot of likely places for them to rob. And I need a few typists to feed the information into computers.

"I want you to write down or put on a tape recorder whatever you see: descriptions of trucks or vans including license plate numbers; truck tracks down dirt roads, anything that looks out of place. Report any gossip you hear about persons who have suddenly become very self important or very busy or who have more money than usual. If you have a camera, take pictures. If you have a portable phone, call in immediately with anything that looks important.

"Remember, you are citizens, not sheriff's deputies. Don't put yourself at risk; we're trained for that, so let us do it. I have a map for each of you, showing the roads, the year-round residents and vacationers." Maggie took them and passed them around and he asked, "Any questions?"

Pauline asked, "Sheriff George, shouldn't we organize an information network? If we find reasonable suspicions, we should share them. Then everyone could be on the lookout for the suspicious characters and their vehicles."

"Good idea. How do you want to do it?"

"I could call five people with the information and each of them could call five others and they could call five more."

"That would work. Do you want to discuss that,

vote on it, what?"

Everyone agreed on the plan, so Pauline passed along a sheet of paper for them to sign and give their phone numbers. She'd make a chart and let them know who to call.

Dave offered some information. "A few weeks ago, a new fellow showed up at Squig's Bar." Pauline recognized the name of one of the nicer bars. "He didn't seem quite right. His shirt and pants looked casual enough, but they were brand new and expensive. He looked about sixty, but one of the guys spilled a drink and when he jumped, he acted more like thirty. He asked a lot of questions, about golfing and fishing for instance. But not only did he ask where the best trout fishing was, he also wanted to know when we went. Maybe he just wanted to buddy up to us, but I couldn't help wondering what he was really fishing for."

"What did he look like?" asked sheriff George.

"Kind of average."

"Average height? Weight?"

"Well, maybe a little under six feet tall, not fat or skinny, some gray in his dark hair, good looking I guess, but . . . yeah, his eyes were close together -- made him look shifty." Dennis and Grant thought they'd seen the same curious man at their bars.

George asked, "Dave, Dennis and Grant, could you stop in my office tomorrow morning? I'd like to have a sketch made up of this fellow."

They could. The meeting ended.

After the meeting, Sharron put a special program into the sheriff's computer. Then she and Teresa would type the daily reports into the computer; it would check all the license plates, identify the owners and determine if the cars belonged where they were seen. It would print out any information that needed checking. The secretaries could eliminate other vehicles, for instance, a plumber's van, seen near a house where the plumber had done repairs.

As they left the meeting, Pauline told Maggie, "I think I'll ask Vern Fitzelditz to come to my house

177

tomorrow morning. I want to talk to him."

George went back to his office and called up a dozen bartenders, men respected in their communities, men who respected the law. George's message was simple, "Please come see me tomorrow afternoon in my office."

By ten the next morning, he had a sketch of "Pete Jenkins," which he showed to each bartender that afternoon. The bartenders came from all over the county; two of them had seen "Pete." None of them knew anything about Pete, not even where he was staying. They would tell George if they heard anything.

That same morning at Pauline's table, Vern nervously drank his highly sugared coffee and scratched at his haphazardly shaved chin. Pauline thought he probably looked at sobriety like a poor kid looking at a candy jar in the store: what he saw was desirable but beyond him; while a storekeeper might give the poor child a piece of candy, nobody could give Vern sobriety. Pauline said, "You know, Vern, I had the strangest dream last night. I dreamed I ate a great big marshmallow. When I woke up this morning, my pillow was gone."

Maggie laughed and then Vern caught on and laughed, too. After a moment, he asked, "Did you hear about the drunk who had the shakes real bad. He finally went to the doctor. The doctor asked him if he drank much. He said 'No, I spill most of it.'"

When they finished laughing, Pauline said, "Vern, we need your help. There's a gang of thieves working this area and we want to know if you've heard anything that might help us catch them."

Vern sat a little straighter. He'd been expecting a lecture on drinking. "Well, uh, I don't know . . ."

"Have you seen any strangers at Guzzler's in the last three weeks or so? We think the brains of the outfit recruits locals, steals for a few weeks and then moves on. Have any of the regulars been missing a lot or sporting more money than usual?"

After some thought, Vern's face lit up. "Yeah, there was a guy, a city weasel if I ever saw one. He was

178

talking to Nimrod and his buddies. It was strange, cuz Nimrod never listens to anybody but himself. They was talking hush-hush, like they was up to no good."

"One weasel recognizes another," Maggie thought.

Pauline asked, "What did the stranger look like?"

"I dunno, normal I guess."

Bit by bit, Pauline arrived at a description: dark hair, a little taller than Nimrod, no beer belly, ordinary clothes, no glasses, about forty. It sounded like Pete Jenkins except for no gray hair.

Maggie asked, "Which of Nimrod's friends were there?"

"They was crowded around that big table. Seven maybe. There was the stranger, Nimrod, Bleek and Zeke, Nels and Nork, . . . is that seven?"

"One more."

Vern tried again. "Nimrod, Nels, Nork, Willard, Zeke, Bleek."

Pauline told Vern, "You're doing great; this will be a big help! Can you think of anything else?"

The praise embarrassed him; he thought some more and then continued, "Yeah, Nimrod and the others weren't at Guzzler's for about a week. When they came back, they was worse than ever, bragging themselves up, pushing everybody around."

"You don't like him, do you Vern?" asked Maggie.

"No, Ma'am. He's a bully and he's mean to women. I ain't much, but I know to respect a woman."

Pauline asked, "Are Nimrod and his gang usually in Guzzler's every day and night?"

"Pretty much."

"Don't they have jobs?"

"Nimrod's an electrician. He works when he feels like it. Maybe a coupla days a week. I guess he does a lot of hunting out of season and stuff like that. Some of the guys work with builders sometimes. I think Willard lives off his wife. Bleek, too."

Maggie wanted to know what they drove.

"Nimrod drives a van with his electric stuff. Zeke has a van for his tools. Funny, they don't have company

179

names on the vans. No, they probably use them for illegal hunting."

Maggie asked, "What about the others?"

"I think the other guys all have pickups."

Pauline said, "Vern, we really appreciate all your help." She wanted to give him some money and a bath, but knew he'd be insulted with either. She gave him her warmest smile and saw by his smile that her approval was all the thanks he wanted. When Maggie saw the glow of his smile, she knew there was a dear old man hiding inside the shabby drunk with his missing teeth and worn, wrinkled clothes.

Pauline called sheriff George with the information. He called back a little later with the license plate numbers they should watch for. Then she called her helpers to pass along the facts.

# 24

That was Friday morning. Friday evening Pauline's Chicago and Colorado relatives came to Pauline's for a visit before the party; since they hadn't seen each other for many years, they had plenty to talk about. Saturday morning, the New York group came to her house.

Saturday noon, Pauline sat near the entrance at the community center and welcomed her relatives to her birthday party. A hundred of them came, her eighty-four-year-old sister, her three-month-old great-great nephew and all ages in between. They came in their spring finery, carrying bowls of hot food or trays of desserts or vases of flowers for the tables. Stuart brought chocolate marshmallow bars; Mary had stayed Friday night with

Dorothy so they could cook up a four-bean casserole and a mammoth meat loaf; Alec provided a most unexpected huge leafy green salad; Sara brought store-bought dinner rolls.

Pauline's granddaughter showed her the cake she'd made. "I wanted to put 'Happy Birthday' on it, but I couldn't get the cake into the typewriter."

Pauline laughed, "Yes, that would be difficult."

As is proper at a potluck, Pauline tried to sample as many dishes as she could, so she ate too much. It was a very proper group, so they all ate too much.

After the tables were cleared, Stuart announced, "All of us here are descendants or married to descendants of Minnie and Karl Peterson. Some of us look like Minnie or Karl. Most of us are hard-working as they were. I doubt if any of us are as poor as they were, but many of us share their love of books and music. All of us have their strong belief in God and great love of family." For a moment, the family bond felt so tangible to Stuart that he choked up, which completely flummoxed the very unemotional man. He turned his back to his family and coughed, to hide his embarrassment.

Then he continued, "We'd like for everyone to get to know each other. My mother, Pauline Johnson had eight brothers and sisters. We'd like for one person from each of the nine to introduce everyone from that family. I'll start with Pauline's. When we're finished, we hope all of you will stick around and talk. We have the hall until five."

When the introductions were over, the people broke into small fluid groups. Pauline had a nice chat with her sister from Minnesota and her brother from Iowa. Nephews and nieces brought their children over. At first Pauline tried to remember everyone and everything, but she gave up and determined to just enjoy them all. Which she did.

During a lull, Pauline thought, "I wish my other three brothers and sister could be here, too, to see all these fine people who have descended from us. We had some hard times. Sometimes I was so unhappy or discouraged that I could hardly go on; all of us felt that way sometimes. But when I see our family here, I know it was worth it. What's that saying, 'You get what you pay for?' We paid a high price, but we got *more* than our money's worth, much more! Oh, I hope Minnie and Karl are looking down from heaven and see us here today."

Then, at Dorothy's instigation, another family came to talk with Pauline. Dorothy was good; she kept them coming.

Sunday, they all met at a restaurant for brunch after church; some left for home afterwards. Stuart and Mary's families, with Alec and Dorothy, visited at Pauline's for a few hours before leaving for the Cities. A dozen of them sat around the dining room table, the rest were in the living room. At the table, Stuart's son Andy said, "You know Dad, what you said yesterday set me to thinking. We have a lot in common with our relatives. For instance, all of us first cousins like playing baseball in one form or another."

"My baseball memories," said Stuart, "go back to when I was a kid, growing up right here. Dave and a bunch of his brothers and sisters used to come over here for a game of ball. Mom would sit on a kitchen chair with little Dorothy on her lap; she was our umpire, which meant we didn't dare fight."

Mary remembered the ball games too. "I was so small when those games started that I could barely swing the bat. That made me mad; I worked so hard at it that in a few years, I could hit the ball almost as far as Stuart could."

"You could not!"

"You used to hit them over the fence sometimes and I finally hit them to the fence!"

"Yes, I guess you did," Stuart admitted.

Mary's daughter Anne said, "Most of us cousins have gray eyes and that funny Peterson nose."

Pauline commented, "My mother read to us when we were young. The only book we had was the Bible, so that's what she read. My sister Rose married a man who did quite well; when she asked what she could send my

182

children for Christmas, I said 'Books!' I read them to my children and now Maggie and I are reading them all again." Speaking about her mother brought on a slight accent.

"Mom read to us and I read to my kids," said Mary's daughter Jean. "I'll bet I read some of the same stories you did, Grandma, Winnie the Pooh, Charlotte's Web and Pippi Longstocking. Then there are newer classics The Cat in the Hat and the Berenstein Bears. And future classics like Dream Snow and The Owl and the Pussycat."

Stuart's George and Mary's Anne read to their children, too. "Just think," Anne said, "fifty years from now, maybe our children will gather like this and tell each other about the books we read to them when they were little."

"I just thought of another trait we have in common. Have any of you ever listened to the way we laugh? If you heard that laugh in a crowded room halfway around the world, you'd know it was a relative, but you wouldn't have any idea which one."

Jean said, "Grandma, tell us a story from when you were a kid." A momentary pause in the living room conversation let those people hear the request and they stayed quiet to hear what she said.

Pauline was a good storyteller, but nobody had been interested in family stories before. "Ja, sure; all right, then." She pulled her thoughts together and said, "My father, Karl, was a farmer. This land isn't too good and the growing season here is short, so he worked odd jobs in the winter. He was a carpenter and a woodcarver so there was plenty of work he could do, but people didn't have any way to pay him during the Depression.

"One winter, there were no paying jobs; he spent his time carving a set of figurines depicting the Nativity. As he finished each figure, he set it in place on a shelf which he had put up. On Christmas Eve, he told us 'Tomorrow is Jesus' birthday. We must each give him a present. I give him my pipe.' My mother gave him her fanciest handkerchief. My brothers and sisters dug out their treasures, a slingshot, a few marbles, a homemade jump-rope and I gave him my beautiful red ribbon. On Christmas morning, the gifts were gone and a smiling baby Jesus lay in the straw." Everyone savored the story silently.

Then Mary said, "Times were hard when I was little too, but Mom always saw to it that we each had a nickel for church every Sunday. She saw to it that we went to Bible classes and Confirmation classes and all that too."

"If I used a bad word without knowing it was bad," Stuart said, "Mom told me not to use it again. If I said it again, she washed my mouth out with soap."

"One of my early memories," said Dorothy, " was when Mom married Tom. She was all dressed up and she was so pretty I wasn't sure she was my mom." Then Dorothy asked, "Mom, was it your parents or your grandparents who came from Norway to the United States?"

"Both," Pauline answered. "My grandparents brought five children over; their sixth and last, Minnie, was my mother who was born not long after they arrived in this area. An Indian midwife helped with her delivery. Not long ago, I had a lovely visit with her nephew who is now a hundred years old and still lives by himself. My father Karl came with his parents. I think they all immigrated around the turn of the century. Both my parents spoke English well enough, but they had accents until the day they died. Everyone could tell they had come from Norway.

"Minnie's father had a farm in Orange Township. In the winter he worked with a logging crew. This area was mostly forest in the early 1900's. He grew potatoes because it was one of the few crops that did really well here, but farmers didn't rotate crops back then or fertilize so they quickly depleted the soil and the market went bad -- I don't remember all the problems, but they did have a starch factory near Cranberry Town for a while." Pauline had an afterthought, "Just think, our family has been in the United States for a hundred years. It has been hard sometimes, but it has been good."

Because of her party, Pauline had arranged for others to keep up on the patrol work over the weekend. She didn't even read the reports until Monday evening. Saturday's report showed three robberies at homes near Riverside while the owners were at work, at 2:00 p.m. One of George's bartending friends reported that Pete Jenkins had spent an hour at his Cranberry Town bar Saturday night. He had two drinks and asked a lot of questions. Sunday morning after church, retirees returned to their Owl Lake homes -- the robberies had them hooting their anger. Sunday night Pete Jenkins went to a bar near A and H.

Monday evening, Alec called his mother. "The Pinch boys have been absent for over a week, which apparently isn't too unusual, but it might connect with the burglaries." They chatted a bit and said good-bye.

Pauline immediately called Doris Doppler. Due to the marvelous effects of the water exercise, Doris only devoted ten minutes to moaning about her back problems. Then Pauline asked, "Have you heard anything recently about Adele and Horace Pinch?"

"Hm. What did I hear, just a few days ago? Yes, I know. Horace quit his bartending job. It was quite peculiar. I heard he was talking to some slick-looking fellow at the bar one night and he didn't show up for work the next night. Dick called his home and Adele told him Horace quit. She said he'd found a much better job, but wouldn't say what it was. Dick was mad but he was surprised, too. Horace had been working there nearly ten years."

"Very interesting. Any news about Adele?"

"Well, she quit her card club about the same time, because she had more important things to do, so I heard."

Pauline asked, "What are they driving these days, do you know?"

"I've seen her at the grocery store in a blue pickup with a white cover."

"Thanks, Doris."

"Anytime."

Pauline called the sheriff, who looked up the license plates. She called her network.

Tuesday morning, Pauline and Maggie found the first potatoes peeping up. They planted squash, cucumbers and carrots. Working with the life force of nature was soul-satisfying labor.

While they were busy in the garden, the thieves burglarized three retirees' homes around Coon Lake. That evening, Pete drank and questioned at Devil's Lake Inn. Wednesday afternoon they robbed three places at Cranberry Lake. A bartender reported seeing Pete at O'Hara Lake Pub. Thursday McKenzie Lake residents felt the sting of being robbed. Shortly after the robberies, Adeline and Mary spotted Bleek's van nearby.

Tuesday, Wednesday and Thursday, Pauline and Maggie read the reports, passed on information, and patrolled their assigned area; they decided that they were on the busywork end of sleuthing only it wasn't very busy. Kathleen and Princess loved all the rides. Kathleen sat on the back seat behind Maggie and watched every approaching car as it came and went, whipping her head around until Maggie wondered why she didn't hurt herself. Princess perched on the ledge behind the back seat, where she could watch over everything. All four of them were delighted to be out in the beautiful spring weather; otherwise, they might have found it boring.

Friday morning, Maggie greeted Pauline, "Happy birthday! Do you have any energy left after last weekend?"

Pauline's smile reached all the way to her heart. "All right, so I slept most of the day Monday. It was worth it! But I'm all rested up now; I have plenty of energy for celebrating my birthday. It's supposed to be hot today, so how about a picnic at Circle Lake Park? We could have fried chicken, potato salad and a tossed salad."

"We should have a birthday cake too. The ones last weekend don't count because they weren't on your real birthday. What kind do you want?"

Pauline answered, "I think my favorite dessert

today is your French silk pie. We could make one for lunch and finish it for supper. After lunch, we could drive around Crex Meadows for a while and pretend we're looking for criminals when we're really admiring all the birds." She thought of something else she wanted. "One more thing. You said once that the library has my favorite movie, The Sound of Music. We could pick that up and watch it tonight. That would make a perfect day."

"If that's what you want, that's what we'll do. Since it's your birthday, you get to sit while I do all the work. Right?"

"Wrong. I should not have to work today, that's right. But since when is cooking and baking with you considered work?"

After their delicious picnic, they drove to the wild life refuge. As Maggie turned on a road into Crex Meadows, a teenager rode up on a bicycle, followed by two dogs. He gestured for her to stop.

"I'm Cal Dowling and I'd like to follow your car and see if I can get a picture of a goose attacking your car." His voice and smile were pleasant, a far cry from his former attitude.

"This is Pauline Johnson and I'm Maggie O'Neill. Aren't you the fellow who takes all those great pictures for the Mackerel High School newspaper?"

"That's me. Am I becoming famous?"

Maggie answered, "World famous, at least. Is there anything special you want us to do?"

"No. When you stop to let geese cross the road, sooner or later there will be a gander that thinks he should protect his family from your car. While you wait, I'll sneak around and snap pictures."

About twenty minutes later, Maggie braked quickly as a goose family started across the road about ten feet ahead of the car on Pauline's side. The geese knew they were protected; they strutted right in front of the slow-moving car. Maggie was only going about fifteen miles an hour so the geese were safe. But the gander didn't like the monster. It flapped it's wings and hissed viciously. The goose and goslings ignored them all and walked right on.  Cal told the dogs to stay and snuck around the driver's side of the car.  He raised his head above the hood and snapped.  He crawled out in front of the car and snapped.  The geese were off in the weeds.  The gander ignored Cal -- he was teaching that car a lesson it would never forget.  Cal stood up and walked behind the gander to take a few more photos.  The gander finished terrorizing the car and waddled proudly after the goose and goslings.  Cal took a picture of the reunited family and walked back to his dogs and his bicycle.  "Good dogs."

Pauline called quietly, "Cal."  He walked his bicycle alongside the car.

"Cal, you probably have some excellent pictures.  Why don't you send them into the Bear County Journal?"  Pauline had taught the editor of the local newspaper and she knew she could get him to take a serious look at Cal's work.  If Cal's photographs were as good as Alec thought they were, that's all it would take.  "They might even pay you for any pictures they print."

"Do you really think so?"

"It's certainly worth a try."

The marsh was filled with ducks, teal, thousands of Canada geese and even a few tundra swans, brought from Alaska several years earlier and doing quite well.  Some of the young were already out and about: ducklings swam after their parents, goslings searched the weeds for food.  Pauline and Maggie saw loons, cranes, herons, red-winged blackbirds and dozens of other kinds of birds, some busily feeding families, others still nesting.

Then they drove along River Road, which wound through the state forest, where the trees were bursting into leaf. Sometimes they could see the river. Although it was only May, it was a gloriously *hot* sunny day.  They explored several side roads, but found nothing suspicious, the same as they had found three or four times a day on the other days they had patrolled; they had seen a few trucks and cars, which were identified as belonging to people who lived around there.

They drove to one of the boat landings and

stopped for a while. No sign of any thieves. They looked at each other. "George did say that we should try to look as though we were doing anything except watching for criminals." They grinned, took off their shoes and socks and walked down the ramp and into the water. Kathleen followed them into the water but turned right around to get out. Princess just looked at Pauline; if Princess had been human, she probably would have scolded her friend for being so undignified. It was *cold,* but they were a couple of kids who were playing hooky and cold didn't matter. Pauline carried her walker along; she used it to steady herself while she kicked water at Maggie. Maggie laughed and kicked right back, until they were both soaked and laughing too hard to continue.

After that, they sat on a fallen tree, to dry off in the warm sun. Maggie said, "Pauline, I'm curious. Your family was poor, but you managed to get enough education to become a teacher. How did you do that?"

Pauline laughed. "The same way I've done everything. Hard work. I went to high school in Cranberry Town. I stayed in town during the week and earned board and room and a few dollars a month by cooking and cleaning for the people I stayed with. A lot of town folks got hired girls that way. It was cheap. When a teacher had to miss school, I was usually the one they put in charge of the class. All my teachers thought I should be a teacher. At that time, the high school offered a one-year course of teacher training. That was the easy year.

"The state had passed a law requiring four years of college for teacher certification, but because all the young men were off fighting in WWII, teachers were scarce. They even let married women teach! We could teach in a one-room schoolhouse with only one year of teacher training, but we had to take classes every year toward a degree. I taught for four years, taking night classes around here and correspondence courses and summer classes. Five or six of us would drive in a dilapidated old car to Mackerel for a history or science course or to Little Fork for psychology or art. I liked learning, the hours of driving gave us some social life and we were young and fancy-free. For me, it was a good time.

"I was never quite sure how we got the extra rations for gas, whether it was because of a high priority for teachers' training or because we gave eggs to our friend on the ration board. If we missed a class because of a flat tire that was too bald to be fixed and no replacement in sight, we had to make up the work.

"I taught for four years and earned enough credits for more than a year of college. I liked my teaching life, that was my second life, but I quit teaching when I married Andy. In 1956, I had to go back to teaching because Andy was too busy drinking to earn enough for us to live on. Night classes and summer school courses used to mean a social time and a time for learning but in 1956, they became time I begrudged being away from my children. I didn't like being poor, but I hated having to hide my earnings from Andy so he wouldn't waste them on drink."

"How much did you get paid then?"

"In 1956, I earned $2800. Back then, they paid a man with my education and experience nearly $1000 more a year, so he could support a family." Pauline shook her head. "Of course, everything was much cheaper then. Gas was twenty cents a gallon. My electric agitator washing machine with its wringer cost $99 in the early fifties."

Maggie interrupted. "The other day, Pat said that she had $25 a week for groceries for a family of four in the early fifties. But you had to feed seven. At that rate, you would have spent almost your whole salary on food with very little left for rent, clothes, heat, gas for the car, insurance . . ."

"We moved back here with my mother, so there was no rent. She kept a few cows, pigs and chickens; she had a garden. We increased the numbers of animals and the size of the garden to help feed all of us. She soon had six-year-old Stuart helping; they would feed the chickens, pull weeds in the garden, wash dishes. Mary helped, too, but Sara! She grew old enough to help, but it was easier to do a job myself than to get Sara working, so eventually, we made her do all the dishes and gave up on other jobs.

"I liked teaching and I didn't mind working hard myself, but I hated seeing my mother so tired. I wanted her to be able to take it easy, but I gave her all our laundry and cooking to do. In the house Andy and I rented, we had electricity and in one of his richer moments, he bought me my electric agitator washing machine, but it didn't help Mother, because she had no electricity. I was very angry with Andy for putting my mother through that. By 1960, though, I had earned enough credits for a big raise. I was up to $4000 a year! Right away, I had electricity put in for Mother. And finally, in 1964, I got my degree."

"Good for you! I hope you celebrated in grand style!" Maggie exclaimed.

"Of course. They even wrote about it in the paper. I'll show you the article when we get home." Pauline smiled. "Tom Johnson read the article; he was my sweetheart in high school. He wanted to marry me before he went off to war, but I wasn't ready yet. I still didn't want to marry him after the war, so he went to Minneapolis where he worked as a car salesman. He earned good money and invested it carefully. By the time he read that article, he was rich. And lonely. I was poor and lonely, only not the same lonely as he was. I had my mother and my children but I wanted someone to take the lead in making decisions, someone to share responsibilities."

Maggie nodded, "I know the feeling. You've proved you *can* carry the whole load, but it would be a lot easier to have help."

"Exactly. Anyway, Tom read the article in the newspaper, which mentioned that I was a widow, and he came back to court me all over again."

Damp but not dripping, Pauline and Maggie walked slowly back to the car, where the cell phone was beeping. "Hello."

"This is Kathy. I just wanted to let you know you

had visitors. The dogs barked so loud I heard them from the garden where I was working. So I stood up and pretended I was on the phone. Even across the field, I could see they were mad. It looked like a man, a woman, and maybe two tall kids. She slammed the pickup door shut and just sat there for a few minutes. I'll bet she was cussing a blue streak."

Pauline said, "Thanks Kathy." To Maggie, she said, "That foolish Pinch woman! I thought she was smart enough to leave me alone, but she learned a little about burgling and became more stupid."

"She tried to rob you again?"

Pauline nodded.

"As much as Princess hates them, it's a good thing George loaned you those two retired guard dogs."

"Well when I realized Adele and her family were in this organized gang, I thought she might try again. I guess she's just so rotten that even salt won't save her." Pauline laughed. "Princess and I both will be very happy when Adele goes to jail so I can return the dogs. George ordered the dogs to leave Princess and Kathleen alone, which they do, because they are well-trained. But cats don't take orders, so Princess has been harassing the dogs ever since they arrived."

Pauline giggled, "Princess reminds me of myself when I was a child -- she knows exactly what she can get away with. When we had an incompetent teacher, I behaved abominably. Looking back, I can see how awful I was. Now that I'm grown up and civilized, I appreciate kindness in myself and others but when I see my cat acting up, I do want to laugh. I guess I'm not as civilized as I like to think I am, but those dogs are *so German!*"

Maggie protested, "Don't be too hard on German's. I have a German grandfather, you know."

"Yes, but you *act* Irish." Maggie wasn't quite sure what Pauline meant by that, but since she was smiling, Maggie assumed it was good.

As she watched The Sound of Music at the end of that wonderful birthday, she loved it again, for maybe the tenth time. Afterwards, Pauline told Maggie, "They say

'The older the fiddle, the sweeter the tune.' I've played a very sweet tune today. Thanks."

Friday, Little Bear Lake residents growled about their losses. Carol and Pat saw the Pinches in the area at the time. Saturday, the thieves stole around Lake O'Hara in the afternoon, while residents were at work.

# 25

Alec had wanted to treat his mother to a special birthday dinner. He was janitor during the week and manager at the drive-in on weekends, Friday afternoons until Sunday night. But business was light on Sunday evenings, so Fred ran the drive-in while Alec took her out to dinner the Sunday after her birthday.

As they waited for their food, Alec said, "Mom, there's something I want to talk to you about." He'd planned to say it just right but he wanted it so badly he just blurted it out, "I want to buy the park from you."

Pauline gasped; she thought she knew her son, but she had no idea this was coming. "I'm listening."

"I want to pay you a fair price and borrow money from the bank and do it up right. I'd run it just the same as we have been doing." He waited for his mom to absorb that and then he continued, "I've had about every job there is, but this one really pulls out the best in me. I'm the boss, I'm an entertainer, I'm wheeling and dealing with lots of people and we're all having fun with it. And I like it so much that the responsibility doesn't bury me. Mom, this job fits me like an old shoe."

Pauline sat there dumbfounded.

"I've thought of making it into a year-round park, but I don't know if you'd want me to do that. I've been saving my money and took on managing the drive-in to earn more this summer. I don't want to buy it yet. I want to prove to both of us that I can manage my sobriety and my finances first." He waited for a reply. "What do you think?"

"What do I think? I have a dozen thoughts for each thing you've said. My mind is racing around in circles." She took a deep breath. "Let's start at the beginning. Do you know why I started the park?"

Alec shook his head. "No."

"Because I wanted to prove to myself and to the world that I was still alive, in spite of the strokes and being in a wheelchair. Now look at me. We didn't bring my wheelchair along or even my walker!" The triumph in her voice was unmistakable.

Pauline continued, "I'm thinking you want to pay a fair price and get a bank loan; I agree. If I were to give it to you, it would be less valuable to you. You want to run it the same and I'm all for that, especially with regard to earning money for the clubs and their projects. That benefits the community and it is good for business. This suits you so well, you want to make a career out of it. That is music to my mother's heart. But no, not next to my house. I've gotten my money's worth out of it. Find a piece of land, put in some water slides and whatever else they like these days and keep it open all year.

"Altogether and absolutely, I think 'yes'. Save your money, plan carefully, and we'll talk more. Maybe you could manage the park next winter and if you're still so enthusiastic next spring, you could buy it then."

"Thanks, Mom"

"Thank *you*, Alec."

The food came and since they were exceptionally pleased with each other, it tasted extraordinarily good. As they finished, Alec saw four people come into the restaurant, Cal and Patty, Jim and *Joan*. She was listening carefully to what Jim was saying. They saw Alec and Pauline and walked over to their table. Greetings flew and then, "We're celebrating Patty's birthday."

"We're celebrating Mom's birthday," Alec said. They exchanged birthday wishes and then the four moved on.

Alec looked perplexed.

Although she knew the answer, Pauline asked, "Are you still seeing Joan?"

"Yes," he answered sadly.

"You know, if you're becoming a somebody for her, it won't work. You have to do it for yourself."

Alec had no idea what she was talking about.

After they ordered, Joan, Jim and Cal gave their presents to Patty. Joan and Jim gave her a card telling her they had parked a bicycle in her garage. Joan had found a used one and they had fixed it all up so it looked and ran like new. Cal gave her a photo album with pictures of her favorite things: pizza, track shoes, a bowling ball, a Robert Frost poem, her English teacher, a lake, a goat, Sunny and King, and one of himself and dozens more; the rest of the album was filled with copies of her favorites among his other photographs.

Patty looked at a few pages and realized what an effort Cal had made to please her. Suddenly she couldn't see too well. She closed it and said, "I'll look at this later," and smiled a huge wet smile for Cal.

Jim said, "I thought Alec's mother had to use a wheelchair."

"She did," Joan responded, "but she's been exercising in the water for months and hardly uses it at all now." Then she asked him, "How many drunk drivers have you salvaged?"

Jim answered, "Time will tell if they're salvaged or not. Don finished his community service hours with Mrs. Green. I wouldn't guarantee he'll never drink and drive again, but his attitude has improved to where he can see some consequences he never admitted before. I have two more men working now. It's sad though, how few of our county's drunk drivers are willing to admit to the judge that they're guilty and willing to make amends, even if it gets them off jail time."

"Oh Cal, I don't think I congratulated you on your photographs in the Journal," Joan said. "You told a story in those pictures, a family of geese crossing the road, the Don Quixote gander defending them from the car and then the family together again, safely across the road. Very well done."

"Thanks." He tried to sound nonchalant but he still wasn't used to compliments and he squirmed until Patty grabbed everyone's attention, as she talked about her job at the drive-in. "Fred is a good boss but he's old and I think maybe he's sick. It's a good thing Alec manages it for him on weekends. He says he'll do it full-time once school closes. Alec is fun. If everything is cleaned up and there aren't any customers, he tells us crazy stories. We never know if he's making them up or not, but he's really funny. If a car pulls up, it's the end of the story until we wait on the people." She was working weekends until school was out, then she would work full-time earning money for college.

Cal had surprised everyone when he got a job at the drive-in, too. He had a busy summer ahead of him: working, studying, Polly, the dogs, photography.

"Here comes our food."

As they ate, Jim looked around at the others and thought, "Such an odds and ends group of people, unrelated, different ages, yet we are so comfortable together." He was grateful for that.

Alec knew Joan had been seeing Jim, knew they were longtime friends, but seeing them together and with the kids, they looked like a happy family and the more he thought about it, the less he liked it; the less he liked it, the more he thought about it.


Monday morning, Maggie drove Pauline into town to see Jim.

"Jim here's my will. I want to add something to it," Pauline told him. "Alec wants to buy the park in about a year, when his finances permit. That's fine if I'm alive, and I expect I will be. But I've had several strokes, so I don't want to leave this to chance. If I die, I want him to have it, free and clear."

Jim read the will and asked her a few questions. She decided on two minor changes. "I'll have it ready in a few days."

"Thank you."

"You're welcome."

When they got back to Pauline's, they put on their grubby gardening clothes and planted the rest of the vegetable seeds. They worked slowly, silently, savoring their labors and being gentle to two aging bodies. Then they went on patrol.

That afternoon was warm and sunny; Cal and Patty sat in the swings facing the water at Circle Lake Park. They were the only ones there, so Sunny and King romped around, in and out of the water, back and forth chasing squirrels, vigorously enjoying life.

Cal felt good. He had finished the algebra in a few months and was more than half way through geometry. Mrs. Koenig was still a good teacher even though she was seventy years old. He and Patty were making progress through the ACT material.

When he had started raising his hand in class to volunteer answers, he shocked his teachers and the students; he aggravated the shock by giving the right answers. The kids teased him; sometimes it almost became ugly, but Alec's determination made a protective coat for him. When the kids realized they couldn't make him mad, they backed off. Sparked by Alec's eagerness in his classes, many of the kids perked up too, much to the teachers' delight.

"Are you sure you want to mess up your summer with that ACT junk?" he asked Patty.

"How often do I have to tell you that I *want* to do it?"

"Okay." Then he changed the subject. "You know that old lady, Mrs. Johnson? She said I should send the gander pictures into the <u>Journal</u>. Well, she sent me the paper with the gander photos in it. She wrote that I should keep copies of all my pictures that are printed or used in any way. That will help me get into college or get a job. Did I tell you that the editor said I should send him more photos? He'll use them whenever he can."

"Yes, you told me about the editor. That's cool."

Cal asked Patty, "Do you still think you want to be a teacher?"

"Of course. I make up my mind and stick to it. Haven't you noticed?"

"Do you know where you want to go?"

Patty looked thoughtful. "Most places have good teacher training courses, but I'm leaning toward the university at Eau Claire."

"They have a good journalism course there; maybe we'll both go there. That would be cool." Then he said, "Sometimes I don't feel real to myself any more. Sunny, all my studying, getting A's in school, Jim adopting me." His voice wobbled, "And you."

Patty responded, " I think you spent all those years with your mother, thinking you were like her, when you're really like your father. And since women tend to pick the same type of man over and over again, your father is probably a lot like Jim."

Well that was something for Cal to think about!

"What I mean is, once you get used to the new you, I think you'll find it's a good fit."

"Do you really think so?"

"I do!"

After a bit, he said, "You're a really good friend, Patty."

She grinned. "I'm glad you've finally realized that." She reached down to take her shoes off. "I'll race you down to the water." He had longer legs and rode his bicycle everywhere, but she ran the 100, 200 and 500 meter races for the track team. She won.

After work Monday, Alec stormed over to Joan's house and told her, "You've got to stop seeing Jim!" He didn't acknowledge the surprise and hurt on her face. "It's him or me! I've had enough of this!"

"I'll get us a cup of coffee," Joan said to give herself a moment to understand what was happening.

Alec repeated his demand as they sat down at the kitchen table.

Joan was shaking, but she calmly told Alec, "You have absolutely no right to demand that."

"But . . ." He knew she was right, but that didn't solve his problem. It wasn't at all the reaction he'd expected. What to do? What to say? "Well then, let's get married."

Joan was speechless. She didn't know whether to laugh or cry or throw him out. "You want to marry me so you can order me around?"

"Yes. I mean no. I don't know what I mean." He was as shocked as she was by his proposal.

"Let me make it very clear: I don't take orders from anyone, not friends, not husbands, not even my boss. I will work *with* my boss but not *under* him."

They sat across the table from each other, glaring, afraid of what was coming. Joan looked down. "I tell you what. Let's go for a walk. You go west and I'll go east for half an hour; maybe we can calm down enough to talk to each other."

He nodded. They walked outside, leaving their coffee behind them.

They were both still determined when they returned, but much calmer.

"Joan, you're always controlling our relationship and it's driving me crazy. You won't even let me kiss you. And then I saw you having such a good time with Jim and the kids and I went nuts and I can't imagine you controlling him the way you do me. Why do you always keep me at a distance? Are you afraid of men? What's going on?"

"First, I want you to understand that no matter what our relationship is, I don't take orders from you."

Alec didn't like that at all. But she was obviously adamant about it. "All right."

"I'm not sure how to respond about the controlling. I explained to you before why I didn't want a sexual relationship with you. Do you think you're ready to make a commitment now?"

"No," he said sadly.

Quietly Joan spoke. "I think you're not tall enough to see your whole self in the mirror yet. You can see the old Alec, who was a mess, but you still can't see the man you are becoming. You're still living in the shadow of your old worthless self. I think if you knew your worth, you wouldn't need to order me around. Maybe we shouldn't see each other for a while until you sort yourself out."

"So you can marry Jim?" Alec asked bitterly.

"No, Jim and I are friends. We have no interest in marrying each other, but we will be friends for the rest of our lives, whether or not either of us ever remarries."

"What then, you don't care about me at all?" Alec cried.

Her look was so full of pain he couldn't stand it. "Please leave."

He left.

# 26

Monday's report showed no robberies in the county; there were three in Wolf County, which was the next county over. They saw Pete at McKenzie Lake Bar.

Tuesday, Maggie pushed Pauline's wheelchair down the long aisle of the Little Fork grocery store. Pauline saw a familiar face. "Myrna?!"

Myrna looked and grinned. "Pauline! And Maggie! I haven't seen you in years! How are you? What are you doing in a wheelchair? How are all your kids?"

"Myrna, it's so good to see you! I'm fine. I just

use the wheel chair because then we can loiter around until we find just the right foods for our gourmet cooking." She looked at Maggie. "I used to teach with Myrna at Lilac. We even took night classes together. She and her husband were two of the card players at our Thursday night '500' games at Queen's bar. Tom and I played cards there when we were courting, back in the sixties. Myrna, why don't you and Les come over to my house this Thursday and we'll play '500' just like we used to. Not quite like we used to, without my Tom. You knew he died -- yes you came to his funeral. Maggie, would you join us?"

"Sure, I'd love to."

Myrna finally got a word in, "I'd love to come, but my Les has died too, three years ago."

Pauline nodded, knowing all that a husband's death meant. "I'll ask Brownie to be our fourth. She and her husband used to play cards with Andy and me back in the fifties."

Later, Pauline said to Maggie, "I just realized Myrna knows you, too. How did you meet her?"

"I worked with her daughter as a waitress my first summer up here, more than twenty-five years ago and got to know the whole family. I even went to Myrna's college graduation and took pictures of her huge smile as she walked down the aisle in the middle of all those bored youngsters."

Tuesday at 3:00 p.m., three weekenders' cabins on Devil's Lake successfully tempted the thieves. Bob and Verna, citizens on patrol, saw Nimrod's van heading north on C at 2:20 p.m. No report on Pete.

Wednesday the robbers zigzagged around Ziggett Lake at nine in the morning, while their owners were at work. Pauline's friend, Betty, saw the Pinch's covered pickup nearby, twenty minutes after the robbery. Ralph, a patrolling citizen, found tracks of several van or pickup sized tires and tracks of semi-truck tires in the county forest near Swamp Lake. That night, Pete was at the Webb Lake Bar.

Thursday evening, as Pauline shuffled the cards, she announced, "I expect that we will all be quite serious about this game, just like we always were."

Brownie snorted. "The only one who was ever serious was old Clark Clapquist and he was so ornery that the bar owner finally told him not to come back." Pauline and Myrna laughed. They knew that Brownie could chew the fat with the best of them and still come out with the high score; they knew Brownie's skills because they could match them. Maggie, being very astute, sized up the situation: the four of them could easily play a very tough game and enjoy it, but tonight was for enjoying people, not skills.

"I remember one night when we all acted so silly that even Clark let loose." Pauline said. "Stuart, who was our only child at the time, had almost died from whooping cough. Andy and I were terribly afraid. When Stuart finally came home from the hospital, we were so relieved, we wouldn't leave him for a while. When we came back for the card games, we were so silly, we ended up tied for low score for the evening. That was a first for Andy! But even when they announced the winner and the losers, we were grinning like children with new bicycles. Everybody there was grinning right along with us, even Clark."

Myrna bid seven clubs, Maggie bid seven hearts, Brownie passed and Pauline bid eight hearts. The blind was kind and they made it.

As Myrna shuffled, Pauline asked, "Myrna, wasn't there quite a story behind your job at Lilac school?"

"Oh, yes. I had graduated from the two-year teacher training program at Carlstown and went to summer school, too. Lilac school hired me as an aide that fall. The day before school started, the phy ed teacher quit. So I substituted for her until October. Then because they couldn't find anyone else, they finally hired me. I taught kindergarten through fifth grade boys' and girls' phy ed and sixth through twelfth grade girls' phy ed. I went to summer schools and night schools for thirteen years to earn my bachelor's degree."

Pauline responded, "I took a one-year training

course in 1942 and finished my degree in 1964. Nine years of that time, I was at home with my family."

Maggie passed. Brownie bid seven diamonds, Pauline bid seven no-trump, and Myrna bid eight hearts.

"Oh, Myrna, you shouldn't have bid that," Maggie said, very seriously. When Myrna took her eighth trick, she looked at Maggie and gloated, "Hah!"

Maggie grinned and said, "I'll get you next time."

As Maggie shuffled, Brownie said, "Maggie, all of us except you grew up here. What brought you to this neck of the woods?"

"Fate. I'd been living in the Cities for quite a few years and felt an itch. So I took a Minnesota map (that was when maps were free) and cut it up along the fold lines. The eastern Minnesota border curves so the map showed a bit of western Wisconsin. I mixed up the pieces and drew one, which was about half Minnesota and half Wisconsin. I cut that into eight pieces and drew one; it was this area, so I drove up and spent the afternoon moseying around. Back then, this area was much less developed; the population in this county has nearly doubled in the past thirty years."

Brownie said, "Yes it has, but 15,000 people in about 600 square miles means we are still pretty spread out."

Maggie continued, "I saw a 'for sale' sign in front of a modern log cabin. I bought it. I even changed my name when I moved up here. I had always been Margie, but I changed it to Maggie. It sounded more like a take charge kind of name. About ten years later, I found out that was my great-grandmother's name, too"

"You were single then?" Brownie asked.

"Yes. I married a few years later, but he died of a heart attack in '90."

"Do you think you'll ever remarry?"

Maggie grinned. "Not me! Marriage is just too darned hard! Would you marry again?"

"I'm not divorced and I'm not looking!" exclaimed Brownie.

"Myrna, what about you?"

"Oh, I don't know. I suppose I might, if the right man came along. But I like my life as it is, with my grandchildren, my art and my friends. It's simple, with no one to answer to but myself. I still miss Les, even after all these years, so it would be pretty hard to find a man who could take his place."

Maggie asked, "Pauline, would you remarry?"

"At my age, who'd have me?" When they stopped laughing, Pauline added, "I buried two much-loved husbands. That's enough."

"Your husbands were so different, Pauline. What happened?" asked Brownie.

"I married Andy for his charm, but charm doesn't buy groceries, especially when it's swimming in beer. As any good teacher knows, you have to learn from your mistakes. I learned. I married Tom."

Brownie bid seven diamonds, Pauline bid eight spades, Myrna and Maggie passed. Pauline went down by one trick. Brownie thought it was such fun setting Pauline and Maggie that she overbid the next hand. Then Maggie bid eight diamonds because she had joker, both bowers and the ace, even though she had little else. She went down.

Brownie said, "Pauline, after you called to invite me for cards, I started thinking about some of the good times we had together. Remember the Halloween dances at Log Gables? We used to put them on to raise money for the fire department."

"Oh, yes. Tell them about your corn stalk costume."

Brownie liked telling stories -- she needed no persuasion. "That was in the early '70's. I made a vest out of burlap and sewed a dozen corn stalks to it with binder twine. I stuck a foldout owl in the stalks. Eileen and I went together. She went as a pumpkin. She had green stockings on her arms and legs (for the vines). We put a Styrofoam ring on her shoulders, strung wires down from that and covered them with orange cloth; we had balloons underneath to keep it billowed out. Luckily our friend lived across the road from Log Gables, because we never could have ridden in a car in our costumes. We dressed up at her house. Dale was selling tickets at the door. He said, 'Jesus Christ, what won't they think of next!' Our costumes won first prize, $100."

Pauline remembered the occasion; she had greatly admired Brownie, thinking at the time how brave she was. Brownie had raised their six children pretty much by herself, because her husband was always gone, working on construction or cutting pulp out in Montana. That Halloween, she had children at home to take care of and she was working as a waitress, yet she still had the imagination and sense of humor to go to a party in that ridiculous costume."

Myrna asked Maggie, "Do you still play volleyball?" They had driven together to the Wednesday night games for adults at the Lilac School gym.

"No, I had to quit because of arthritis, which I hated to do. I had a lot of fun smashing that ball around. I never did learn how to set it up and all that fancy stuff you used to do."

Myrna thought that was funny. "I never felt like I did it very well; I had to learn to do it so I could teach it in phy ed. But we had a fun group of players there."

"We sure did."

Pauline asked, "Brownie, do you still play softball?"

"No, I quit when I was sixty-nine; I was afraid that I'd hurt my leg again and have to quit that *and* bowling."

Maggie looked at Brownie. "I'll bet you were good."

"Well, I had my moments." Brownie laughed. "One of my more spectacular nights was when I was about forty-five. We played slow pitch at the Lone Pine Bar. I hit my way to first base. Bonnie came up next and hit the ball way out into left field. I ran for second base, but somehow, my head went faster than my feet and suddenly I flew headfirst into the sand. My teammates were yelling 'Brownie, get up!' and 'Bonnie, don't run over her!' All I could do was spit out sand and laugh. Fortunately, Bonnie had hit it so far that I managed to get to second base in time."

205

Maggie said, "You should see Pauline swim. She's up to a hundred yards at a time now, plus doing the water exercise routine for an hour. I think that's amazing for someone who's had three strokes." Brownie and Myrna agreed.

"I can do everything better now, because of the water exercise and the best part of it is that it's so much fun," Pauline added.

Whenever the scores dipped below -1000, they would pay attention to the game for a few hands, but most of the time, they were busy catching up with each others' lives. At nine o'clock, the score was -780 for Pauline and Maggie and -780 for Brownie and Myrna, still on the first game. Pauline announced, "Since both sides appear to be unable to win this game, I suggest we call it quits and continue talking around a snack." The others agreed.

Maggie put four pieces of zucchini chocolate pecan cake on a cookie sheet and smothered them with vanilla ice cream while Pauline beat up a brown sugar meringue. They buried the cake and ice cream in meringue and put it into the oven. After a few minutes, they served the Baked Alaska. Eating halted the conversation for a while, but when they finished their sweet treat, they talked on until the wee hours.

Thursday, the robbers bit Mosquito Lake residents at two in the afternoon, while owners were at work. Jenine and Catherine saw Nimrod near the scene of the crime. Ralph found more truck tracks at Swamp Lake. Pete went to the Yellow Lake Tavern that night.

The next day, Pauline and Maggie agreed that they could start planting the flowers. Maggie dug holes and Pauline removed the plastic containers to plant rose bushes, phlox, lily of the valley, butterfly weeds and mums. It took both of them to handle the day lilies. They barely had energy left to plant the tomato plants.

Driving around on patrol with Kathleen and Princess, seemed very easy after their planting. Pauline and Maggie did their duty, but missed out on all the action. At 10:00 a.m., the thieves ducked in around

Webb Lake. A bartender reported seeing Pete at Rice Lake Bar. That afternoon, Jo found truck tire tracks in the county forest near Frog Lake.

Their bones ached Saturday, but Pauline and Maggie planted the flower seeds; the warm sun eased the ache. The dirt felt good as they made a shallow trench with a finger for the alyssum seeds or pushed nasturtium seeds into the soil.

As they drove around that afternoon, Pauline and Maggie welcomed the rain. They were well satisfied because their planting was finished. It was time for the sun and rain to do their part.

Saturday afternoon, the thieves gambled on robbing three retirees homes while the owners gambled at the casino. Laverne and Lois saw Nimrod's van near there shortly afterward. Pete went to the Birch Island Inn that evening. Sunday the robberies occurred at Rice Lake, 11:00 a.m. while the owners were at church or work. Bleek's pickup was seen nearby. Ralph found more tire tracks at the same place near Swamp Lake. Monday the thieves worked west of Crex Meadows at weekenders' homes, in the early morning. Pete drank at Hank's Bar near highway 70 and county road H.

Sheriff George's nightly meetings with the leaders were brief. He would share the new information and remind them not to give the thieves any indication of being watched. George added up what they had discovered: they could identify all the thieves except the driver of the semi and they knew two out of three of their rendezvous points. Good. But he worried that they wouldn't have enough information to lay a trap before Pete Jenkins disappeared.

On a hunch, Ralph went to Swamp Lake at dawn on Tuesday, hid his car and walked through the woods. He found the semi and set up his video camera. While he waited, he drank coffee and ate sandwiches. He knew he wasn't supposed to be there, but he was over seventy and wanted a little adventure before he checked out permanently. At ten that morning, the thieves robbed homes at McKenzie Lake. A patroller saw the Pinches near there.

At 10:25 a.m., the Pinches drove up to the clearing near Swamp Lake, followed a few minutes later by Nimrod and his cronies. Ralph recorded the vehicles, their license plates, and the ten people emptying their cargo into the semi. He took shots of each face as they quickly did their work and also caught Pete and his driver on film. After they left, he had another cup of coffee. He was grinning.

At that night's meeting, he showed his little movie. Everyone was proud of Ralph, except George. He was proud and mad. "What if they had caught you?" But it was done.

Ralph asked, "George, does this mean you can just arrest all of them?"

George decided to watch the tape again. He realized that the camera was at a distance that made the faces fairly recognizable, but were they clear enough for positive identification? The driver of the semi came through clearly; that was the first time they could identify him. But, was the movie proof that they were handling stolen goods? Probably not.

George said, "I still have to catch them giving the stuff to Pete." Everyone left, except Pauline, Maggie, Bob, Verna, Ralph and George. George stared at the map on the wall, marked with colored thumbtacks wherever there had been a burglary. "Most of the robberies have been between highways 70, 77, 35 and the county line on the east. I can get help from the neighboring counties and state police and Mackerel, Lilac and Cranberry Town police. I could have a force of a dozen patrol cars and a helicopter. But when and where? Where is pretty simple, in that square, but when? There is no discernible pattern that shows where he will strike next, in the robberies themselves or in where he drinks his whiskey the night before. I can get all that help, but I can't call them out for a week at a time. I have to decide soon because Pete will be moving on in less than a week."

"George, can you get that help three days in a

row, if necessary?" Pauline asked.

"Maybe. Two, probably."

"Over half the robberies are in that square. The longest time out of that square is two days. Chances are you'd have them there in the first or second day you tried."

George grinned, "You're right." He thought a moment. "Ralph, is there only one way out of that place?"

"The road goes on past the clearing, so there are two ways by truck, plus they could run away through the woods."

"What about the rendezvous near Frog Lake?" George asked.

"Only one way out by truck."

"There's probably another rendezvous, around Gull Lake or Loon Lake or thereabouts. I'll get my best woodsmen at those three spots by dawn so they can find the semi." George looked at the map. "I could spread half the patrol cars along A, ready to move north or south, with the other half at the rendezvous with the semi. All right, then, we'll run the trap Thursday. I'll want all the patrollers out of the way, so pass the word along to stay home that day."

When they left, George called all those who had promised to help and asked them to meet him at 4:00 a.m. Thursday so he could explain the plan and get them in place before the robbers were about.

The robberies Wednesday were in Wolf County.

Early Thursday morning, George explained the plan and sent half the unmarked patrol cars to positions along A. He showed the rest how to get to their positions at rendezvous sites one and two. He gave what information he could about the third site. Just after dawn, his phone rang. He called his deputies at Swamp Lake and Loon Lake to tell them to go to Jo's house, which was where they were to meet if the semi was at Frog Lake.

"All right, lady (there was one policewoman there) and gentlemen, let's go." The five of them went in one car, north on 35, east on 77 until they reached Jo's house, less than a mile from the Frog Lake rendezvous.

They parked out of sight, to wait until the car radio announced that the robbers were at work. The three deputies who had scouted for the semi were already there. They chatted quietly, drank coffee and ate some of Pauline and Maggie's cinnamon rolls. At six o'clock, Jo came out and said, "I suppose you have to listen to your radio. But why don't you take turns doing that while the rest of you come inside?"

So the youngest of them, Bill, stood first watch, with a hot cup of Jo's coffee. Inside, Jo started a poker game, playing for ten chips a penny. They put aside a set of chips for Bill, for when he came in.

While she dealt the first hand, she asked the men if any of them knew the difference between an elephant and a loaf of bread. None of them knew. "Well, I'd hate to send you grocery shopping!"

When Bill finished his half-hour watch, he received his chips and Dennis set his aside for when he came back. An hour later, half the chips were in front of Jo. The men realized they'd have to get serious or they'd be wiped out. They held their own for the next hour, but it was hard, because they kept distracting each other with crazy jokes.

At noon, they ended the game, so they could eat and stretch. Jo won $3.65, Bill won $.36, George was five cents ahead; the others all lost money. The game had distracted them from the anxiety of waiting, but it hit hard after lunch. They all went outside. Some walked, some did stretches, some muttered. Finally at 2:00 p.m., the car radio announced that burglar alarms had gone off on Birch Island Lake. That was their signal.

They followed a trail through the woods for half a mile, then they spread out and crawled on their hands and knees until they were in a half circle, close to the semi but hidden by newly-leafed brush.

The other eight would follow the vans twenty minutes after the burglar alarm announcement and form the other half of the circle. If anyone tried to escape, they would shoot at tires or legs. The gang had no history of fighting back, but they hadn't been trapped before.

George and his men and woman waited again, for about ten minutes. They watched the efficient transfer of goods into the semi.

Then a helicopter flew into position above the semi and a voice called out, "Raise your hands above your heads. This is Sheriff Jackson. You are surrounded." The circle of officers stood up with guns pointed. They gave up without a fight, but Pete Jenkins looked wildly around. George told him, "Pete Jenkins, look at me. I am watching you. My gun is pointed at you. Lie down on the ground. Keep your hands above your head." He kept eye contact with Pete and repeated his message until Pete gave up, too. Nimrod was in the semi when he heard the announcement. He thought he might just hide there until they were gone and then get away, but Dennis yelled at him, "Nimrod, come out of the semi." He came out. When they were all handcuffed, George read them their rights, loud and clear.

George felt good. They all felt good.

# 27

Maggie waltzed into Pauline's house. Pauline was already in the kitchen, starting breakfast; she greeted Maggie with a big smile.

Maggie grinned back. "I'm feeling Tookish today. How about going up to Grand Marais?"

Surprised, Pauline gaped at her friend and quickly decided. "Yes, it's a grand day for an adventure, but why go to Grand Marais? That's hundreds of miles from here."

"Because the drive along Lake Superior has great scenery and we can get a cabin to stay a night or two and it's May and maybe we'll see a moose and hear some wolves." Pauline was nodding excitedly. "And my friend Teresa says there's a place up there that has just finished making maple sugar candy."

"Oh." Pauline's eyes grew big at the thought of that delicious treat.

Maggie let Pauline savor that thought for a moment before she asked, "Do you want to go?"

"Yes."

"Good, because I reserved a cabin for us for tomorrow night and Friday night. I figure that gives us time to get organized and pack. You'll want to let your kids know you're going; we have to take our own bedding and food. I'm thinking I'd better ask Joan if I can leave Kathleen with her while we're gone. I don't know how well she'd deal with skunks and porcupines and other wild creatures. Maybe you want to leave Little Princess with her, too."

"Yes, that would probably be better."

"I thought we could make a good soup and take fruit and oatmeal . . ." They had a busy day. Maggie went home to get a few things; she stayed with Pauline overnight so they could leave right after an early breakfast.

Near home, dandelions and lilacs danced in the spring sun; farther north, they found trilliums, millions and millions of trilliums, most of them white, a few turning pink. Pauline asked, "Maggie, I'm delighted to be going, but why did you wait until the last minute so that we had to rush around all day yesterday?"

"I've been asking around, trying to find some place that still makes maple sugar candy because you said you haven't had any since you were a kid. I called all the maple syrup places around home, but no candy. Yesterday, Teresa told me about this place near Grand Marais, so I called them. By the time I had all the information, it was too late to call you, so I arranged everything and hoped you'd like to go."

"Oh."

Maggie stopped for scenic overlooks, lighthouses,

and waterfalls. Pauline used her walker so she could get a good look and Maggie clambered around to take pictures. They found the maple sugar candy and went to their cabin. By the time they started a fire in the wood stove, ate and unpacked, they were ready for bed.

After breakfast, they planned their day. Pauline had read a book by Justine Kerfoot and wanted to drive up to see the Gunflint Lodge. At an open area by a lake they spotted a picnic table so they stopped for a leisurely lunch. The lake housed ducks, loons and beaver. Because they saw and heard no sign of man except the table, they felt less intrusive being silent. Two Canada jays landed nearby, begging for food. Pauline and Maggie threw a few scraps to the birds. Back at the cabin, they took a nap. That evening, they drove out on a lonely gravel road to look for moose. They were just about back to the cabin when Pauline pointed to her right. A huge bull moose lumbered to the road. He glanced at their car, which had stopped a few hundred feet away, plodded on across the road and disappeared into the woods.

"Wow! I wouldn't want to disagree with him," exclaimed Maggie.

Pauline said, "I think *that* was a horse put together by a committee. Whoever thought of that description for a camel never saw a moose."

Back at the cabin, they built a camp fire in the fire pit; it was jacket-cool as the moon rose. They munched on maple sugar candy. Maggie asked, "Well, Pauline, what do you think of your seventh life?"

"What? Oh." She nibbled on her candy. "My seventh life had a very bleak beginning. Then you brought good food, good music and swimming back to me. Have I ever thanked you properly for that?"

"Proper thanks, I think, is more a matter of real appreciation than of words. And your appreciation has always been abundant."

"Yes, you're right." Pauline paused thoughtfully. "But really, what jerked me out of my self-absorption was when Alec needed me. That was quite a challenge, to get *him* to prove his innocence."

Pauline laughed, a long hearty laugh. "I was so busy manipulating him into taking charge of his life, I didn't even realize I was once more taking charge of *my* life. Alec is doing so well -- did I tell you he isn't seeing Joan any more? He seems to be throwing all his energy into work now, which is a fine temporary solution. I'm hoping that in another year or so, he will grow up some more and . . ."

Maggie let Pauline's words drift away, then said, "Dixie's death changed a lot of lives, yours and mine, Alec's, Jim's, Cal's, Joan's. We should nominate that wasp for a Nobel Peace Prize!"

"Let's do!" Pauline agreed. "Starting the park was another grand challenge. I enjoyed that immensely. When the excitement died down, I reveled in cooking, cleaning and gardening. A good adventure adds spice, but the meat and potatoes in my life have always been the homemaking chores. Because I was unable to do that work for over a year, I find it even more satisfying now. 'You learn the value of water when your well goes dry.'" After a moment, Pauline said, "I like my seventh life."

Then watching the fire became more important than conversation. They heard frogs, loons, the crackling fire, the wind in the trees. After a while, the wolves sang their mystery, their loneliness, their wildness. Pauline and Maggie listened until the fire burned down to coals. Then they carefully put it out and went to bed, well satisfied. Spring was ripening and life was good.

**The Attic Was an Unused Room**, by Katy King, is a five-generation novel about Wisconsin women, based on family stories. $17.00 includes tax and postage.

**The Seventh Life of Pauline Johnson**, by Katy King, is a Wisconsin novel about a woman who is crippled by strokes, but then . . . $14.00 includes tax and postage.

Make checks payable to

Katy King
4521 Morningstar Dr.
Danbury, WI 54830

_____

Name

_____

Street address

_____

City              State          Zip

Katy is available as a guest speaker

## About the author

Katy King has lived in Shawnee, Kansas, in Rochester, Austin and Minneapolis, Minnesota and for the last thirty years in the Wisconsin woods near Danbury, with her husband, her dogs and herself; she lived in the convent, in apartment houses, in a trailer tent and in her own home. She has taught high school math and science, owned and operated a group home, kissed the Blarney Stone, been a home health aide and a lifeguard. Her next book will continue the adventures of Pauline and Maggie.